Close to a Father's Heart

A NOVEL

Non-fiction Books by Neva Coyle

Abiding Study Guide
Daily Thoughts on Living Free
Diligence Study Guide
Discipline tape album (4 cassettes)
Free to Be Thin, The All-New (with Marie Chapian)
Free to Be Thin Lifestyle Plan, The All-New
Free to Be Thin Cookbook
Free to Be Thin Daily Planner
Free to Dream
Freedom Study Guide
Learning to Know God
Living by Chance or by Choice
Living Free
Living Free Seminar Study Guide
Making Sense of Pain and Struggle
Meeting the Challenges of Change
A New Heart . . . A New Start
Obedience Study Guide
Overcoming the Dieting Dilemma
Perseverance Study Guide
Restoration Study Guide
Slimming Down and Growing Up (with Marie Chapian)
There's More to Being Thin Than Being Thin (with Marie
    Chapian)

9606

NEVA COYLE

A love so aloof.
Why could the words
never be spoken?

Close
to a
Father's Heart

A NOVEL

BETHANY HOUSE PUBLISHERS
Minneapolis, Minnesota 55438

Published by Bethany House Publishers
A Ministry of Bethany Fellowship, Inc.
11300 Hampshire Avenue South
Minneapolis, Minnesota 55438

Printed in the United States of America.

Library of Congress Cataloging-in-Publication Data

Coyle, Neva, 1943–
    Close to a father's heart / Neva Coyle.
        p.   cm. — (Summerwind ; 3)
    ISBN 1-55661-548-5 (pbk.)
    I. Title. II. Series: Coyle, Neva, 1943–   Summerwind ; 3.
PS3553.0957C58   1996
813'.54—dc20   96–25231
                                                CIP

Summerwind Books

A Door of Hope
Inside the Privet Hedge
Close to a Father's Heart

NEVA COYLE is Founder of Overeaters Victorious and President of Neva Coyle Ministries. Presently she is the Coordinator of a prayer ministry in her church. Her ministry is enhanced by her bestselling books and tapes, as well as by her being a gifted motivational speaker/teacher. Neva and her husband make their home in California.

Prologue

A hush fell across the crowd gathered in Summerwind's outdoor amphitheater for the Class of 1957's graduation exercises. Amy Weaver was lost in her own thoughts as Pastor Jim Henry spoke to God about the graduates seated across the wide cement platform of the open-air pavilion. Amy was impressed that Jim, whom she knew casually as her next-door neighbor, was as informal and friendly with God as he seemed to be with everyone else he knew. She scanned the front row of faces, wondering how her mother would have reacted to Jim's informal prayer of invocation.

In her weakened condition, Amy's mother had been unable to attend the ceremony. Finding her father, Amy saw the same everyday expression on his face. Most people didn't see past John Weaver's stoic exterior, but Amy's mother had taught her to read her father and had reassured her of the love he never expressed with words.

"A man says he loves you in other ways," Charlotte Weaver told Amy repeatedly. "Your father says it through the way he provides for us. He comes home after work, takes good care of the house and the yard, and makes sure we have everything we need. That's how a good man says he loves his family."

Still, Amy often longed to hear words of love from her father. Now she felt only sadness and disappointment that he didn't show joy about the full four-year scholarship she had earned with her straight A average. Her mother had been so proud she had cried when Amy received word she would be attending a four-year nursing program in the city, but her father had looked at the prized letter and with only a hint of emotion had said, "It'll be a lot of work, daughter. I hope you won't let the people down who believe in you as much as I do."

In the middle of the ceremony, Amy was called to the po-

dium to give her speech as class valedictorian. She had neither wanted nor sought this honor, but hadn't been able to
think of a way to get out of it. She had chosen every word carefully, staying away from controversy and cleverness and em-
phasizing challenge and responsibility toward God, country,
and "those who believe in and count on us." While she didn't
expect her father to be openly proud of her, she prayed he
wouldn't be embarrassed, either. Her delivery, thanks to
hours of practice, was flawless, and conviction rang in her
firm, clear voice. She was a strikingly beautiful young woman,
and as she stood confidently at the podium, her long blond
hair streaming gently in the breeze, the audience remained attentive to her every word. At the end of her speech, she took
her seat accompanied by the enthusiastic applause of her
classmates and their parents.

Finally, the last of the more than three hundred graduates
received their diplomas. Now the class stood in the traditional
darkened silence as the carillon in the church four blocks
away played the alma mater in their honor. The tall palms
swayed gently in the warm evening wind.

The graduates, full of promise and hope, were eager to get
the momentous ceremony over with and move on with their
lives. Many, like Amy, looked forward to college; others were
heading out into the work force. Suddenly cheers erupted as
the classmates threw their caps high into the air.

The graduates filed off the platform into the arms of waiting families and friends. Amy found her father standing at his
seat, waiting.

"Wonderful speech, Amy." Pastor Henry's vivacious, young
wife, Linda, extended her hand in congratulations.

"You did a great job," her husband added. "You're off to
college soon, right?"

"In September," Amy said quietly.

"Got a summer job?" Linda asked.

"No, I'll be home with mother," Amy said. *As usual*, she
thought to herself.

"You must be so proud, Mr. Weaver," Jim said, trying to in-
clude the solemn man in the conversation.

"Her mother would have liked it," John Weaver said flatly.

Only Amy caught the moist twinkle in his eye.

"I'm sorry she wasn't up to coming," Linda said. "I offered to—"

"The night air isn't good for her," John interrupted. "Otherwise she would have been here."

"Hey, Amy," called a friendly classmate. "We're going to Sandy Peterson's. You coming?"

"Daddy?"

"Go ahead, daughter. But remember, be home by midnight. You don't want to worry your mother."

Amy joined several others and left Jim, Linda, and John looking after her. "She really did a great job tonight, Mr. Weaver. Don't you agree?" Jim asked.

"There's more to life than making a good speech, Mr. Henry," John said, concealing his pride.

"I just meant that—"

"I know what you meant. Amy's got a good head on her shoulders. She'll do all right. We're very proud of her." John stuck out his hand toward the young minister. "Good night, sir," he said, then nodding toward Linda, he wished her a good night as well before turning and walking away.

Jim slipped his arm around his young wife's waist. "I wonder if she knows he's proud of her."

Linda shook her head. "I never met a more—well, how do I say this nicely—*reserved* man in my life. It's hard to imagine he would even have children," she said.

"Our kids will know, won't they?" Jim whispered, pulling his wife nearer.

"That we love them? That we're proud of them? Oh, yes. From the very minute they're born."

One

"Hi." Amy Weaver's eyes burned from sleeplessness as she walked into her college dorm room and flopped on the bed.

"Hi yourself," said Kristina, her roommate. "You look beat. Have a hard night?"

"Yeah, the Morans' baby has a cold and was up almost every hour or so."

"You were babysitting again, huh?"

"Didn't I tell you? Both of them were called in to pull duty last night. It must be tough to have two doctors in the house."

"You were there all night?"

"Yup, just me and that cranky baby."

"And Teddy?" Kristina asked, referring to the Morans' four-year-old.

"He slept straight through, thank goodness." Amy sighed heavily and turned to face the wall. "And I've a big test in pharmacology today. I'll never make it."

"Oh, sure you will." Kristina grabbed her sweater off the chair near the small student desk. "Want me to get you something to eat? You could nap for a little while. Why not skip your first class and—oh, hey, I almost forgot. Somebody named Linda Henry has been calling. She wouldn't leave a message. Just said that you were to call her as soon as possible."

"Hey, Amy!" a young woman's voice bellowed down the empty hallway. "Telephone!"

Amy dashed out the door and grabbed the phone at the end of the hall. "Hello? Hi, Linda. I just got your message." Amy tried to sound cheerful and alert.

Kristina had followed her and stood, waiting.

"Tell her I'll be there as soon as I possibly can." Amy's face was drained of color, and she leaned weakly into the wall as she said good-bye and hung up the phone.

"Amy?" Kristina moved closer to her roommate and friend.

"It's my mother. She's had an accident. I have to go home."

"Is it serious?"

"She broke her hip. She's in surgery right now. Oh, God, Kristina!" Amy's voice underscored the look of panic on her face. "She was alone for hours before Linda found her!"

Amy raced down the hall and into their dormitory room, and immediately began pulling her clothes from the dresser drawers. "I have to go home."

"Listen, why don't you let me do this? I can send the rest of what you need later."

"No," Amy said firmly. "I'm going home."

"I know," Kristina offered, "but you'll be back."

"No, Kris, I won't. Not this year, anyway. Listen to me. My mother was all alone. Who knows how long it will take for her to recover? She doesn't have anyone else, don't you see that? No one else but me."

"I see that this is a handy excuse—that's what I see," Kristina retorted.

"Come on," Amy defended herself. "My mother needs me."

"And who can object to your coming home to take care of her, right?"

"Kris," Amy pleaded with her friend.

"Well, Marshall will love to hear this, at least," Kristina quipped.

"Oh, Marsh," Amy said quietly. "I'll phone him and have him pick me up at the train station. Listen, Kristina"—she turned to her friend—"would you really mind helping me here? Who knows if or when I'll be able to come back and get the rest of my stuff? I have to go to the administration office. Call Marsh, and—"

"Speaking of Marsh . . ." Kristina tilted her head and raised one eyebrow.

"I wasn't speaking of him," Amy said, wishing Kris wouldn't be so persistent.

"When are you going to break up with that guy?"

"I haven't decided."

"What, haven't decided to break it off? Or haven't decided

to tell him? You're not about to marry him, and you know it."

"Kris, we've been through this before."

"And we'll probably go through it again. Do you expect me to stand by and watch you make the biggest mistake of your entire life?"

"Are you going to help me out here or not?" Amy didn't try to hide her frustration. Kris hadn't hidden her opinions of Marshall Jennings. After meeting him on a couple of social occasions, she hadn't hesitated to tell Amy she thought her choice for a husband was a poor one.

"Go on," Kristina said. "I'll do this. Listen, if you want to catch the train, you've got to be ready by three at least. But you'll have to tell him sooner or later—sooner gets my vote."

While Kristina hastily packed her things, Amy stopped by the administration office to make her explanations, then called and left a message with Marshall's secretary. Barely making the four-thirty train, Amy settled back in her seat and tried to anticipate what it would be like when Marshall met her at the station. Pulling into the Summerwind station, she found the usual emotions surfacing. Almost immediately she wished she had taken a cab. From the moment they got into his car and pulled into traffic, he began to pressure her to put her mother in a nursing home and move ahead with wedding plans.

Amy fingered the expensive engagement ring she had worn since the week after her father's funeral, barely six months earlier. "Maybe it's not that you want to wait until after graduation, but that you're having second thoughts altogether." Marshall's biting remark echoed Kristina's oft-repeated words.

"Please, Marsh," she begged, "I can only think of my mother right now."

"As usual," Marsh complained as they turned into the hospital entrance.

Amy's thoughts once again drifted back to her mother's condition.

"Well, do you or don't you?" Marshall's voice held an impatient edge.

"I'm sorry, Marsh," Amy said as the car came to a halt in

front of the small-town community hospital. "This will just have to wait."

"Shall I come in or not?"

"I'd better see her by myself. If I can't get a cab later, I'll call."

"Okay by me," he said, reaching across her and opening her door from inside. "I'm not much for the hospital scene anyway. And Amy," he said, catching her hand as she turned to step from the car, "don't forget what I said."

Without a word, Amy pulled away from his clasp and got out of the car.

"I'll drop your things off at your house." Did Amy imagine it, or was he actually in a hurry to leave?

"Thank you," Amy said curtly, anxious to get to her mother's bedside. Then, remembering her mother's little dog, she asked, "Will you get Princess? She's next door, at the Henrys'." Without giving Marshall the chance to say another word, she turned and hurried through the entrance. Only when the automatic doors swung closed behind her did Amy slow her steps and glance over her shoulder toward Marshall. *I can't put this off much longer*, she scolded herself. *It's not fair to him and it's not good for me.* Then, shutting him out of her mind, she made her way toward her mother's room.

"The doctors couldn't wait," the nurse explained as she walked with Amy to her mother's room. "Her hip had to be set. She was in so much pain and with her heart condition, and then laying on that floor all day—well, they had no choice but to operate right away. She's still in pain, but not as much as before. The surgery went well."

"And her heart?" Amy asked.

"Seemed to do fine. She's pretty weak. But all in all, she actually did better than—well, let's just say it could have been much worse. Are you Anna?" the nurse asked just before opening Charlotte's door.

"Anna? No, Amy."

"Has Anna been notified of your mother's condition?"

"No, you misunderstand, I'm Amy—I'm an only child."

"Oh, I see," the nurse said, her eyebrows raised. "I guess I did misunderstand."

But later, beside her mother's bed, Amy realized that the nurse hadn't misunderstood. More than once, the heavily drugged Charlotte called out for Anna.

"It's me, Mama. It's Amy."

"Amy, my darling, Amy. Did you see Anna? She was here, wasn't she?"

"Sleep now, Mama," Amy soothed. "It's going to be all right. I'm home now."

"Is my Anna all right, Amy? Did you see her? I heard her cry, but they took her away before I could see her. Go find her, Amy. Go find your sister."

"It's the drugs, dear." The nurse tried to convince Amy to dismiss her mother's ramblings. "She's just having dreams or hallucinations. That's not unusual. She probably won't remember a thing about this later on."

It was almost eleven-thirty when Charlotte finally seemed to be almost fully awake. "Amy," she whispered to her dozing daughter sitting in the chair beside the bed. "Amy, I must talk to you," she insisted, her voice heavy with emotion rather than drugs.

"Mama? You need the nurse? Are you in pain? I can call and get you something."

"Amy, I have to talk to you," Charlotte said. "Before I get another pain shot. Please, let me tell you . . . before you call the nurse."

"Tell me what, Mama?" Amy whispered as she moved closer to her mother.

"I hadn't wanted you to find out like this," Charlotte said. "I intended to tell you a million times. But—"

"Mama, you're tired. Let me call the nurse."

"In a minute," Charlotte protested. "First let me tell you about Anna. You see, darling . . ." her voice faltered. "Two years before you were born, there was another baby. I gave birth to your older sister, Anna."

"What are you saying? Where is she now?"

"Dead," Charlotte whispered sadly. "My baby died right after she was born." Charlotte cried, "I can still see my sweet baby's face."

Amy stood in shocked silence. "Why didn't you ever tell me?" she whispered at last.

"Your father wouldn't let me speak of it. He said it was best to put it all behind us. Then two years later you came, healthy and so beautiful. You were such a miracle."

"But why didn't you tell me?"

"She—I mean, it seems like she's been here." Charlotte lay back on her pillow and tried to shift to a more comfortable position. "Amy, we'll talk about this later. I promise. But now I think I need a nurse. I'm having such pain. Can you get the nurse, honey?"

Amy found the call button pinned to her mother's bed sheet. Numbly, she pressed it and then bent toward her mother's face. "Mama, please . . ." She searched her mother's pain-filled face. "I want to know about Anna. What happened to her?"

"Honey, I promise, I'll tell you everything. I've wanted to for so long. But now, I'm . . . I can't."

"That nasty hip hurting you?" the nurse asked as she approached with a hypodermic.

"It hurts so bad," Charlotte said.

"No need of that," said the nurse. "Not when we've got something to take care of it."

Amy stepped back while the nurse gave Charlotte the injection, then she sat in the chair and watched as her mother dozed once again.

Charlotte drifted in and out of a drug-induced sleep, rousing only slightly from time to time. Amy saw a frown crease her mother's forehead. "Anna, my baby Anna," Charlotte had whispered more than once. "My poor little baby Anna."

"Mama," Amy whispered, bending over the guard rails on the high bed to place a gentle kiss on her mother's cheek. "Mama, it's me, Amy. You're having a dream. It's only a dream."

"Amy?" Charlotte said barely above a whisper. "Amy? Why aren't you in school?"

"I came to take care of you, Mama."

"No. You have to finish school."

"We'll talk about it later, Mama. When you're better. Right now, we have to get you well."

"You mustn't let this keep you from finishing school," Charlotte said. "Please, Amy, promise me you'll finish school. I can go to a nice nursing home for a while. Daddy left me plenty of money. You go on back to school."

Amy couldn't tell her mother she had already decided to withdraw from the nursing program. She wasn't about to put any thoughts into Charlotte's head except hope and healthy dreams of getting well.

"Sleep, dearest Mama. We'll talk about school later," Amy whispered into the semidarkness of the hospital room.

"Amy," Charlotte said, rubbing her chest. "Amy?"

"I'm here, Mama."

"Go home, honey. Get some sleep. We'll talk in the morning."

"She's going to sleep," the nurse said, taking Charlotte's pulse. "You go on home and get some rest."

Amy bent and kissed her mother lightly on the lips. "Good night, Mama."

Charlotte managed a slight smile, and Amy slipped quietly away from her mother's bed. Anna's story would have to wait until later. But Amy was determined it wouldn't wait until much later. She would see to that. As soon as her mother was awake, Amy would learn more about her sister Anna.

Unable to sleep, Amy tossed back the handmade quilt covering her bed and sat up. In the darkness, she searched with her feet for her slippers and found her robe on the chair nearby. *Almost twenty-one*, she said to herself. *I'm certainly old enough to know that I'm not cut out to be a nurse.* Then a familiar pang of guilt stabbed at her rib cage. *Mama*, she thought, *she wants this so bad. It's not her fault*, she scolded herself silently. *She means well.*

Without turning on the hallway light, Amy headed for the kitchen. A cup of coffee was just what she needed to bring warmth to the inner chill she felt. Her mother's little dog, Princess, followed cheerfully behind, and Amy opened the back door to let the cherished pet out into the yard.

She glanced out the kitchen window over the sink, and even through the thick oleander hedge she could see the light on in Linda's cheery kitchen. Not that much older than Amy, Linda was already happily married—to a good-looking minister, no less. *Nothing like Marshall,* she thought. Amy shut her eyes against the loneliness and tried to keep the jealousy from stealing its way into her heart.

The sun began to streak the October morning sky with shades of pink and yellow. Dawn. A new day was supposed to bring promise and light, yet Amy's heart was heavy with darkness and pain.

She glanced at the large clock on the wall as she settled the coffeepot on its usual place on the back burner. Not quite six. If she tried, she could get to the hospital just in time to help her mother eat her breakfast. But as much as she willed herself to go, she couldn't seem to make her body respond to the commands necessary to get ready.

Waiting for the coffee to perk, she slumped into a chair by the small kitchen table. Resting her head in her hands, she recalled her visit with her mother the evening before.

You had a sister . . . Anna, Charlotte had said. Amy's mind flooded with thoughts of a sister she never knew.

Princess scratched on the back door, bringing Amy back to the present and to an awareness of her familiar surroundings—her mother's small and homey kitchen. The energetic Pomeranian began her usual morning jumping and running in circles as Amy filled her dish with food. She couldn't help but smile as she set the dish down on the pink gingham place mat by the refrigerator. "I'm surprised it isn't a lace tablecloth," she laughed. "You're one spoiled dog."

Princess gulped eagerly at her food, and only the small flicker of her bushy tail told Amy she had heard the comment.

Filling a china cup with coffee, Amy sat back at the table. She winced slightly as the hot liquid touched her lips. She glanced at the large diamond solitaire on her left hand. There was no question as to what Marshall Jennings wanted her to do about her mother's care and her own education. As adamant as her mother was that she finish school, Marshall was just as insistent that she give it up. The one thing both parent and fiancé agreed on was that her mother would be moved into a nursing home as soon as the doctor thought it was possible.

"You've got our life to consider," Marshall had said repeatedly during the last few months. "Let's set the date and get on with it."

"Two more years," Amy said aloud into the empty kitchen. "That's all I wanted. Just two more years." She wasn't sure who she wanted to hear those words, Marshall or her mother. If she didn't return to school within a week, she'd surrender the rest of her full scholarship. Yet how could she go back? Her mother needed care and there was no one else to see that she got it. Marshall wanted her to leave school and marry him. Her mother needed her but wanted her to go back. If she stayed home to care for her mother, Marshall's insistent attitude would have to be reckoned with. If she returned to school, her own guilt would nag her. *Perhaps Kristina was right*, she reflected. *As awful as it sounds, I've been handed a perfect excuse.* And now this shocking news about Anna, a sister—something she had longed for all her life. If handling Marshall and dealing with her injured and frail mother weren't enough, now Amy had this mystery to deal with.

Absentmindedly, Amy pulled a half-loaf of bread from the painted tin bread box on the kitchen counter. Slipping her hand inside the waxed paper bag, she pulled out two slices to drop into the Toastmaster. She paused when she noticed the small, green, moldy areas on the bottom crust and threw the whole loaf into the trash. "Oh, well," she said to Princess. "Guess I'll have something else."

She opened the refrigerator and discovered an unopened bottle of milk. She removed the top and sniffed the milk. Noticing the slightly sour odor, she poured it down the drain. In the small freezer she found another loaf of bread and examined it before slipping two frosty slices into the toaster. While the bread was heating, she took another look inside the refrigerator. "Not much here to choose from," she said to Princess. "Guess I'll stop by the A & P on my way home this afternoon."

"Good idea," Princess seemed to say with an enthusiastic

wag of her tail. Moving around in her mother's kitchen, Amy noticed how close the little dog stayed to her feet.

"Get away, Princess," Amy scolded. "You'll trip me and—" Amy stared wide-eyed at the dog. "That's what happened, isn't it, Princess? She tripped over you." Scooping the little pet up in her arms, Amy buried her face in the soft fur.

Amy shuddered to think of the hours Charlotte lay clad only in her nightgown on the cold kitchen floor before Linda Henry found her. "If only I had had the courage to tell her when I was home for summer break. I would have been here." Amy carefully placed her empty coffee cup in the sink. "On the other hand," she muttered, "I would have had Marshall pressuring me even more. It just seemed easier somehow," she confided to the pet. "I'm not a very nice person, Princess," she confessed. "Now look at the mess I'm in." She shrugged off the realization that sooner or later she would have to face decisions about her future as a nurse and about her relationship to Marshall. But not today—today she had her mother to consider. Her mother—and Anna.

Turning from the kitchen sink, Amy checked the wall clock again. Six forty-five. She still had time to get dressed and make it to the hospital in time to help her mother eat breakfast. As she headed toward the bedroom, the telephone began ringing and she detoured into the living room to answer it.

Pausing with her hand on the receiver, she took a deep breath. She had thought he might call early, but this was unusually early, even for Marsh. She knew she would need all her strength to persuade him to stay away today. She needed this time with her mother. Today she would learn about Anna—her mother had promised.

Calling on all the inner strength she could find, she took another deep breath and prepared herself to hear Marshall's voice before lifting the receiver to her ear.

Two

Linda glanced across the table at her young husband and caught him eyeing her closely. She tucked her short brown hair behind her ear and rested her face in her hand.

"What was that all about?" Jim asked, his face breaking into a broad smile.

"What was what all about?" Linda couldn't help but smile back at him.

"That big sigh."

"Did I sigh?"

"You didn't sleep well, did you?"

"No, I'm afraid not."

"Something on your mind?"

"It's just that I feel so sorry for Charlotte. If only I had checked on her earlier."

"It's not your fault, Linda. You had no idea—"

"Oh, but I did," she interrupted. "I was backing out of the driveway on my way to the women's Bible study and I had this little thought that I ought to—"

"Come on, Linda." Jim's forehead wrinkled into a frown.

"I'm not kidding, Jim. It's just that I was running a few minutes behind. I realized that her porch light was still on from when she let the dog out in the morning. I knew then something must be wrong. I feel so bad about it, that's all. Going about my day when she was lying there. Can you imagine what that must have been like?"

"You couldn't have known, Linda."

"No, I didn't know—but I think the Lord was trying to get me to—"

"Listen, honey, you can sit here all day and beat yourself bloody for what you didn't do. But look at what you *did* do. As soon as you found her, you did all the right things. You called for an ambulance. You put in a call to Amy. You went to the hospital and sat with her all that first night and then after only a few hours sleep, you went back as soon as they called and said they couldn't wait to do the surgery. Then you stayed with her until you knew she'd be all right and that Amy was on her way. You're too hard on yourself, Linda."

"It's not what I did for Charlotte that I'm questioning, Jim. It's that I didn't listen to that inner voice that was nudging me to go to Charlotte's door that morning. After all, she's become one of my best friends. But I thought I had too much important stuff to do for God to take a detour or risk running a little late. Even for Charlotte, and even when I knew it was probably His voice speaking to me to do it."

"He could have told Mattie. Isn't she one of Charlotte's best friends too? God's work doesn't just hinge upon you, you know."

"Oh, Jim," Linda's voice tightened. "I didn't mean to imply that God depends on me to get His work done. But if He can't use me . . ."

Jim sat back in his chair, never taking his eyes from his wife's face. "He does use you, Linda. Listen, honey, God isn't up there waiting for us to mess up once so He can toss us out because we're unusable. You've got it wrong. Didn't He keep urging you to check on Charlotte? Did He give you a second chance?"

"Yes, but—"

"It's your sense of compassion and the depth at which you feel for others—that's what's going on here. You're not perfect, sweetheart—no one is. We're all learning how to hear His voice and to respond accordingly." Jim scooted his chair back and came to his wife's side. Squatting beside her, he gently stroked her short, dark curly hair, then pulled her around to face him. "Linda Henry, you are a wonder to me. You serve God with your whole heart and it devastates you if you think you have let Him down—even when you're doing your best. But don't you think the God who told you to help her also had the strength to cover her with His mercy and grace until you got there?"

"Yes, of course," Linda agreed, wiping her tears with the

back of her hand. "I just love that woman so much. She's become such a friend to me. I want to be just as good a friend for
her."

"I know you do. You will be. Next time you'll have this experience to fall back on and you'll see, God will trust you
again. He'll give you another chance very soon."

"He already has," Linda said quietly.

"Oh?"

"I think I'm supposed to clear my day and be available to
Amy."

"That's not a bad idea. Any special reason?"

"He's not saying what the reason is—at least not yet. Just
to be available."

"Hmmm. You going over there then?"

"After you're gone. I'll just do the dishes and a few things
around here first."

"Thought you said you were going to clear your calendar,
not the table. Can't these things wait?"

"I just thought I should take care of my primary responsibilities first."

"That's just my point." Jim smiled at his pretty wife.

"Okay, I get the message. But then don't you complain
when you come home and the place is a mess."

"Only to the whole church." Jim laughed.

"You going to answer it?" Linda asked when the phone
rang.

"I guess I have to, don't I?" Jim smiled as he walked to the
center hallway and lifted the receiver to his ear.

Linda took the opportunity to move the dishes to the sink
and decided to get dressed and go on over to Amy's. She
stopped in the middle of the room when she saw the look on
Jim's face as he returned.

"It was the hospital. Honey, Charlotte got a blood clot this
morning." Jim hesitated, then said simply, "She just died.
The doctor is calling Amy now. You'd better get over there."

Without even thinking, Linda tightened the belt of her robe
around her waist, spun around, and bolted toward the back

24

door. "Call Mattie," she ordered as she yanked the door open. "She'll know what to do."

"Wait, Linda!" Jim called after his wife. "You're barefoot!"

Linda didn't even turn around.

Three

"No!" Amy heard her own voice screaming at the dangling phone receiver. "No!"

Linda didn't even approach the front door of the Weaver house but headed straight toward the kitchen door along the driveway. Without knocking, she opened the door and moved quickly through the kitchen to Amy's side in the living room.

"Oh, God, please!" Amy cried, unable to do anything other than stare at the phone receiver swinging at the end of its cord.

Amy felt Linda's arm around her before she saw her; she watched numbly as Linda picked up the receiver with her other hand and put it to her ear. "This is Linda Henry. I'm the Weavers' neighbor. Who's this, please?"

Amy stood frozen in place, her hand clasped tightly across her mouth. She searched Linda's face for some evidence that she had made a terrible mistake, that she had misunderstood the doctor—that her mother wasn't dead.

"Yes, I understand. No, I just got here . . . I see . . . I know, I just saw her last night." Linda paused in the conversation, and the stricken look in her eyes told Amy the awful truth. "I see," Linda continued. "Is there any reason for Amy to come to the hospital? No, I have no idea. How soon do you have to know?" Amy leaned against the strength of her friend. "Okay, I'll have someone call you back as soon as we can. Thank you, doctor." As Linda gently replaced the receiver on its base, Amy felt her knees buckle and she collapsed in Linda's arms.

"Linda?" Jim asked softly from the kitchen doorway.

"She's gone, isn't she?" Amy forced the words out from behind the hand still firmly covering her mouth. "She's dead. Oh, Linda, my mother is dead!"

Once again Amy sagged against her friend, and Jim

quickly came to slip his arms around both young women.

"Here, Amy." Jim urged the two toward the sofa. "You'd better sit down. Tell me what the doctor said."

"He said she was doing all right." Amy could not control the trembling overtaking her whole body. "Last night everything looked like she had come through the surgery just fine. Then this morning—I don't know, something about a blood clot—I can't remember. . . ."

"He said it was a pulmonary embolism, Amy. A blood clot formed somewhere in her leg and without warning broke loose and went to her heart. He said her weakened heart just couldn't handle it. She died almost instantly."

"I can't believe it!" Amy cried. "This can't be happening." Amy's head throbbed as she dissolved into tears. Sandwiched between her friends, Amy didn't resist when Linda pulled her close. Burying her head in Linda's neck, she released deep, pain-filled sobs of grief.

"Amy, who should we call for you? A relative or someone?" Jim asked when Amy's sobs subsided.

"There's no one." Amy pulled away from the comfort of Linda's embrace but held on firmly to her hand. "My father's only brother died a few years ago, and my mother's parents are . . . well, I never knew them. You two are the closest to family we have."

Linda touched the large diamond on Amy's hand. "What about Marshall? Hadn't we better call him?"

"No!" Amy almost shouted as Jim stood to go to the phone. "I mean—not yet. Please, I need a little more time—not right now."

"Hello, Amy dear," Mattie said tenderly. Amy looked up to see a large woman with gray hair and a kindly face standing in the living room doorway. She had come in through the kitchen following the same route taken by Linda and Jim just a few minutes earlier.

"Amy, do you know Mattie?" Jim asked. "She's a lady from our church who's been calling on your mother recently."

"Oh, Mattie, yes. My mother has spoken of you in her letters. How did you know to—"

"Pastor Jim, here—he called me. I'm going to stay with you

for a little while if you don't mind. You shouldn't be alone during a time like this."

"Linda?" Amy turned and begged Linda with her sorrowful eyes.

"I'm only going home long enough to dress. Then I'm coming back here to stay with you. But right now, we've got an important decision to make. I know this is difficult, Amy, but do you know what funeral home you'll—"

"Oh, my gosh, this is really happening, isn't it?" Amy looked into the eyes of the three dear people surrounding her, offering their friendship and support. "My mama, she's really gone."

Linda held open her arms and Amy once again collapsed against her friend and gave way to her sobs.

"I'm going to make some coffee," Mattie whispered to Jim. "And then, I'll take charge of the kitchen. This will be a busy place before long, considering how well her father was known in the business community. No doubt all sorts of people will be dropping by to offer their condolences."

"Thanks, Mattie," Jim whispered back. "Linda said you'd know what to do."

"That poor girl has a mighty rough few days ahead. Let's see what we can do to make it easier for her," Mattie said quietly before slipping into the kitchen.

"Linda," Amy said at last, trying to compose herself. "I guess we should call Chet Ramsey—he's the manager down at my father's store. He should be told. He helped us when my father died. He'd want to be here; I'm sure of it."

Jim headed for the phone as Amy continued. "We took my father to Donavon and Morgan—or something like that. Donahue Morgan—that's it. But Linda, do I have to go through what we went through for Daddy?"

"You don't have to make any more decisions just yet. Let's wait until someone asks you for something, okay? Right now, let's just see if we can get you dressed—how's that?"

Linda helped Amy find something to wear, knowing that Mr. Ramsey would be by shortly. She glanced at her own bare feet and remembered she, too, still wore her robe.

"How're you two doing?" Mattie asked quietly from the bedroom door.

"Mattie, can you stay with Amy while I go home and dress?"

"Of course, my dear."

"Will you be okay, Amy? I'll just be a minute," Linda said, realizing Amy was clutching her arm tightly. "I promise, I'll be right back. Jim will come be here to answer the phone and get the door when Mr. Ramsey arrives. I'll hurry as fast as I can."

Mattie gently pulled Amy into her ample arms, and once again the beautiful young woman gave way to her grief and shock, releasing deep, heartrending sobs.

Linda ran home, and Jim called the hospital to give the name of the preferred mortuary. Then he called the mortuary and began the painfully familiar process that occurs at the time of a death. "I hate this part of my job," he muttered as he reached once more for the phone.

"I know Amy said she didn't want to, but don't you think we should call Marshall Jennings?" Linda asked upon her return.

"I already did," Jim said.

"Did Amy agree to that?"

"I just called him on my own. He is her fiancé, after all."

"And?" Linda was confused by the disgusted expression Jim wore.

"He said he had an important appointment. That he'd call his mother to come over and he'd be by as soon as he could tactfully break away."

"At a time like this? You're kidding!"

"No. I'm not."

"Where's Amy?"

"In the living room with Mr. Ramsey and Mattie. Better go on in, I guess. Coming?"

Jim and Linda quietly took seats across the comfortable living room from Amy and Mr. Ramsey, who were seated on the sofa. Mattie glanced gratefully at Linda, then wordlessly headed for the kitchen.

Seeing the pleading look in Amy's eyes, Linda crossed the room and sat close to her on the sofa.

"I was just telling Amy here," Mr. Ramsey said, glancing at Jim, "that I'll do everything I can to keep things running smoothly. We've got only five employees at the moment, and I'm sure they'll want to come by and also attend the funeral. I think it's best to close the store on the day of the funeral. Out of our respect for Mrs. Weaver—Mr. Weaver would have wanted it that way, I'm sure."

Chet Ramsey stood to go, then turned to Amy. "If you need anything, or want anything from me, please don't hesitate to call. I'll be in touch," he said. Turning more to Jim than to anyone, he added, "Let me know if there's anything she needs."

After Chet Ramsey left, Amy looked at the ring on her finger. "I guess I have to call Marsh."

Jim and Linda exchanged glances. "I already did," Jim said.

"Oh." Amy's tone was flat.

"I'm sorry, Amy. I just thought he ought to know. He'll be by a little later," Jim said, wishing Amy would look at him so he could read her eyes.

"He told me last night that he was going to have a heavy morning," Amy said listlessly. "And that if I needed anything—you know, with my mother in the hospital and all—I could call his mother."

"His mother?" Linda asked before she saw Jim's warning glance.

"I suppose she'll be by before too long," Amy said. "I'm sure he's called her."

"Yes, he said he would," Jim nodded.

"Then, would you mind talking to her, Jim? I think I'd like to lie down for a while." Amy stood and headed for the bedroom.

"Amy," Linda said, "do you want me to come with you?"

"I'd really appreciate it. Do you mind?"

"Not at all," Linda replied. "I'll be right there."

After Amy left the room, Linda turned to Jim. "What kind of love match is this? Your own fiancé can't leave work and sends his mother? Criminee—you'd think he'd bust his you-know-what to be with her right now."

"Calm down, Linda," Jim warned. "She'll hear you."

"Do you know the Jennings family?"

"No, but I'll bet Mark Andrews does. He knew Amy's dad from Weaver's Building Supply. Being a contractor, he seems to know everybody." Jim glanced out the living room windows just in time to see Marshall Jennings' mother, Adele, pull her large Lincoln into the modest driveway of the Weaver home. "Go to Amy. Let me handle this."

"Be careful," Linda warned.

————

"She's resting, you say?" Adele Jennings' tone reeked of superiority and false concern. "Poor darling. This must be such a shock to her. You're the neighbor? How nice of you to come right over like this."

"I'm not just her neighbor, Mrs. Jennings." Jim wondered just how much to say. "I'm—well, I'm more a friend of the family, really. I'm the pastor of River Place Community."

"A clergyman. How nice. It won't be necessary for you to stay, you know. I will call our minister now."

"I appreciate that, Mrs. Jennings, but Amy asked me and my wife to stay. My wife is with her now."

"I see." Adele Jennings looked at Jim critically.

Jim glanced down at the Levi's and flannel shirt he had thrown on earlier this morning. He was supposed to be working for Mark Andrews today. The small church wasn't able to pay their young pastor much, and Mark often saw to it that part-time jobs came Jim's way. However, tarring the roof above the print shop downtown would either have to wait or be done by someone else. Amy needed him now. When it came to pastoring or taking a job for extra money, Jim didn't even hesitate to make his decision. Noticing Mrs. Jennings' negative appraisal of his clothes, Jim fought against feeling awkward.

"It's my day off," Jim apologized. "I was about to—"

"You don't have to explain, Reverend." Adele's smug emphasis on *Reverend* told Jim she certainly didn't approve of a minister dressing in Levi's—even on his day off. "Marshall explained to you, didn't he, that he'd be here just as soon as possible?"

"Yes, he did."

"Good," she said, refolding the gloves she held daintily in her lap. Jim watched as her long, manicured fingers unhooked the small mink collar that trimmed her light-colored suit.

"Mrs. Jennings, would you care for a cup of coffee?" Jim asked, trying to alleviate the tension in the room.

"I—please, don't go to any bother."

"It's no bother. Really, I'm sure there's a fresh pot by now." Jim hastily retreated to the kitchen, grateful for even a moment's reprieve. Upon his return, he noticed Mrs. Jennings looking around the small but comfortable room. "Mattie will bring it right in."

"Mattie?"

"Yes, she's—"

"Here we are," Mattie said, producing a tray with not only coffeepot, cups, cream, and sugar, but a plate of her own homemade oatmeal cookies as well.

Jim couldn't help but think that Adele Jennings probably hadn't had an oatmeal cookie since she was a child. Ladyfingers, petit fours maybe—but oatmeal?

"How kind of you, thank you." Mrs. Jennings looked at Mattie with some curiosity. "I'm sorry for staring, Mattie," she said, delicately balancing her cup and saucer in one hand. "But I didn't know Mrs. Weaver had anyone. How long have you been with the family?"

"With the family?" Mattie shot Jim a puzzled glance.

"Yes, have you been here long? No one mentioned it to me."

Jim smiled at Mattie and started to say to Mrs. Jennings, "Oh, Mattie here is a longtime—"

But before he could get the word "friend" out of his mouth, Adele interrupted. "Well, never mind that now. I'm glad you're here, Mattie. I'm just surprised that Charlotte never said anything to me about it."

Mattie winked at Jim, then turning to face Mrs. Jennings, she said with dignity and a slight bow, "Why, thank you, ma'am." As Mattie returned to the kitchen, Jim wanted to laugh out loud over the ludicrous assumption of this impatient woman before him. He felt a little guilty not saying any more, but Mrs. Jennings would just have to figure out the truth for herself.

"I'm glad there's a woman here," Adele said, interrupting his thoughts. "I was wondering how I'd manage the funeral and all. I know Amy will need my help managing all the details. This takes quite a load off my mind. But I'll have to speak to her about having something other than oatmeal cookies to offer visitors. I'll stop down at the bakery and have them send over some things. You know, to have when people come to call."

"Do you think there'll be that many, Mrs. Jennings?" Jim doubted that the woman had ever paid a social call on Charlotte. Otherwise, she would have known Mattie was a friend, not a servant. *And what's more*, he observed silently, *she certainly seems eager to be in charge now.*

"Mr. Weaver was quite an important merchant in our small town, Reverend. I'm sure many will want to come and call. Mrs. Weaver, though, wasn't too much for keeping up on social responsibilities. But Mr. Weaver, he was quite well liked. I think I'll go take care of a few things now—that is, of course, if you think Amy will be resting for a while yet."

"She's had a long night. She was at the hospital until quite late. And I don't think she slept very well after that. I can tell her you were by."

"Oh, I'll be back." Adele's condescending tone irritated Jim. "We'll also need a guest book, and I suppose I should make sure Mattie has enough napkins on hand. Oh, well, I'll just get what I think is needed. By the looks of the dear woman, her estimate would be a shot in the dark at best. I'll be back later."

"And Marshall, when will he be here?"

"Just as soon as he can break away, I'm sure. Poor Mrs. Weaver couldn't have picked a worse day. Marshall has been working on this contract for months. Now that he's finally got all the parties together, he couldn't very well not show up, now could he? But don't you worry. He said himself he'd shorten it to nine holes instead of the usual eighteen. But then, you know men. Once they get to talking business—it really is very important, Reverend, or he'd be here by now. But for the moment, Amy's in good hands with you and your wife here. I can't tell you how much we appreciate your taking such an interest in her right now."

Jim thrust his hands deeply in his pockets and watched the elegant woman guide the sleek luxury car out into the street and drive away.

"Is she gone?" Mattie whispered from a partially open kitchen door.

"That she is," Jim said. "That she is."

"Is she coming back?"

"I'm afraid so, Mattie."

Four

"Amy, darling," Marshall Jennings said several hours later as he crossed the living room to embrace Amy.

"Marsh," Amy said, "you're finally here."

"I came as soon as I could. I sent Mother, didn't I? Didn't she come first thing this morning?" Amy involuntarily stiffened at his patronizing tone.

"Yes," Linda offered from the other side of the Weaver living room. "She was here."

"There, you see? I didn't desert you entirely, now did I? I'm here now. That's all that matters."

"What matters, Mr. Jennings, is that Amy's mother died this morning." Linda's tone was angry. "You—" She stopped abruptly when Jim gently squeezed the base of her neck and shot her a warning look.

"Yes, thank you for coming," Amy said, but her words sounded empty.

"Now, about the arrangements. Mother will help you with whatever you need." Marshall ignored Linda's comment and overlooked Amy's lack of enthusiasm. "There will be quite a few people at the funeral, I would guess. I'm sure you would like to have it at our church. I'll call Reverend Mercer. He'd be glad to handle the service. It will be very nice."

Amy pulled away from Marshall and turned to face Jim and Linda.

It was Linda who saw Amy's panicked expression first. "I don't know that she's decided for sure. Have you, Amy?" *Say what you want, Amy,* Linda's face pleaded.

Finally, Amy found her voice and spoke quietly. "I haven't thought it through yet, Marsh. I'll let you know in the morning. I'm too tired to make any decisions tonight. I'm not sure yet what I should do and—"

"Well, that's obvious, isn't it?" Marshall retorted. "Your father was a very influential man in this town. You remember how many people streamed by his casket and came to pay their respects when he died, don't you? It hasn't been that long, only a few months—surely you remember that, don't you, Amy?"

"Yes, I do. But this is my mother, not my father." How could Amy forget the funeral that had added to her mother's distress rather than relieved it? Even though Amy hadn't even accepted Marshall's proposal yet, Adele had taken over the entire affair—and that's exactly what her mother had called it. *This isn't a memorial—it's a social affair*, Charlotte had commented. *Your father would be appalled.*

"But it was too late," Amy explained to Jim and Linda after Marshall left. "By the time we got to the funeral home, it was all in place."

"But why in the world did your mother allow such a thing to happen?" Linda asked.

"Daddy's death was so sudden," Amy felt her throat tighten. "We didn't know anything about arranging a funeral. Mama was so overcome by it all that she thought Adele was just being helpful. She had no idea anyone would overrule her wishes." Amy paused, then continued. "My mother wasn't one to make a scene or cause a fuss about anything. I just remember how she gripped my arm the whole time. My parents were quite simple people, really. There's always been more than enough money, but they never felt any need to spend it on more than just the bare necessities. My mother's family were plain people—you know, in upstate New York."

"Plain people?" Jim asked.

"Immigrants from Germany—they had very strict beliefs about material comforts, conveniences. My father was a Lutheran, but he respected my mother's beliefs. I think he felt he had asked her to give up quite enough just marrying him. She was shunned for that. Her family disowned her entirely. Even my father's family was against the marriage. That's why they came to California. They had no one—just the two of them. They had hoped to start a family of their own. My mother's dreams began to crumble when she didn't—well, she was in her early forties when I came along."

"So, is that why there's no TV in the house?" Linda asked.

"Or radio, except the one in the kitchen. Father insisted on that only to hear the weather and the news each morning before he went to work. After he left, Mama immediately turned it off."

"How did she keep in touch with the outside world?" As well as Linda knew Charlotte, this private side of her hadn't been discussed.

"That's just the point," Amy said. "She didn't. At least not the way most people do. She was well read, however. Her room is loaded with magazines and several newspaper subscriptions. She wasn't in contact, but she was well-informed."

"You know, I wondered about that from time to time. She was such an interesting conversationalist on so many issues. She seemed to enjoy discussing world events, politics, and even literature. I assumed she had a TV in another room." Linda crossed the room to stand beside Amy. "She was a remarkable woman; I liked her very much."

"So did I," Amy said quietly. "She was very involved in my schoolwork. She was only allowed a sixth grade education. But she knew more than most of my teachers—at least that's what my father used to say. He admired her so much. She was never very strong physically. As a child she suffered from rheumatic fever, and it left her heart somewhat damaged. She did what she could around the house—too much sometimes. But then she didn't have to spend her energies on outside activities. She loved her fruit trees, sewing her quilts, and making a home for Daddy and me."

"Amy, in all those years when you stayed home all summer with your mother—well, didn't you ever resent it?"

"Sometimes," Amy admitted. "But life was so interesting with Mama. By the time I was in the ninth grade I knew how to sew, cook, and even can fruit, vegetables, and meat. When I went to home ec class in high school—at my father's insistence—I was entirely bored. I already knew how to do everything. Oh, yes," Amy smiled at the private joke between her and her mother, "except one thing. I didn't know how to sew using a store-bought pattern. We always made our own.

Mama could have been a designer, Daddy said."

"How did your parents feel about Marshall?" Jim asked.

"My parents had been deeply hurt by their families when they married. They both said they had reservations about him, but that choosing a mate was something one did for life and it was far too important a decision for anyone else to make but me. They assured me that they would stand behind my decision. They just kept repeating that this was my decision and that I was the one who would have to live with it."

"Did they give you a reason for their caution about him?" Jim asked.

"My parents wouldn't say a bad thing about anybody. They answered most of my questions about this with philosophical statements."

"Like what?" Linda asked.

"Oh, like, 'a man is as a man does' and 'beauty is only skin deep.' Oh, yes, my father used to always say, 'You can't judge a book by its cover. There's a lot of trash printed inside some leather-bound editions.' "

"Wouldn't it have been easier if they had come right out and told you what they thought?" Linda asked.

"Oh, but they did," Amy said defensively. "They thought I had enough sense to make my own decisions." Amy stood and rubbed her back as she paced the living room floor. "You know, there's something else my father said. 'If you poke at a man's reasons long enough, you might find nothing more than a bag full of excuses.' " Amy stared at the ring on her left hand.

"Do you know what he meant by that?" Linda asked.

"I'm beginning to," Amy said thoughtfully.

"How about something to eat, Amy?" Linda said. "I'm sure Mattie left something in the fridge. Come on, let's find out what it is."

"I don't think I'm hungry," Amy said as they went into the kitchen.

"Well, I am," Jim said as he helped himself to an oatmeal cookie.

Soon the three were gathered around the kitchen table, and Mattie's hot vegetable stew was filling the room with the pungent aroma of homegrown vegetables and spices. Before long even Amy was spooning warm stew into her mouth.

"I guess I was hungry," she said.

"Listen," Jim said to his wife after finishing a tall glass of milk, "I'm sure you'll want to stay here with Amy tonight."

"Oh, Linda, I couldn't let you do that," Amy said with surprise.

"I'm sorry, Amy. If you'd rather be alone, then I understand—"

"No, it's not that. I would really be grateful for the company. It's just that I don't want to impose."

"It's no imposition. I'd want someone to be with me at a time like this. After all, what are friends for?"

"Not having many, I couldn't say," Amy replied. "Please stay."

After Jim said good night, kissed Linda on the forehead, and let himself out the back door, he headed for the quietness of the small house he shared with Linda. Puzzled about Amy and Marshall, he wanted some time to pray about the situation. Time alone was in order.

After straightening up the kitchen together, Linda and Amy headed toward Amy's bedroom and the twin beds covered with Charlotte's handmade quilts.

"I've never been in here before," Linda said, running her hand appreciatively over Charlotte's handiwork.

"You've seen my mother's room, haven't you?" Amy asked.

"No, I've only been in the living room. I must say I was quite taken with her braided rugs. I never had a clue she did them herself, until one day when I came over she was working on one to give Mattie."

"Come on." Amy quickly led the way to her mother's room. As she entered the room, she was suddenly overcome with the realization of why Linda was there and engulfed by the fact that her mother would never come back to this room again. She sank to the floor in tears as her grief overwhelmed her once more.

"Oh, Amy," Linda said, her own eyes filling with tears. "It would be so much better if you had some family. A brother or sister . . ."

Suddenly, Amy's sobbing stopped and she swung around to face Linda. "Anna!" she said. "Linda, my mother promised to tell me about Anna. Oh, no!" she cried, covering her face with her hands. "Now I'll never know what happened to Anna."

"What are you talking about?" Linda asked as she gently pulled Amy's hands from her face.

"Last night," Amy began, wiping the tears from her eyes, "she was calling for Anna. I thought the nurse was mistaken; then I went into my mother's room and heard her myself. I asked her about it and she told me I had an older sister, Anna, but that she died. I never heard about this before and questioned her more. But she was so tired and wanted to sleep. She was rubbing her chest and I was afraid her heart might be bothering her, so I let it go. But she promised to tell me later—this morning. This morning I would have learned the whole story. But she's gone—oh, Mama!" Amy's voice gave way to deep sobs. "Mama . . ."

Linda scooted closer to Amy and gathered her in her arms. Together, the two young women sat tightly together on the braided rug in Charlotte Weaver's bedroom. After a few moments, Amy let her eyes wander about her mother's simple but tastefully decorated bedroom. "What other secrets lie within these four walls?" Amy wondered aloud. "How will I ever find out about my sister now?" she whispered.

———

After a few hours of needed sleep with Linda nearby, Amy was able to regain some of her strength both physically and emotionally.

Mattie arrived the next morning just as the two young women were about to tackle a file box in search of Charlotte's birth certificate the funeral director requested, saying it was necessary to establish Charlotte's identity, a requirement of law. Amy would also have to select the clothes Charlotte would be buried in.

"I just came by to see if I could be of any help," Mattie offered. "Do you mind?"

"Thank you, Mattie." Amy hugged the older woman. "I'm

so glad you're here." Distracted, Amy ran her hand across some of her mother's clothes. "I'll have to pick something for Mama to wear . . ." Her voice broke, and Mattie slipped an arm around the young woman's waist.

Mattie perused the closet. "I remember my own Ben's funeral," she commented. "He had but one good suit." By the looks of the modest selection in Charlotte's closet, Amy wouldn't be given much of a choice, either. "You still have a little time, dear. You don't have to decide this minute."

John Weaver's closet stood pretty much the same as the day he died. Charlotte had simply sent one of his suits to the funeral home, closed the door, and never opened it again. Now Amy would have to contend with it all. Mattie shook her head and returned to the kitchen.

"Look," Amy said as she took a square box from the top shelf of Charlotte's closet. "This must be it."

Sitting on the large bed, Amy sank into the softness of the thick featherbed topper hidden beneath the quilt. Linda joined her, and the two began to examine bits of family history written on slips of paper and an occasional certificate of one kind or another.

"Look at this!" Amy held up a yellowed parchment sheet for Linda's inspection. "This is my birth certificate."

"Look how tiny your feet were, Amy. Aren't they sweet?"

But Amy's attention was suddenly drawn elsewhere. In her hand she held another birth certificate with *Anna Weaver* scrawled across the top. Little inked footprints were at opposite bottom corners. Amy ran her fingers across the tiny spots where each toe had been carefully pressed against the parchment document. Uninvited tears ran down her cheeks and one fell on a footprint. Amy carefully blotted the wetness with the sleeve of her sweater.

"Oh, Linda, I'm not an only child," she whispered. "I had a sister." The bittersweet discovery was almost beyond comprehension.

"Oh, Amy, darling." Adele's voice rang with false cheeriness from the hallway. Amy's chest tightened. "May I come in?" But without waiting for a response, Adele Jennings, fashionably dressed in a lightweight woolen suit and matching pillbox hat, entered the room. "Oh, my," she said, glancing around the room and across the paper-strewn bed. "What is going on here? I can help you with this, darling. Surely you don't want outsiders looking over family matters—"

"Look, Adele," Amy said, trying to deflect the impolite reference to Linda's presence. "Look at this." Amy held the certificate for Adele to see.

"What in the world? Who, pray tell, is Anna Weaver?"

"My sister!" Amy said. Though true, the fact sounded so strange.

"Your what? For heaven's sake. Where in the—I mean, why hasn't this come to light before now? Where is she?" Adele's voice rang with as much alarm as interest.

"She died," Amy said.

Adele's shoulders relaxed, almost as if she were relieved.

"Oh, thank goodness," Adele said, bringing both Amy's and Linda's faces quickly around in shock. "I mean," she attempted to explain, "thank goodness you found the family records. You know the funeral director needs your mother's birth certificate—or some other legal form to establish her identity." Adele reached for the document in Amy's hand. "How sad that she died, dear. When did all this happen?"

"She died at birth. I only found out about her when I went to see my mother."

"You mean she never told you about this?" Adele asked.

"No, not until I saw her in the hospital."

"Then, my dear, you had better return this to your mother's file immediately. If she didn't tell you, she must have had good reason. Let her secrets go with her, Amy. That would be the best, most respectful thing you could do." Adele took Amy's arm and tried to escort her away from the file box and out of the room. Amy pulled from her grasp and stepped away.

"You're right, Adele. Outsiders have no business seeing all this." Strength from an unknown, untapped inner place surged through the young woman. "Would you mind waiting in the living room? I won't be but a minute."

"I'm sorry, Amy," Linda said, obviously embarrassed. "I didn't mean to intrude."

"I'll be in the living room," Adele said coolly, leaving the room as abruptly as she had entered.

"I'm not talking about you, Linda," Amy said to her friend. "I don't want Adele in my mother's things. She didn't understand Mama at all, but I'm beginning to see that my mother understood her, even though she wouldn't say a bad word against her."

"Listen, we can continue this later if you'd like," Linda offered. "That woman makes me feel like a first-class snoop."

"You're not a snoop. Would you do me a favor, Linda?"

"Of course," Linda said.

"Keep looking through here for anything that would legally identify my mother. The marriage license—anything. I'll go deal with Adele. I don't want a full-blown production with this funeral, and if I don't step in right now, that's just what it will be. I'll only be a few minutes."

Linda tried not to listen to the conversation between Amy and Mrs. Jennings, but their raised voices made it difficult. It was obvious that Adele Jennings wasn't going to be happy with Amy's decisions.

"How'd she take it?" Linda asked when Amy came back into the bedroom.

"She's an interesting woman," Amy said. "At first she thought I was completely wrong by wanting to keep things simple. That my father's business connections and acquaintances would be offended. Then she did a complete about-face." Amy was pacing now; Adele's reaction and turnabout wasn't easy to figure out. Linda waited.

"I don't follow you," Linda said after a few moments.

"Suddenly she said it might create even a better impression with the community if Mama's funeral was smaller, quieter—private. Understated elegance, she called it."

"What?" Linda didn't even try to hide her shocked expression.

"Everything that woman does is for effect—even funerals." Amy continued her pacing. "You know she wants to make sure my father's business is presented in a favorable light. 'You don't want the town thinking he left your poor mother destitute.' Those were her exact words. I went along with her when my father died. I really had no say in the matter. After all, I had my mother to think about and take care of. His death was very hard on her. But, I swear, I'll not make that mistake again. She'll not make a circus out of my mother's death for her own reasons."

"Her own reasons? You think she has reasons?" Linda asked.

"I'm sure she does," Amy said. "I just don't know what they are—just yet."

"How in the world did you get mixed up with—" Linda started, then stopped. "Never mind, it's none of my business."

"It's a question I've been asking myself lately," Amy admitted.

"Know the answer?"

"I'm working on it." Gesturing toward the papers scattered around, she asked, "Find anything?"

"Just this," Linda said, holding up a small book printed in German. "It appears to be a prayer book of some kind. Inside—look here." Linda pointed to a few pages of family records in the center of the book.

"My mother wrote this," Amy said. "It's her hymnal."

"But there's no music . . . ."

"Not on the page," Amy said. "But Mama told me about the way they were sung in meeting. She said the music was written on the heart and passed on for generations. She was sad I'd never hear it for myself."

"She ever sing to you?"

"No, she said it was forbidden. She was cast out. She said her sister slipped the hymnal in her things when she left with Daddy."

"She was so quiet and—I don't know—peaceful. No one could ever guess she had such pain in her past." Amy heard the emotion in Linda's voice.

"Maybe she didn't have a birth certificate. It may have been against what they believed in. Not registering with the government in any way." Amy wandered over to her mother's dresser and began opening first one drawer, then another.

"You think so?" Linda stared at the prayer book.

"She didn't have a social security card; I know that for a fact."

"And your father?"

"He did. He didn't believe the same as her. She wouldn't sign the tax forms or anything. And he didn't make her. I'm surprised they have a marriage license."

"A marriage license! Amy, maybe they'll accept a marriage license and this hymnbook as her identification."

"They should. It certainly tells the story of her life, doesn't it?" Amy turned to see Linda still sorting family mementos on the bed.

"You looking for something else?" Amy asked.

"I just thought that Anna's death certificate would be here, too. See? Here's your father's birth and death certificates. Your mother put them together. And the marriage license is here. But," Linda paused, then continued, "wouldn't you expect anyone as orderly as your mother to put the baby's death certificate here too?"

"Maybe I'll find it when I go through the house."

"Oh, Amy!" Linda exclaimed, dismayed. "You have to do this all alone?"

"I guess I do. But I don't have to do it now, do I? I mean, if I have my mother's identification papers—"

"That's quite enough for one day, I'd say," Mattie said from the doorway. "I'm fixing the two of you a little lunch. Goodness knows if you ate any breakfast or not." The generous-sized older woman came to stand beside Amy and slipped an arm around her slender waist. "Did you pick out the clothes you want your mother buried in, Amy dear? Maybe something needs pressing?"

"It won't be hard to decide. Mama always liked to wear her plain blue cotton dress on the Lord's Day. And whenever she read her Bible, she always wore her prayer covering. I think she'd like to be buried in that." Amy quickly opened the top dresser drawer and produced her mother's small, gauzelike prayer cap.

"Oh, Amy," Linda said, coming to stand beside her friend. "I think you're right."

"She may have been banished from her community—but she kept her faith. All these years, she still believed."

"She was quite a woman, Amy," Linda said tenderly.

"Yes, she was," Amy said softly. "I will miss her so much."

Five

"Oh, Amy, you can't be serious!" Marshall's expression underscored his immense disdain when Amy told him what she was planning.

"Oh, but I am," Amy said quietly, sitting at the small kitchen table and fingering her coffee cup. "I'm very serious."

"But Mother went to a lot of trouble. She made almost all the arrangements."

"Without asking me," Amy said flatly.

"She's only trying to help."

"She's interfering." Amy swiped at the tears that once again threatened to overtake her, tears not only of grief but of her growing frustration and anger over Adele's meddling.

"Look at you," Marshall said. "You're not up to handling these decisions and details. You're a mess."

"My mother just died, Marsh."

"My point exactly," he retorted. Glancing at the clock on the wall above the refrigerator, Marshall continued. "It's less than twenty-four hours until the funeral. How do you think you'll manage without my mother's help?"

"There won't be a funeral," she said quietly.

Marshall paced Charlotte's shining kitchen floor. "You don't mean it. That's not what you want."

"Are you two having a private conversation? May I come in?" Adele's crisply cheerful voice preceded her graceful body as she entered the kitchen balancing a tray laden with coffee cups.

"You'll never guess what Amy has just told me, Mother."

Amy hated the whiny tone Marshall's voice took on when he spoke to his mother this way.

"Oh, really? Well, never mind. Amy dear, where do you keep the coffee? And where is your woman?"

"My woman?" Amy asked with surprise.

"The one who was here yesterday. Martie? Mattie? Yes, that's her name. Why isn't she working overtime during these few difficult days?"

"I can't believe this!" Amy didn't even try to hide her anger.

"Hold your voice down," Marshall ordered. "You have guests in the living room."

"And you really do need to come out and greet them, dear." Adele's searching through Charlotte's immaculate cupboards yielded the coffee. "These are very important clients of Marshall's father. They've come to extend their condolences."

"I don't even know them," Amy snapped, refusing to allow any more tears to surface.

"Oh, but you will." Adele put the percolator on the burner to cook. "Once you and Marshall are married—"

"Oh, please!" Amy said, standing up and turning her back to Marshall and Adele Jennings.

"You're right, dear. There's plenty of time to talk about the wedding a little later. But for now, come on, Amy, be a good girl and make an appearance."

"I'll go," Marshall said, heading for the door. "You try to talk some sense into her, will you, Mother?"

"Men don't understand women at a time like this, darling." Adele's cheery tone soured with false comfort. "What about the funeral, Amy? Even the smallest memorial service has endless details to attend to. Now, about your mother's clothes. I know this is difficult, but if you'll just go with me now we can pick out something nice. She has something nice, doesn't she?"

"I've already sent her clothes to the mortuary."

"You have? But I wanted to see—"

"No, Adele, you don't."

"I don't understand," Adele said, a touch of irritation in her voice.

"Seeing wouldn't change that, believe me."

"Amy, what's gotten into you?"

"Didn't you hear me yesterday?" Amy fought the impulse to scream at the overbearing woman. "I've already made the arrangements for my mother."

"I heard you, dear. But certainly—I thought that by today you might have changed your mind."

"There isn't going to be any public funeral service," Amy began again. "Only a small, private graveside service. You're welcome to come, of course. And your husband, too. But other than myself, Marshall, and a couple of other friends, it's closed—private."

"You can't be serious!" Adele said incredulously. "No chapel service at all?"

"That's what *I* said," Marshall said, returning from the living room.

"Please, both of you," Amy pleaded. "Can't you understand? I will handle my mother's burial in the way I think suitable for her."

"Well, you may be right," Adele said, sounding suddenly thoughtful.

"I know I'm right."

"Mother, I hardly think after all you've done—the arrangements you've made—"

"No, Marshall, I think Amy's right. The more I think of it, the more I think it's really the perfect plan after all."

"Plan?" Amy said, unable to hide her sense of shock. "You talk about my mother's memorial service as if it's supposed to fit into some sort of a plan."

"Well, I didn't mean it like that, really," Adele said, obviously trying to placate her while sending a pleading glance in Marshall's direction.

"You just don't understand, sweetheart." Marshall took Amy's hands gently in his own. "Our family, well—honey, you have to know that when a family holds a certain place in the community—"

"I don't want a place in the community," Amy said, struggling to maintain her composure as she felt her anger rising. "I just want to bury my mother in a manner fitting to her. She didn't care about making a great impression, nor did she have a lot of friends."

"But, darling," Adele insisted, "perhaps she didn't, but we certainly do."

"What's this got to do with you? This has only to do with my family—not yours."

"But you're my fiancée, Amy," Marshall said.

"Look, dear," Adele said, taking her arm. "Maybe if you rested awhile. It's still a couple of hours before dinnertime. Why don't you lie down? Is Mattie scheduled to come and fix dinner?"

"Mattie!" Amy couldn't hold her temper any longer. "Look, Mattie is a friend. She was one of my mother's closest friends. She's not my hired woman—she's a friend."

"Oh, I see," Adele said, embarrassed. "I just thought that since she was here and working in the kitchen she was . . . oh, I'm so sorry. I didn't understand."

"Listen to me, Marshall. For the last time, listen to me." Amy made little effort to keep her voice down. "I'm not having a big, showy funeral for a woman who wanted to live her life in privacy and loved her seclusion. She had a few close friends like Mattie and Linda Henry, who came by a couple of times each week and had tea with her. They read the Bible together and discussed literature and gardening. Linda brought her so much joy, and my mother loved telling her all my news from school. I'm not going to open her funeral to people who didn't care about her when she was living and don't care a whit about her now. I'm not going to have people passing by her casket staring down smiling at her—it would have made her very uncomfortable when she was living, and I'm not going to force this on her now."

"But, Amy," Adele coaxed, "people mean well—"

"No," Amy said flatly. "I've already contacted the funeral home and given my instructions."

"Amy," Marshall said sternly, "this is not like you at all."

"I've made my decisions." Amy tried to sound resolute and firm even though her knees were shaking.

"Well, then," Adele said. "I guess I should inform the minister of the change in plans. I'm sure he can—"

"I've already called him," Amy said. "Jim Henry is handling the service."

"Jim Henry?" Adele said. "But he's not of our faith—"

"And your minister is not of mine," Amy interrupted.

"Please, Adele, cancel any other plans you may have made. It will be a simple graveside service. Simple and befitting my mother."

"Then afterward," Adele persisted, "maybe afterward—"

"Afterward, I'm coming home to be with my friends. If you care to join us, you're more than welcome. But certainly, we won't be needing a caterer."

"But you'll need—"

"I'll have all I need. I'll have my friends." Amy glanced at the clock. "Now if you'll excuse me, I have a four-o'clock appointment at the lawyer's office."

"Alone?" Marshall seemed incredulous that Amy would attempt to handle legal matters without him.

"Do you want to come along?" Amy regretted the invitation immediately.

"Of course, darling," Marshall said, taking her arms and turning her to look at him. "I can't let you face this by yourself. A funeral is one thing, but business is quite another."

He sounded almost tender, but something in his tone of voice sent chills of warning up Amy's spine. "There's nothing to face, Marshall," she said. "Mr. Carlson has been a friend of the family for years. He just has some papers to go over with me. Some items in my father's will go into effect now since my mother—" She bit her lip, unable to go on.

"He should have called me. I'm sure this could have waited until another time."

———

"As you know, Amy," Mr. Carlson said after she and Marshall were seated in his office, "your father was a very simple man. He lived much simpler than his means would've allowed, but that was his way."

"I know."

"And," the lawyer continued, eyeing the young couple above his half-glasses, "he was also a very generous man. He lived as though his wealth was a trust. That it was only placed in his hands to benefit others."

Amy felt, more than saw, Marshall shift in his chair and

lean ever so slightly forward at the mention of John Weaver's wealth.

"I won't go into all the details at this time," Mr. Carlson continued. "That can wait. But there is one matter that won't wait."

"Yes?" Amy said.

"Morningside." The lawyer's simple statement held immediate understanding for Amy. Marshall, however, was completely in the dark.

"Oh, yes," Amy said. "Morningside."

"Morningside?" Marshall asked politely.

"It's a home for . . . well, for those less fortunate than ourselves," Mr. Carlson explained.

"I see. And Mr. Weaver was somehow . . ." Marshall looked confused.

"John Weaver was a great benefactor for the residents of Morningside Home, Mr. Jennings. For years he has relieved a great deal of suffering and provided an enormous amount of comfort for some very deserving, yet very denied people. And he encouraged others in the community to do the same."

"And what does this have to do with Amy? And why does she have to deal with this now? Her mother's funeral hasn't even—"

"I'm sorry to have to bring this up now, Amy," Mr. Carlson apologized, addressing her directly. "If it could've waited, I would have put it off until after—"

"It's fine, Mr. Carlson. Go on." *Poor Marshall,* she thought, *you'll never understand about Morningside.*

"Your father's will states that Morningside's needs would be handled just as he prescribed as long as your mother was alive. But he added that at the time of her death, Morningside's needs would be handled at your discretion, my dear. All decisions no longer follow a prescribed protocol—they fall squarely upon you."

"I see," Amy said quietly.

"Well, I don't see," Marshall said curtly. Amy stiffened at Marshall's impatient tone.

"And," Amy asked, "is there a need that must be tended to immediately?"

"I'm afraid so," Mr. Carlson said. "One of the boys living there had . . . well, had a problem last week. He's not injured, but a window was badly damaged."

"And it needs repairing?"

The lawyer nodded.

"Anything else?"

"They could use a little extra cash this month as well. Since your father died, his absence in the community has caused other contributors to slack off in their giving. It's been pretty difficult for the home to continue to make ends meet."

"He didn't make provision for repairs to be covered?"

"Not within the stringent guidelines of his will. He made it out some years ago, and while I'm sure he intended to amend it, like so many others, he put it off—then, well . . . then it was too late."

"Then why do it now?" Marshall interjected. "If he had wanted to make such provision, why didn't he just endow the place or set up some sort of trust fund?"

"He wanted his daughter to handle it when he . . . when the time came." Mr. Carlson found his patience being tried by Marshall's obvious lack of concern for the home.

"Mr. Carlson," Amy said, "Morningside was something my father spoke of only on rare occasions. I knew he supported it, and we gave clothes and toys once in a while. But I really knew very little beyond that. How can I make a decision—a good one—based only on what you've just told me?"

"And on your trust in me," Mr. Carlson urged. "I've been out there and have seen the need myself. I wouldn't have called you down here if I thought it could wait. I'm asking that you authorize me to—"

"Maybe I should go out and take a look, Amy." Marshall looked directly at Mr. Carlson as he made the offer. Amy didn't misunderstand the thinly veiled threat in his expression.

"Maybe you should, Mr. Jennings."

"I don't think that's necessary," Amy said. "For now, handle things the way you think my father would, Mr. Carlson. After my mother's service, and well, after some time to sort things out, then I'll make other decisions. Until then, will you just take care of this for me?"

"I'd be glad to." Mr. Carlson seemed relieved.

"Call Chet Ramsey if you need anything. I'm sure he'll be glad to—"

"He's already been alerted. We just needed your authorization."

"Well, then, if there's nothing else, Mr. Carlson," Marshall said, standing up.

"We need you to sign this temporary authorization, Amy." Mr. Carlson passed a prepared document to her and handed her a pen. "And we do need to meet again."

"Of course," Amy replied.

"I'll drop by in a few days to see how you're getting along. And you know without saying, if there's anything I can do for you. Anything at all . . ."

"Thank you, Mr. Carlson. I'll call you if I need anything."

———

"I can't believe this," Marshall said once they were sitting inside his car.

"Can't believe what?"

"First you cancel all my mother's efforts to spare you the details of the funeral, then you just hand that man a blank check to spend any way he chooses. God only knows what he is up to."

"I'm counting on that," Amy said quietly.

"You are so trusting, Amy. You should be more careful."

"Really? Can I trust *you*, Marsh?"

"That's different."

"Really? How?"

"We're planning to be married." Marshall pulled his car into traffic and headed toward Amy's house. "There's no reason to put off the wedding any longer, is there, darling?" he said after they were moving with traffic.

"Marshall, please."

"I mean, you don't have any excuses left, do you? Your mother isn't going to need a nurse any longer. You have no reason to finish school now. Your father left you plenty of money. Why would you even consider it?"

Amy turned her head away from Marshall's demanding

glances. Suddenly, he pulled his car to the curb and turned off the motor.

"I mean it, Amy. I want to take care of you now. You're facing so much—your father left you not only a great deal of money, but a tremendous load of responsibility as well. Why can't we be married? It would take a big load off you. I'm a good manager, have a growing business of my own. Can't you see? It makes perfect sense to stop putting off our marriage any longer."

"Marshall . . ." Amy felt smothered. "I can't talk about this right now."

"That's what you've said for the last six months."

"Our engagement happened so soon after my father's death. I told you then I thought it was too soon to make such decisions—I only agreed when you said you'd wait until I finished school. Nothing's changed."

"But, honey, everything's changed. Now you're alone." Marshall's tone didn't conceal his frustration. Amy knew he would continue the pressure to convince her to marry him as soon as possible. He had already suggested an elopement, saying the social obligations could be taken care of later.

"I'm not alone."

"Of course you are."

"Please, Marsh," Amy pleaded, "let me get through the next few days. Give me some time to think through what I should do next. Can't I at least bury my mother without pressure from you?" Why did she feel that same smothering tightness in her chest? "This isn't the right time to make any decisions. Surely you know that."

Without a word, Marshall once again guided his sleek car into traffic. Silence or pressure—Amy didn't know which she hated the most. Lately, it seemed as if it was either one or the other. Glancing at Marshall's clenched jaw, she knew it wasn't only the difficulty of her mother's death that made him appear like a total stranger to her. In a few days, certainly within a few weeks, she'd have to be truthful with Marshall Jennings. Fear squeezed her insides into knots.

"I want to be alone," she said quietly after they were inside her house. "Please."

"Have it your own way. It doesn't have to be like this. I can stay with you if you'd like." Marshall tried another approach. "I do care for you, Amy," he said huskily as he pulled her within the tight circle of his arms. "I thought you might need me tonight."

Amy stiffened at the implication of his words. "I want to be alone."

"I won't be put off much longer, Amy. I'm being patient now, but after the service, after tomorrow, we will have a talk." Marshall Jennings then turned and left Amy standing in the middle of the room.

She cringed at the finality and determination in Marshall's statement punctuated by the solid closure of the front door. Perhaps she wished he'd soften and just hold her. If only he'd stop being so interested in the marriage and be more interested in her. If he'd just do something to prove that her growing uneasiness had no foundation—that she was wrong about him and that he was, after all, a good choice for her.

"This isn't right," she whispered into the silence. "This just isn't right." Fighting back tears of frustration, loneliness, and fear, she wrapped her arms tightly around her middle. "I've really dug myself a pit," she moaned. "Using Marshall as an excuse to stay in school, and using school as an excuse to stay away from Marshall. It would have all been so simple if I had only been honest with him—and with Mama."

The wall furnace in the hallway whooshed to life, startling her. Standing perfectly still, she pushed thoughts of Marshall from her mind and listened to the sounds of the silent house. The ticking of her mother's pendulum clock, the humming of the refrigerator in the kitchen, even the faint sounds of the delicate wind chime outside the back door didn't bring her comfort tonight. Home was just a shell without her mother's presence.

"Mama," she cried aloud. "Mama." Amy slumped onto the couch and gave way to the tears that she had been fighting against all day.

————

A while later when Linda Henry came in, Amy was sitting on the living room floor.

"Amy?" Linda called softly from the kitchen as she stepped quietly toward the swinging door that separated the kitchen from the dining room. Shoving the door open, Linda walked quietly toward the heartbroken figure on the floor. "Oh, Amy," she said, dropping beside the young woman and gathering her in her arms. "You go right ahead and cry. Go ahead, Amy. Let it all out."

Amy buried her tear-covered face in Linda's shoulder as soul-shattering sobs tore from deep inside her. Linda patted her head and kissed her forehead lightly. "That's right, honey. Let it go. You've got every reason to cry."

"Oh, Linda," she said between sobs, "I'm so scared."

"Of course you are," Linda said.

"I can't believe she's not coming back. I can't believe she's gone."

"I know."

"She was my best friend. What am I going to do without her?" Amy buried her face in Linda's shoulder and didn't fight the sobs racking her slender body.

When Amy eventually quieted, Linda smoothed her silky blond hair back from her tear-swollen face. "Come on, honey," Linda said. "Let's get something in that stomach."

"I'm not hungry," Amy protested. The thought of food made her stomach turn.

"No, but you're empty." Linda gently pulled the grief-filled young woman to her feet. "Just some tea and toast, how's that? Will you at least try?"

Amy followed Linda obediently to the kitchen just as Jim came through the back door. "I thought I'd find you here. How's—"

"We're just about to have some tea," Linda interrupted.

"Good idea," Jim said, glancing at the clock. "It's almost seven. I could use something in my empty stomach."

"Sit down, Jim," Linda invited. "This will only take a minute."

Jim sat opposite Amy and then extended his hand across the table to cover Amy's. "It's difficult, Amy. I know it is."

She looked up at him through puffy red eyes.

"We're here for you, you know that."

"I know," she said.

"And Marshall, I thought he'd be here with you—"

"I asked him to leave me alone."

"Alone?" Linda said, setting cups and plates on the table. "Amy, if you'd rather be alone—"

"No." Amy said quickly. "I'd just rather be alone than with him. Please," she said, looking from Linda's face to Jim's, then back to Linda's again. "Please," she said simply. "I don't want to be by myself."

"Good," Linda said, "because Mattie left an entire refrigerator full of food here. You couldn't possibly eat all this by yourself."

Jim saw the look of concern in Linda's face and forced himself to relax in his chair. His empty stomach wouldn't be empty much longer. Mattie's meatloaf and homemade bread would take care of that. He looked at Amy and saw the same angry pain he had seen on other faces in times like this. Certainly the issue of Marshall Jennings would have to be addressed, but there was more. Somewhere deep within Amy's eyes was a question, or was it more of a longing? She seemed so very alone. Jim silently prayed for wisdom as he ate his sandwich. He wasn't in favor of exploiting times of grief for evangelistic purposes, but he certainly didn't hesitate to answer questions and introduce Christ to those inquiring under any circumstance. He would wait, being available to both the Lord's direction and Amy's. In the meantime, he would plan his remarks for the memorial service carefully. *Simple, straightforward,* he decided as he finished his meal. *Nothing less would do than honest simplicity for Charlotte.*

———

After Amy made her decisions and convinced Marshall and his mother that she was firm in those decisions, everything else fell into place. Charlotte's body was not put on public display, and only Amy, accompanied by Linda and Jim, saw her. "Good-bye, Mama," had been the only words Amy whispered after standing in tearful silence for more than ten minutes before the simple wooden casket was closed and taken to the cemetery for the graveside service.

At the graveside, Amy controlled her emotions as she looked around at the faces of the small group gathered to say their last farewells and honor her mother. "From the words of Psalm one hundred four, verses twenty-seven and twenty-eight," Jim said. " 'These wait all upon thee; that thou mayest give them their meat in due season. That thou givest them, they gather: thou openest thine hand, they are filled with good.' "

Jim's voice soothed Amy. She took a deep breath and closed her eyes. Regardless of Adele Jennings' opinions, this was right—right for her mother . . . right for her.

"Charlotte Weaver was our mother, friend, and sister in Christ," Jim said. "Her faith, like her life, was simple. She believed in God and His goodness. If I may be so bold, even presumptuous, perhaps, I believe that God also believed in her. Always trusting, never demanding, Charlotte carried out her trust and relationship with Jesus Christ in private. Only those who took the time to know her discovered the inner strength and depth of character she possessed. These words from Proverbs thirty-one describe her perfectly: 'Who can find a virtuous woman? For her price is far above rubies. The heart of her husband doth safely trust in her, so that he shall have no need of spoil. She will do him good and not evil all the days of her life.' And these words as well: 'Strength and honor are her clothing; and she shall rejoice in time to come. She openeth her mouth with wisdom; and in her tongue is the law of kindness. She looketh well to the ways of her household, and eateth not the bread of idleness. Her children arise up, and call her blessed; her husband also, and he praiseth her. Many daughters have done virtuously, but thou excellest them all. Favor is deceitful, and beauty is vain: but a woman that feareth the Lord, she shall be praised.'

"Charlotte Weaver had a secret," Jim continued, then to Amy's relief, hurried on. "She knew the secret of contentment. She knew the secret of private prayer, and she knew how to wait on God. She had few close friends, but great influence in the lives of those who knew her best. Charlotte chased not after happiness or pleasure, but preferred deep moments of quiet and solitude before the Lord. Those of us who knew and loved her face life with an empty place that will never be filled again, for Charlotte Weaver was a rare and wonderful person. We'll not likely meet anyone like her again.

"We've come to commit her body back to the earth from which it was formed, for the Bible says, ashes to ashes and dust to dust. But we've also come to reestablish our belief that those who are dead in Christ will arise again in the day of resurrection when the Lord himself shall descend with a shout and those who are alive and remain will also be caught up together with Him in the air.

"And in the days and weeks to come, when we come to grips with our grief and loss at Charlotte's passing, she will be experiencing the sweet presence of the Lord in a new and deeper way—in a way that even she has never known before. We celebrate that fact for her."

Amy closed her eyes again, recognizing every word as words she had heard first from her mother.

"Let us pray," Jim said. Then in his own open, spontaneous, familiar way, he prayed earnestly for Amy, her future, and the friends Charlotte left behind. "Amen," he said at last.

"Amen," the small group repeated in unison.

"God bless you, Amy Weaver," Jim said taking her hand in his. "And keep you in His will."

Silently, Amy could only nod. Linda was by her side, as was an unusually sober Marshall Jennings.

Six

"What do you think?" Jim asked his wife several mornings later.

"About what?"

"Marshall Jennings."

"You really want to know?" Linda asked.

"I wouldn't have asked otherwise."

"I wish I had a better word. The one I'm thinking of isn't very nice." Linda glanced away and sipped her coffee.

"I have to admit I'm struggling with my own attitude toward the man. I just can't understand anyone who has behaved like he has during this whole thing. It's not as if Amy's helpless, or even friendless. She's just going through a bad time right now."

"He's really putting on the pressure," Linda said.

"I thought he might be—"

"In the week since the funeral, he's been by to see Amy every day. He's not offered to take her out, to help her with her father's affairs, or anything. All he can say is—"

"You mean, he's not taken her out to dinner, or offered a show—or anything?"

"Even if he had asked, she would probably have refused." Linda drained her cup and reached for the pot. "There's not much left here. You want me to make another pot?"

"No, thanks, honey. I've had enough."

"I'll finish it off then," Linda warned.

"All right by me." Jim smiled at his petite wife. Linda's short brown hair curled haphazardly around her face. Her dark eyes sparkled with enthusiasm for life. Only when she was as concerned for someone as she had been for Amy did that sparkle diminish slightly.

"What are you looking at?" she asked shyly.

"You."

"Well, don't."

"Why not?"

"You make me nervous when you do that."

"You're lying." Jim shook his head. "The pastor's wife lying to her husband. Now, what do you think we ought to do about that?"

"Stop it, Jim. I'm worried about Amy."

"I love you, Linda," Jim said. "C'mere."

Linda rose and willingly went to sit on her husband's lap. "Now tell me," Jim said in a low voice into her ear, "just what are you so worried about?"

"She's been at it for a solid week, night and day. She spends most of her time out there in her father's office behind the garage."

"What's she doing?" he said, nibbling at her neck.

"Going through files, making notes. She's exhausted, I can tell."

"Have you offered to help?" Jim asked huskily, still nuzzling Linda's ear.

"Jim" she scolded. "Stop it. I'm serious. Listen to me, will you? Otherwise, I'll go back to my own chair."

"You wouldn't."

"I would."

"Okay," Jim said, raising his face to get a closer look at his wife's expression. "What's on your mind?"

"I told you—Amy."

"So, what happens when you go over?"

"She's so busy and preoccupied with everything. She says she can't believe how in order everything is. Her father left perfect files, complete instructions, and everything. It's as if he knew he was going to die and wanted this to be as easy for Amy and her mother as possible."

"Did he?"

"Did he what?"

"Know he was going to die?"

"How could he? You know yourself what happened. He had a stroke on top of a ladder at the store. If it hadn't been for the fall, he might not have died at all. No one can predict those things. Can they? You don't believe in premonitions, do you?"

"I don't think it would take a premonition for a sixty-five-year-old man with a semi-invalid wife and a twenty-year-old daughter to know he needed to have his affairs in order. From what I hear, he lived his entire life that way."

"I can't help but wonder," Linda said, "what it must have been like for a man like John Weaver—so quiet and private—closed, really—to know that someday Amy would be going through all the stuff he never discussed with her. That someone would be looking in all his personal affairs so closely."

"You mean there's more than just business files out in that office?"

"I don't know if there was a difference between business and personal for Mr. Weaver."

"Has she discussed any of this with you? Has anything more turned up about Anna?"

"Not really. She has said she wants to talk to the two of us whenever we could spare a few minutes."

"You got time now?" Jim asked.

"I guess so. I was going to tackle that pile of shirts over there, but you know me. Don't iron today what you can put off indefinitely."

"I'm free all morning," Jim said. "Mark is coming by later with the preliminary sketches for the new church. We can leave him a note. He won't mind coming over to Amy's to find us. He knew her dad, you know."

"He did?"

"From the building supply store."

"What does he say about John Weaver?"

"Not too much. Liked him though; he did say that much. I think he'd like a chance to extend his sympathies."

Jim and Linda found Amy engrossed in papers behind a stack of files waiting to be refiled and another waiting to be read. The long, narrow office took Jim by surprise. "I had no idea this was back here."

"It's where my father did most of his work."

"I thought he worked at the store," Jim said as he visually explored the room.

"Not for the last few years. He trusted Chet Ramsey completely. He had his office downtown, but when I left fo school . . . I think he liked being near Mama." Amy replaced one waiting stack of files, then motioned Jim and Linda to nearby chairs.

"Wow," Jim said again, "this really takes me by surprise."

"Yeah," Amy said smiling, "I guess it would." She followed Jim's gaze to the recliner chair and television set in the corner.

"I somehow got the idea that TV was something he didn't approve of," Jim said.

"No," Amy explained, "it was just something my mother didn't want in the house. He often teased her saying he had to watch TV outside like other men had to smoke their cigars. Whenever he wanted to watch something, he would say he was going out back for a smoke." Amy laughed softly. "It was a joke between them. Mama would say, 'Watch where you put the ashes. I don't mend burns.' "

"Linda tells me he left everything in pretty good order."

"More than pretty good, Jim. Perfect, in fact."

"That's good." Jim glanced at Linda, who frowned in his direction and nodded toward Amy. "I understand you wanted to talk to us. Is this a good time?"

"Oh, yes," she said, "it's a very good time. But am I keeping you from something?"

Linda avoided Jim's smile and quickly said, "A pile of shirts. I hate ironing with a passion, so it's perfect. You've saved me."

"I've discovered some interesting things going through my father's files," Amy began. "This office has been locked ever since he died. Mr. Carlson had to get something one time, but Mama just gave him the key. She couldn't bring herself to come out with him. We were planning to do this together on my Christmas vacation. She was sure she could manage it by then."

"What can I help you with? You know," Jim said, "I'm not a lawyer or financial advisor or anything like that."

"No, Jim. I think this comes under pastoral counseling or ministerial advice. You see, in this last week I've discovered that my father was worth much more than I thought. There's several pieces of real estate I didn't even know he owned. And now this is what I need to ask you about. He had made several donation pledges that haven't been paid—because he died before he could do that. I'd like to make good on those pledges, of course. But do you think that's okay? I mean, why shouldn't I?"

"Can you be more specific?" Jim asked.

"My mother was an avid reader. She ordered books by the dozens each year. Some she kept, and others she donated to the library. You know, they wanted her to serve on some sort of advisory board or council—I had the letter here, somewhere—here it is, see?"

Jim examined the letter from the librarian, then turned to the reply stapled on the back. Scanning it, he handed it to Linda.

"Why did your father refuse to let her?"

"Oh, he didn't refuse. She refused. It was her decision. I remember her asking him to write a letter in her behalf. He never refused her anything. This was her decision, I'm sure of it."

"But this looks like—"

"I know what it looks like. I'm sure my mother had no idea that it would put my father in a bad light. But, I assure you, he didn't make her decisions for her. Anyone who thinks that didn't know my mother very well. She was perfectly capable of making up her own mind—and did."

"But then, why?"

"Because she knew if they got a letter from Daddy, they wouldn't be apt to ask again. She was right. They didn't." Amy replaced the letter in the appropriate file. "Anyway, that's not the point. My father pledged a large amount to the new wing at the library. See?" Amy produced another letter on the library's letterhead.

"So, what's the problem?" Jim asked.

"Marshall."

"Marshall?" Jim tried to sound surprised.

"Marsh thinks that what my father pledged has nothing to do with me. He came right out and said they couldn't make me pay it, and he didn't think I should. He stated that if I was determined, I should wait until after we were married, then make a much smaller donation. 'After all,' he says, 'we have a life to think of now, too.' "

"I see," Jim said thoughtfully.

"Have you set the date?" Linda asked.

"No," Amy said. "And Marsh is furious. He can't understand why I just don't sell everything, put the money in the bank, and run off and get married."

"In a joint account, of course." Jim's comment was barely audible.

"Run off? Oh, Amy, you mean elope?" Linda sounded panicky.

"That doesn't sound like a real Jennings family wedding to me," Jim said.

"It isn't," Amy replied. "That's why I'm . . . well, let's just say I'm tired of having all these second thoughts."

"Hallelujah!" Jim said, barely under his breath.

"You mean about the elopement? I should hope so," Linda quickly added. "You should have a wonderful and grand wedding." Her eyes shone with excitement. "Amy, you'll make such a beautiful bride."

"No," Amy said, studying her hands now nervously twisting a paper clip into a straight piece of wire. "I don't have anything against a small, private ceremony. Without my parents—"

"Oh, Amy! I'm sorry. I didn't think . . ." Linda quickly slipped an arm around her friend's shoulder.

"Linda," Amy said quietly, "Jim . . . I've decided not to marry Marshall Jennings at all."

"Are you sure?" Jim asked.

"Yes, very." Amy stood and walked to stand behind her father's recliner chair.

"Can you tell me why?" Jim inquired.

"Because it was a mistake from the beginning. I rushed into this—I don't know, perhaps it was because I knew that someday I'd have to face this." She glanced around at her father's files and papers. "Maybe it was just easier to say yes than to say no. Marshall can be very persuasive."

She caressed the well-worn place where her father had, no doubt, taken many Sunday naps while a football game was in progress on the small TV. "Daddy always said, 'If in doubt, don't.' He believed that a good decision today is a good decision tomorrow. He often said that the best, most important decisions of all are not usually harmed by a thoughtful delay."

"I wish I had known him better," Jim said.

"He didn't let too many people know him, Jim. Mama knew him better than anyone. I learned most of what I know of him from her." Amy searched for the right words to tell Jim and Linda the rest.

"Is there something else?" Jim urged.

"Yes," Amy said softly. "I'm ashamed to admit it, but as much as it appears Marshall was using me, I think I was also using him."

"I don't follow," Linda said, wrinkling her nose. "You were using Marshall?"

"Kind of a safety net, I guess you could say."

"Keeping you out of circulation?" Jim asked.

"Something like that," Amy admitted. "I didn't see it until—well, let's just say I have a very perceptive roommate."

"And how will you break this news to Marshall?" Linda asked.

"Straight out would be my guess," Jim said.

"That would be best, wouldn't it?" Amy said, more than asked.

The sudden sound of a knock on the door and the squeak of a rusty hinge made them all turn their heads. "Hello!" Mark Andrews stuck his head through the partially open door. "Your note said you'd be here."

"Mark! I'll be right with you," Jim responded. "Amy, listen, give this some more thought. Let me pray about it, okay? Marshall Jennings isn't about to be put off because you have a feeling or even a doubtful intuition. You may have very good reason for your decision. If you don't rush it, that reason may be made very clear to you. Okay? Can you give it some time?"

"Yes, of course," Amy said before she walked to the doorway to greet Mark Andrews. "Mr. Andrews, please come in. I haven't seen you since—well, when was the last time I saw you?"

"At your father's funeral, Amy. And, may I say, I'm terribly sorry to hear about your mother. No one can possibly know what this means to you."

"I'm sure you can, Mr. Andrews. It must be difficult for you, even now. I mean, of course, about your son. We were all shocked by the news of Michael's death."

"Did you know his wife was expecting a baby when he died?"

"I did hear something about that. Karissa's remarried, isn't she?"

"Yes, and I couldn't be happier about it. She married Holden Kelley. Your father knew him. A landscape architect here in town. And little Katie, my grandbaby. Here, I carry a picture. Would you like to see?" Mark didn't wait for Amy's response. By the time his question was out of his mouth, Hope Kathleen's picture was out of his wallet.

"Then, you're still close to your daughter-in-law?"

"Very. I'm Katie's godfather in addition to being her grandpa. She's sort of got me coming and going."

"Ruined him completely," Linda laughed, "winding him around her little finger like she does. Mark Andrews is a man without a spine when it comes to that little charmer."

"I'm sorry," Mark said, nodding toward the stacks of files on John Weaver's desk. "I'm interrupting."

"Not at all," Amy replied. "Please, it's nice to see you."

"We—all of us in the building trade here in Summerwind, especially—we sure miss running into your father down at the store. He was a very respected man, Amy. But then, I'm sure you knew that."

"Thank you, Mr. Andrews."

"Are you going to take up where he left off?"

"No one can do that," Amy said. "Anyway, I'm just trying to find out where that is." She motioned toward the stack of files.

"Saw that young fiancé of yours at the planning commission meeting last night. I was sorry to hear that you're planning to sell the downtown properties so soon." Mark leaned against the doorframe. Somehow, Amy Weaver wasn't at all what he expected—at least, not from the picture Marshall Jennings painted of her.

"Marshall was there?"

"Oh, yes. And fully representing your interests."

"My interests?"

"Excuse me, Amy," Mark said. "I thought he was speaking for you."

"No, he wasn't. I've not authorized anyone other than Mr. Carlson to represent me or my father's interests in anything."

"I feel I've talked out of turn," Mark said apologetically, then cast a look in Jim's direction.

"I don't think so," Jim said. "After all, the meetings are public, are they not?"

Mark nodded.

"Well, then, what was on the agenda last night?"

"The downtown shopping mall."

"What downtown shopping mall?" Amy asked.

"You don't know?" Mark asked in reply to her question.

"No, I don't. But I have a very strong impression that I should, don't you, Jim?"

"Mark Andrews, once again you may be the answer to my prayers," Jim said. "Can you spare a little time—and perhaps a ton of information for Amy?"

Seven

During the next few weeks, Amy found herself comforted by spending her morning hours in her father's office. For the moment, Anna's story was put aside as Amy methodically approached her father's files. His penchant for perfect order began to reveal to Amy the serious manner in which he perceived his accountability for his wealth. She began to be drawn to the office earlier each day until by mid-November, she was out there most mornings by five-thirty or six and staying until almost lunchtime.

Princess had settled into the daily routine with Amy, eager to take her morning naps luxuriating in John Weaver's recliner.

Amy reached for the files in the section marked "L." "We're almost halfway there," she said to Princess. Each day had held a few surprises along with the usual collection of receipts, owner's manuals, and various notes penned in her father's familiar scrawl. When she discovered her father's donation receipts were almost always accompanied with annual reports, it became clear to Amy that he tried his best to put his money where it would do the most good and where administration costs were kept to a minimum. Missions, orphanages, and even art museums had benefited from John's systematic generosity. Various hospitals and libraries were also included in John's list of worthy recipients.

"Lander's Landscaping," she announced to an uninterested Princess. "My gosh, here are the landscaping records and receipts for the fountain area behind the library. These papers are ten years old. He never threw anything out."

Amy poured herself another cup of coffee, leaned back in the office chair, and carefully opened the next file. "Leder's Floral Company," she said. Princess, used to Amy's musings by now, napped contentedly, perhaps even comforted by the sound of Amy's occasional comment. "Look here—receipts for flowers." Amy leafed carefully through the thick stack of monthly invoices. "This looks like a standing order, Princess," she said, glancing at the sleeping dog. "As if you care." She smiled at her little companion. "Wait a minute," she said, leaning forward for a closer look. "It *is* a standing order. The last date on these papers is the week just before Daddy died. Somebody's not getting their flowers anymore. I wonder who that is . . ." Amy stood and walked to the window to look out at her mother's fruit trees, now bare. "There's only one way to find out," she said decisively, crossing the room and dialing the phone number on the invoices.

"Good morning, Leder's Floral," the cheerful female voice said on the other end of the line.

"Good morning," Amy responded. "My name is Amy Weaver, I'm calling about the account of John Weaver, my father."

"Well, yes, Miss Weaver, good morning. This is Mrs. Willis. How can I help you?"

"I've been going through my father's files and have come across the standing order for flowers he kept at your shop—"

"Yes," the woman said, "as long as I've been here, we've sent those flowers each month. On the third, if I'm not mistaken. Well, not anymore. Not since Mr. Weaver passed away. And," the woman continued, "I'm so sorry to hear about your mother, Miss Weaver."

"Thank you," Amy said. "Could I renew that standing order for my father?"

"Of course, dear," the woman said. "Let's see here, roses and glads in season, pink and white if I recall. Let me see— yes, here it is. Yes, roses and glads—is that what you'd like?"

"Whatever my father ordered," Amy said.

"On the third of each month?"

"Yes."

"And sent to the cemetery—let's see—to *Baby Anna?*"

"Mrs. Willis," Amy said, struggling to keep her voice even, "I'd like to take them myself."

"On the third?"

"No," Amy said quickly, "I don't want to wait until the third of next month. I've missed several months already. Could I come by and pick them up today?"

"Of course, dear. After lunch sometime?"

"Yes, thank you." Amy glanced at the clock. Eleven-thirty. She had time to change and talk to Linda before going downtown. "And, Mrs. Willis, will you please look up delivery instructions? I mean, can you tell me exactly where they have been delivered before?"

"I'll have it all ready for you, say, about one-fifteen, one-thirty?"

"Thank you." Amy hung up the phone and glanced toward the little dog, now suddenly wide awake. "It's Anna, Princess. I think we've found her!"

"Who was that?" Marshall's voice took Amy off guard.

"Marshall, I didn't hear you come in," Amy said just as Princess sprang from the chair barking ferociously. "Hush, Princess," she ordered.

"That dog has the most annoying yap I've ever heard," Marshall complained.

"What are you doing here?" Amy asked after she let Princess out into the yard.

"I came by to see you, of course," he remarked. "After all, a man has a right to see his fiancée, doesn't he?"

Amy's insides tightened.

"I had some free time, so I decided to take you to lunch."

"I wish you had called."

"Don't tell me you prefer to stay cooped up out here like this over going to lunch with me." Amy detected a tone of arrogant teasing in his voice.

"I've made some plans for early this afternoon." Of all times for him to arrive unannounced. Amy wasn't about to be deterred from her afternoon delivery errand.

"Cancel them." Marshall grabbed her arm and pulled her against his body. "It's time you and I had some quality time together." He crushed her tighter and tried to force a kiss on her mouth.

"Marsh," she said turning her face from his kiss, "you've caught me at a really bad time." Thinking fast, she tried another approach. "Can't we have dinner or something? I mean, look at me. I'm not ready to go anywhere looking like this." Amy gestured toward her jeans and cotton shirt.

"You look all right to me. We don't have to go anyplace where people would see us. We could have lunch here, or if you're afraid of being alone with me, we can just go get a burger. Or, I could wait while you change. . . ."

Amy didn't like the tone of his voice or the smoldering look in his eyes. Taking a step back, she managed to free herself from his embrace. "Not today, Marsh. I already have plans. How about tomorrow?"

"I thought you said dinner," he said, letting his glance wander over the files on John's desk.

"Well, I know, but I'm not sure when I'll be getting home. I've still got work to do out here and—"

"What's this?" he asked, lifting the Leder's file from the desk.

"Marshall, don't." Amy tried to reach the file but with a swift movement, Marshall swung it out of her reach. "Please, it's personal," she said.

"Personal?" he asked, keeping her at a distance with one hand and opening the file with the other.

"Marsh, please. This isn't any of your business." Amy's throat began to tighten with anger and her eyes filled with tears.

"Anything that concerns you is my business," he said bluntly while glancing toward the insides of the thick folder.

"This doesn't," she said. "It concerned my father."

"Oh, I see." He ignored her and looked closer inside the file. "Flowers. Each month. Hey, did your father have someone on the side?"

"How dare you suggest such a thing!" she said, flinging herself toward the file folder and knocking the contents from his hand all over the floor. Quickly falling to her knees, she began to gather the cherished remnants of the once orderly file.

"My, my," Marshall mused, reading one of the invoices. "Are there more skeletons in the perfect Weaver closet?"

"Stop it!" Amy cried. "Stop it this minute!"

"Tell me, Amy, what do you know about all this?"

"These were flowers sent to the cemetery each month for my sister's grave. Now leave this alone."

"So, now you've arranged to have them sent again. Come on, Amy—"

"You heard!" Amy said, her tears flowing unchecked down both cheeks. "You stood right there and eavesdropped."

"You don't even know there was a sister for sure."

"I do so. Mama said—"

"A baby that died before you were even born? Come on, Amy. Your mother was half out of it when she told you that. Even if it were true, I don't understand what that has to do with you now."

"No, I didn't expect you to."

"Listen to me, Amy." Marshall's voice was forceful and firm. "Leave this alone, do you hear me? This has nothing to do with you. It's in the past. Whatever was between your parents is between them still. Let this die with them. Everyone's entitled to their secrets. Why pry into this now?"

"Funny you should say that—" She wiped her eyes with her shirt sleeve.

"Excuse me?"

"No, Marshall, I won't excuse you. You say everyone is entitled to their privacy—then give me mine! Leave me alone. Leave my father's papers alone. Get out of his office. Go on, get out."

Amy physically shoved Marshall toward the office door. "I want you to leave me alone. This is my family, my business. Get out of here." Even Amy was surprised at the angry loudness of her voice.

Marshall spun around and grabbed Amy by the shoulders. "You want me to get out? Don't do this, Amy." Marshall shouted close to her face.

"Do what?" Amy shot back.

"Don't do something you might be sorry for later. How long do you think you can push me around? I'll only take so much from you."

"You'll only take so much from *me?*" Amy's whole body began to shake with anger. Her voice rose to a fevered pitch. "*I'm* the one who's done all the taking, Marshall. *You're* the one pressuring and prodding. You're the one who's shoving and pushing. No, Marshall Jennings, you've got this all wrong. *I'm* the one who's not going to take any more. Listen, you want to know why I won't marry you right away? You wonder why I won't run off and get married like you want?"

"Amy don't. Maybe I was too hasty. Listen, honey, calm down. Okay, we won't have lunch today. Maybe I've been too—" Marshall lowered his voice, trying to calm her.

"No, it's time I told you. It's past time, in fact. I've waited too long as it is. I just wanted some time to think through everything."

Marshall backed toward the door, trying to postpone Amy's emotional announcement. "Amy, this isn't a good time. I've interfered and I'm sorry. Don't say anything you haven't thought through, okay? Listen, honey—"

"No, Marsh. I have to tell you—and I have to do it now. I don't want to be—"

"Married right away, okay. I hear you. You want to give it a little time. Maybe that's best. After all you've been through—"

"Don't finish my sentences for me! You always assume that you know what I'm going to say!" She almost spat the words in his face.

"I'm sorry, sweetheart," he said apologetically. "I just don't want you to do or say anything you'll be sorry for later. Please, Amy, listen to me."

"No, Marshall, it won't work." Amy took a deep breath and then quietly continued. "I don't want to marry you now—and I don't want to marry you later. In fact, I don't want to marry you at all."

"Amy, don't. Give this some time. Give us some time. This is not a good decision. Believe me, this is not a good thing—"

"For who, Marsh? Me? You're wrong. I think this is very good for me."

Marshall dropped into a nearby chair. "I can't believe you said that. In fact, I think I'll just overlook the fact that you did." His voice was soft and his eyes searched Amy's, apparently hoping to find something to tell him that she didn't mean what she had just said. There was nothing in her eyes to tell him she was anything but serious. "You don't mean this. Really, you don't."

"Let's face it, shall we?" she said coming closer, hoping he would be able to see her point. "I've had second thoughts about us almost from the beginning. We're not in love, Marsh. Don't you see that?"

"That's not true!" he protested.

"It is," she said simply.

"I won't let it end like this," he said between clenched teeth.

"You don't have any choice," she said matter-of-factly.

"Give this some more thought," he begged.

"No. I've made my decision."

"Then, give me some time to think it through. Time to—"

"To what? I've made this decision myself. It's over, Marshall."

"No," he repeated. "No, it can't be."

"It is." Her words held a ring of finality.

"Amy, please." Marshall's frightened tone of voice surprised Amy. She had never heard him any other way than confident—even arrogant.

Amy stood and straightened herself to her full five feet six and tossed her long hair behind one shoulder. "I have business to attend to, Marsh. Please, will you go now?"

"Can we talk later?" he asked meekly.

"I don't think so."

"Just to talk, Amy. Please. Toss me out—but please, don't slam the door."

"I want you to go now," she said firmly.

"Amy—"

"I think you heard her." Mark Andrews' voice carried clearly through the doorway, cutting Marshall Jennings' pleading off midsentence.

"Stay out of this, Andrews," Marshall warned. "This is none of your business."

"Well, I've just made it my business," Mark said. "Is that all right with you, Miss Weaver?"

Amy nodded her head and motioned for him to step inside.

"This is between you and me, Amy," Marshall insisted.

"Not anymore," she said. "Please, Marsh—"

"The young lady is asking you to leave, Jennings."

"Amy," Marshall said as he walked quickly toward the door. "This isn't finished—not by a long shot. I *will* be getting back in touch with you. Count on it."

"Marshall!" she called out, stopping him before he could exit the office doorway. As he turned around to face her, she slowly removed the diamond solitaire from her finger.

"No—I don't want it—not yet." Marshall's face registered his personal pain.

"Take it," she insisted.

"No."

"She said take it." Mark Andrews' voice thickened with authority. "Do as she says."

Marshall snatched the ring from Amy's outstretched hand, turned, and quickly left the office. Amy waited while Marshall took long, swift strides down the driveway, got into his car, and backed out into the street. Slumping into her father's desk chair, she put her forehead down on her arms and wept openly.

"You all right?" Mark asked after a few minutes.

Amy raised her face to meet his gaze, her eyes red from crying. "I'll be okay. It's just that . . ." Her voiced trailed off. "How did you? I mean, where did you—?"

"I came by to talk to Jim and I heard your voices. You were really having a go at it. I was afraid that he might—" Mark didn't finish the sentence but turned away from Amy's tear-streaked face and walked across the room. "I can't stand the thought of a man—" Mark gazed out the window, his back to Amy. After a moment, he turned and looked at her, his face filled with compassion and pain. "Amy, did you know my son?" he asked.

"Michael? I knew who he was, Mr. Andrews. Everyone did. He was one of the popular crowd. But I didn't know him—not really." Amy reached for a tissue and blew her nose. Then with another she wiped her eyes.

"Did you know he beat Karissa up the night he died?" Mark asked.

Amy couldn't miss the pain in his voice. "I heard the rumor."

"It wasn't a rumor. I turned my back on what he was doing to Kassy. I won't ever make that mistake again."

"Oh, Mr. Andrews," Amy said, coming to stand facing him. "I'm so sorry."

"You've nothing to be sorry about, Amy. I'm the one with a lifetime of regrets. You're young, with your whole life ahead of you. I'm just glad I came by when I did. I may be sticking my nose in where it doesn't belong—"

"Please, Mr. Andrews, I'm glad you're here."

"Well, I know it may not feel like it right now, but I think you're better off without that—well, without being married to Marshall Jennings."

"Me too," she said. "I've known it for some time. He had no way of knowing, but this was about to happen sooner or later. It's just that today . . . well, he sort of forced it and it happened sooner." Amy Weaver's clear blue eyes clouded again with tears. "You've had a lot of pain in your life, too, haven't you?"

Mark nodded. "You too," he said with tender softness.

Amy's tears washed down her face and Mark opened his arms. "Come here, young lady. I think you need a hug."

Without reservation, Amy welcomed Mark's fatherly, though awkward, embrace.

"Will the pain ever go away?" she asked, pulling away.

"Probably not," he said simply. "But you'll learn to live with it. To balance it out somehow."

"Have you?" she asked.

"Some of the time," he answered. "Most of the time, in fact."

"How did you do it?"

"I had the help of some good friends. Jim and Linda. Kassy and Holden. And Mattie. Sweet Mattie." Mark smiled with appreciation for his church and family. "You know, Amy. You need friends, too. This is too hard to go through alone. Don' t you have some family somewhere?"

"No, I'm the only one left."

"Well then, would you like Kassy to call you? I know she'd

like to. She's been asking about you ever since she found out I met you that day over at Jim and Linda's."

"I'd like that," Amy said. "I really would. Linda's being really great. But I've already taken up too much of her time. I know she's busy."

"I haven't heard her complain," Mark said, "have you?"

"No," Amy said. "It's just that I was so used to being alone—I'm afraid I've latched on to her too much."

"You're too young for that," Mark said. "Much too young. Listen," he said, glancing at his watch, "I've got to go, but I think you need to tell Jim and Linda what happened here today, okay?"

"Yeah, I will. I'll tell them later this afternoon. I'm going out to the cemetery, but when I get back, I promise, I'll drop in on them and tell them what happened."

"You going out there alone? Is that a good idea?"

"It's okay, I'm taking flowers. I'll be fine." Amy didn't want to explain to Mark about the flowers, especially when she didn't have the full explanation herself. Later. She'd explain later to Jim and Linda and maybe even Mark Andrews—if he cared to listen.

Eight

A little after four, Amy turned the Weaver family car between the large gated stone pillars and drove slowly along the winding, tree-lined street directly to the cemetery office. Pulling to the curb, she took a deep breath before opening the door and getting out of the car. She searched inside herself for the determination she knew she needed to get the answers she so desperately wanted. Somehow the thought of her sister helped stem her loneliness. Even though she never knew Anna, she missed her almost as much as she missed her parents. *I wish they had told me*, she thought. *I wish I had known sooner.*

"Oh, my dear," the gentle elderly lady said hurriedly to Amy as she stepped inside the small office, "you almost missed me. I was just about to leave. Is that a delivery you're making? Couldn't this have waited until morning?"

"I'm sorry, I didn't realize," Amy mumbled, turning to leave. "I can come back tomorrow."

"Oh no, dear," the woman apologized. "I'm the one who's sorry. Now let me help you. What is the name?" On the tag perched among the roses were the same familiar words the lady had seen once a month for the several years she had worked at the cemetery. "Oh, Baby Anna. You know, I wondered what happened. All the time I've been here, flowers arrived each month. Then all of a sudden, nothing. Made me feel kind of sad. Let's see, here we are. The Morgan plot. You go right out this door," she said pointing to a detailed map posted on the wall, "and it's only a few places down the path on the right. Here," the woman offered, walking ahead of Amy toward the door. "Let me show you."

Amy followed obediently and walked behind the small, brisk woman toward the spot where her sister was buried.

"Isn't it beautiful here this time of day?" the woman chattered. "It's my favorite part of the day. The shadows stretch across the lawn and the headstones shine so brightly in the afternoon sun. Here we are," she said cheerfully. "Baby Anna. You can put the flowers in the container there." She pointed to a permanent vase built into the small granite marker. "They only last a day or two, but it's the remembering that counts, don't you think?"

Amy stood quietly holding the flowers, almost afraid to step on the soft grass near the small grave.

"My goodness me," said the woman. "Look at the time. I must run. If there's nothing else I can do for you . . ."

"No, this is fine. Thank you." Amy couldn't tear her eyes from the small grave. "Can I stay here a few minutes longer?"

"Of course." Amy felt the woman pat her arm. "The caretaker closes up at five-thirty, though. He'll see your car. Don't you worry; Smitty's never locked anyone in overnight yet. It is kind of heartrending, isn't it? I mean a little baby and all. How sad. I am curious, though," the lady said. "I mean, after all these years. Many of our—well, some of the graves go unattended year after year. But not this one. Each and every month, year after year, the flowers came. Is this someone you know?"

"My sister," Amy whispered.

"I see," the lady said softly. "Well, then, honey, you take all the time you need. You've not been here much, have you?"

Amy shook her head.

"I didn't think so. I would have noticed."

"Why is she buried here?" Amy asked before the woman could leave.

"Pardon me?"

"Why is she buried here in this place?" Amy looked around and made note of the distance between her parents and their firstborn daughter.

"She was here first," the woman said. "I was kind of curious about that myself. It was my guess she was an only child. The Morgans died several years later. See, Mrs. Morgan first, then several years later, Dr. Morgan."

"But she's not a—"

"Oh my. I do have to run. If you have any more questions, please don't hesitate to come by the office another time."

Amy watched through blurring tears as the woman re-treated back into the office. Standing in the long shadows, she remained motionless for several minutes before slowly making her way closer to the small granite block marking her sister's life and death. *Baby Anna*, the stone said simply. *April Third, Nineteen Hundred and Thirty-Seven.*

Kneeling in the grass beside the cold stone, Amy carefully placed the flowers in the waiting receptacle. Silently, she let the tears fall down her cheeks and spill on the grass-covered earth separating her from her sister.

"Amy?" It was Linda's voice calling softly from several feet away. "Amy?"

"Linda? How'd you find me?" Then without waiting for an answer she added, "You saw Mark?"

Linda nodded.

"Look, Linda. Here she is." Amy's voice was thick and heavy. "Here is my sister."

Linda took a few steps closer, then hesitated briefly. "Oh, Amy," she said, closing the distance between them. Kneeling beside her friend, she slipped her arm around Amy's shoulder.

"I don't understand," Amy said finally. "I just don't understand it at all. Mama and I were so close. She told me everything. I just can't believe she didn't tell me about her. I had a right to know. She's my sister."

"Come on, Amy," Linda urged. "It's getting late. Maybe we should go."

"Linda," Amy said, "walk with me over to where my parents are." Amy stood, then turned, waiting for Linda. "Please," she begged.

"Sure."

Linda came alongside the tall, beautiful girl and took her hand as they walked together. Beside the graves of John and Charlotte, Amy was again overwhelmed by grief. And, once again, Linda slipped her arm around Amy's shoulder and let her cry.

Suddenly Amy grew still and thoughtful. Straightening her

shoulders, she turned to Linda and said, "I want them all together. How do I get Anna moved over here?"

"I have no idea," Linda answered. "But I'm sure if there is a way Jim will know about it. Let's go home now and ask him, shall we?" Linda gently guided Amy around and back toward the path leading past Anna's grave and out to the cars.

"Wait," Amy said, pausing once again to adjust the flowers at Anna's grave. "I'll be back, Anna," she said aloud. "I don't want you over here with strangers all by yourself. You need to be with Mama and Daddy."

"Come on, Amy," Linda said gently. "I think they're waiting for us to leave so they can lock the gates."

———

"You should have seen her," Linda told Jim and Mark Andrews a little later. "It's so sad." Linda picked up the dishes from the table. "More pie? How about you, Mark. More coffee?"

"A little coffee, maybe," Mark said rubbing his stomach. "But no more pie, please. You'll make me fat yet."

"Don't blame me," Linda called over her shoulder as she left the two men at the dining room table. "This is Mattie's fault. She's forever making us pies, cookies, and bread. If you ask me, I think she's trying to put a little meat on Jim."

"What do you think, Mark?" Jim asked thoughtfully when he knew Linda was unable to hear him. "It just seems so drastic, moving a grave site."

"She may think better of it as time goes on," Mark said. "But I don't know. If I put myself in her place, I might want my family all together too. I know, I know," he said, holding up his hand in response to Jim's protest. "But think about it, Jim. We have no idea of what this is like for Amy. The only family she had in the whole world is gone. She's all alone now. What in the world must that feel like? Do you know? Do I? Even after Michael's death, I had Karissa and then Katie. I can't imagine being so alone."

"But the Lord can—"

"Oh, yes. He surely can," Mark interrupted his young pastor friend. "You and I know that. But we can't assume that

Amy does. Not at this point. And really, Jim, how can we address her spiritual needs when her emotional needs are so overwhelming?"

"What are you two in such deep conversation about?" Linda teased as she poured fresh coffee into waiting cups.

"Needs," Jim said. "Overwhelming needs."

"Amy will want to know what you two think about the idea of moving Anna's grave," Mark said to the young couple. Linda shifted uncomfortably in her chair and glanced across the table at her husband.

"Jim?" she asked. "Do we even know what we think about this?"

"Honey," Jim said, "I'm at a total loss on this one. What do you think?"

"I think there is nothing more than a little bundle of dead bones in that grave. There's no life there. We know that. But . . ." Linda hesitated.

"But what?" Jim asked, encouraging his wife to continue.

"It's just that maybe it's not what's in the grave that's so important to Amy, but what it represents." Linda shifted herself to rest her chin in her hand. "She has no one. No uncles, no aunts, or cousins. No brothers or sisters. No one."

"And now with her broken engagement," Mark offered.

"What?" Jim's expression clearly registered his shocked surprise.

"I guess I didn't tell you. Well, earlier today, I dropped by to show you these latest changes on the church sketches. You know, I wanted you to see them before I took them back to the architect. And as I was coming up the drive, I could hear an argument coming from over at Amy's place. She was out in her father's office and had most of the windows open. I, well, I wandered on over just in case she couldn't handle things on her own. You know, I—"

"You heard a damsel in distress," Linda winked at Mark.

"And?" Jim insisted. "Go on."

"And she told him to leave, that she didn't want to marry him. He was not about to let her off so easy. Poor guy. He still hasn't a clue that she's questioning his real motivations."

"Real motivations?" Linda asked, looking to Mark then to Jim for an explanation.

"Well, honey," Jim said, "the awful truth is, Marshall Jennings needs the Weaver properties downtown to put together the deal on the downtown shopping mall. He's made some pretty bold statements that Mark overheard."

"No kidding?" Linda began to press a crease in her napkin with her thumbnail. "No wonder."

"And," Mark added, "without that property, the shopping mall is a dead issue, at least for the time being."

"Or they could choose a different location," Jim said.

"Not too likely," Mark continued. "A lot of study has gone into finding the precise location that would enhance the mall's chances for success and make the most desirable impact on the downtown area. She's sitting on a premium piece of land."

"What was her father's position on the shopping mall?" Jim asked.

"Cautiously optimistic, in my opinion. It was pretty hard to read John Weaver. Until he took a firm stand, no one ever quite knew for sure." Mark leaned forward in his chair. "You know, there's something else that's been bothering me. I know that while John was alive his lawyer worked in his best interests. I'd hate to see that change now."

"You think someone could get to him?"

"I'm just hoping it hasn't happened already." Mark scooted his chair back and stood up. "I need to let you two have the rest of the evening to yourselves. I've had a busy day and I'm bushed."

"Mark," Jim said thoughtfully as they walked to the front door, "would you be willing to approach this subject with Amy?"

"You know I have an interest in that shopping mall going through, don't you, Jim?"

"I know you have an honest interest in both the mall project and in Amy's best interests."

"I'd have to tell her my position," Mark said.

"I'd prefer that you did," Jim responded. "The sooner the better."

"My heart goes out to that young woman," Mark Andrews said.

"I know that," Jim answered. "In fact, I'm counting on that fact."

"You know, Jim," Mark added, thrusting his hands in his pockets, "about moving that grave. Maybe it would help her— maybe she needs some way to communicate the fact that she knows about Anna—oh, I don't know. Maybe I'm just guessing. But it seems to me that grief is something you don't just go through. It's more like something you work through. Maybe this is a part of that process. Taking initiative, making a decision all on her own. She has no answers about Anna, and now with their deaths she never will. Maybe this is her way of making peace with that. Perhaps by reburying her sister, she will be able to bury the unanswered questions."

Linda was listening from the other side of the room. "I think that may be true, Mark. But I also saw the look on her face as she measured the distance between the graves. Somehow there is something that she needs—and now I'm just guessing—but it seems to me that wanting to have them all together may be connected to her own feelings of separation and loneliness."

"Boy," Mark said, "you may be right at that."

"I think you're both on to something," Jim said. "It's hard to evaluate the deep needs of the human heart, isn't it?"

"More than you know," Mark said quietly, then turned and walked out into the dark evening.

"He's alone, too," Linda commented, watching Mark cross the front lawn and get into his car parked at the curb. "I wish he could find someone—you know—I just can't stand it knowing people we really care about are so lonely."

"I love you, Linda Henry," Jim said wrapping his wife tightly in his arm. "And one of the things I love about you most is the way you love other people. You're one of the most wonderful people I've ever known."

"Only one?" Linda teased. "Who's the other?"

Jim didn't answer, but instead pulled her even closer and ended the conversation with a tender kiss.

Nine

Linda got up at four-thirty and prepared a sack lunch for Jim to take with him on the construction job he was doing for Mark. "I don't know why you guys have to start so early," she said between yawns.

"It's not that early. Don't forget my coffee jug, okay?" Jim called from the bathroom. "Besides, by the time I get out of here, it will be nearly five." He came into the warm kitchen smelling of soap and shaving lotion. "You seem a little sleepy this morning."

"Morning? It's still the middle of the night."

Jim peered through the sheer curtains gathered generously at the window over the kitchen sink. "Hey, Amy's lights are on," he commented.

"They've probably been on all night. Maybe she just left them on for comfort—you know, it must be pretty quiet in that house all alone."

"She's up," Jim said. "She's moving around in the kitchen."

"I think I'll slip into my jeans and go on over when you leave. Maybe she'd like some company."

"Why not just call her on the phone?" Jim asked innocently.

"Adele Jennings, that's why," Linda yawned.

"I don't understand."

"She's been calling. Amy finally took her phone off the hook. Seems Adele can't understand why anyone would throw her darling little boy overboard."

"If you ask me, she's as much a part of this as Marshall is. He strikes me as being pretty much his mama's puppet."

———

"What are you doing up so early?" Linda asked when Amy responded to her light knock at the back door.

"I couldn't sleep. Something's not right. I'm so confused, Linda. I think I could shake my father for doing this to me."

"Doing what?"

"Look here, everything he ever touched is in perfect order. His clothes are in perfect order, even his car maintenance records are flawless. Both his personal and business records are meticulous. It's been interesting to go behind him and be able to see not just what he did but why. I think I know him better today than I ever have. And, in some ways, I'm even closer to him than ever. But . . ." Amy hesitated as if trying to unravel a puzzle, "but I can't understand how someone so detailed and perfectly ordered could leave out this whole thing about Anna as if she never existed."

"Oh, Amy."

"Every day I'm more confused about this than ever." Amy slumped heavily into a nearby kitchen chair. "Linda, look at this and tell me—what do you make of this?" Amy slid a thick folder across the table at her friend. "Can you make heads or tails of any of this?"

Linda carefully opened the folder marked *Morningside Home* and began leafing through the papers inside. Work orders, repair records, and cash donations were carefully noted, detailing the generosity of John Weaver. Suddenly Linda turned over the last of the papers and her eyes fell on a group of snapshots carefully organized and fastened to loose pages from a scrapbook or photo album.

"I know," Linda said slowly, "that Morningside Home is a group home for mentally retarded people. You can see by this picture that this person is obviously one of the residents. What's so strange about that?"

"Keep looking," Amy said.

"Okay," Linda answered. "But I'd really like you to tell me what I'm looking for. Is there something that's supposed to just leap out at me here?"

"It's all the same person. These pictures are all of the same person. Look, there's more," Amy said, pointing to several more pages beneath the one Linda was examining. "From the time this person was little, until when—now? And why? Why only this one person?"

"Do you think your father could have had a favorite at the home?" Linda asked.

"That's what it looks like to me," Amy said. "And look, see this picture? I remember Mama asking if I'd like to give some of my toys to little children who didn't have any. We did that maybe once or twice a year. Once she asked me if I would give up a favorite rag doll. I couldn't do it. The next year she again asked about that doll—I just couldn't part with it. Daddy gave it to me. And look here—right here, this child is clutching a doll *exactly like mine.*"

"Amy," Linda said coming to sit nearer her friend, "is this a surprise to you? I mean, that your father took interest in one of the children in the home?"

"He just never mentioned it, that's all."

"But was that out of character for him? I'm sorry, Amy. Please don't think I'm talking harshly about your father, but I don't ever recall him being a very talkative man. Am I wrong about that?"

"No." Amy rubbed her forehead. "No, you're not wrong. As I've said, I'm learning more about him going through his papers and files than I ever would have known about him through conversation. I guess Mama told me more about what Daddy thought and felt than Daddy ever did."

"Do you think she knew about this?"

"I have no idea. She loved and trusted him so completely. She talked as though she knew him through and through. I still have no reason to doubt that she did—but I didn't; that's for sure."

Linda looked closer at the picture of the strange child with the doll and noticed that one of the gummed corners that secured the picture was loose. Absentmindedly, she slipped her fingernail beneath another corner, then another, until the picture came loose from its page. As she held it up for closer scrutiny, Amy gasped.

"Amy?" Linda looked at her companion. The color drained completely from Amy's face.

"My God! Oh, dear God!" Amy stared at the back of the photograph in Linda's hands.

"What's the matter?" Linda asked.

Amy could only cover her mouth with one hand and point at the photograph with the other.

Slowly, Linda turned the photo over and stared at the two startling words written across the back. *Anna Weaver.* "What?" Linda jumped to her feet and started pacing the kitchen floor. "Okay, now, there's got to be some explanation for this." Turning, Linda looked with concern at Amy. "Now, Amy, listen to me. There's a reason—I mean, there's just got to be a simple explanation." Linda continued to pace.

"Amy, there's no other way. You have to go out to Morningside and see for yourself. Take these pictures with you. Take the whole folder and ask some questions. Ask to meet Anna—you know, kind of like you knew about her all along."

"What? You can't be serious," Amy cried.

"I'm thinking you'll get a lot more answers that way than if you just—" Linda stopped pacing and faced Amy. "No, forget that—the open and honest approach will be much better. Yes! Just go out there, ring the doorbell, and talk to the person in charge. Tell her everything from the beginning. You can't hide anything anyway. Just look at your face right now. Anyone looking at you would be able to tell you've just seen a ghost or something. I can't believe this, Amy. I mean—" She paused and looked at the picture again. "Anna Weaver."

"Do you think my sister could really be alive after all?" Amy's voice was barely above a whisper. "I mean, after all these years, could she have lived just a few miles away and I didn't even know it?"

"No." Linda's voice was firm. "No. This can't be true. Your mother would have never agreed to such a thing. Would she?"

"I don't think she could. We were too close. We didn't keep any secrets from each other. Even the misgivings I had about Marshall. She knew everything about me and I knew everything about her."

"You're forgetting one thing, Amy. You knew nothing about Anna at all. If she hadn't told you about your sister that night in the hospital, you still wouldn't know anything."

Amy poured her cold coffee in the sink and rinsed her cup before refilling it with fresh, hot coffee. Thoughtfully, she sat down at the table and began to nibble at one of Mattie's cinnamon buns.

Linda studied her young friend. "What are you thinking?" she asked finally.

"I've had quite a month, haven't I?"

"Has it been a month already?"

"It was a month yesterday. And so far I've learned I had a sister who died before I was born—at least according to my mother. I've lost my mother, I've dropped out of school, I've broken off my engagement to Marshall, and now I've discovered that the sister my mother thought was dead might not be after all. No wonder I'm tired."

"But if Anna is living at Morningside, who is buried in her grave?"

"And who are the Morgans?" Amy asked. "And why would my father have sent flowers to her grave every month?"

"Wow," Linda said softly. "For a father who left perfect records and no stone unturned when it came to business files, he really left you a mystery, didn't he?" Linda reached for a cinnamon bun, tore off a generous piece, and stuck it in her mouth. "Do you think," she said after swallowing, "that there is a possibility that your mother only *thought* Anna was dead? No," she answered her own question. "Absolutely not. Nobody would do that—especially John Weaver."

"Well, one thing's for certain," Amy said. "I'll not get any answers until I go to Morningside and see for myself. But that will have to wait until another day. I'm too tired."

"Did you sleep at all last night?" Linda asked.

"No, I'm afraid not. I was thinking about finding all the paperwork I might need to have Anna's grave moved. Guess that will have to wait for now."

"Why not go to bed for a while? I'm going to be around today—all day, in fact. I still have those shirts to iron. Want me to get them and bring them over here? I'll iron and you nap."

"Oh, Linda, you don't have to do that."

"I know I don't have to, silly. But if you'd sleep better with someone in the house—"

"Really, Linda, I'll go back to bed. Just knowing you're close by is good enough. Really."

"Okay," Linda agreed. "Then I'll be back later to check on you, okay?"

"Deal," Amy laughed at her friend. "You're such a mother hen."

"A real pain, right?"

"Not at all. I love you for it."

Amy watched her perky neighbor walk down the driveway, around the fence separating their yards, and enter the back door of her own house. It was strange how close they had become in such a short time.

"Thank God," Amy said aloud as she climbed back in bed, "for such good friends as Jim and Linda Henry."

Ten

Back in her own kitchen, Linda set up the board and iron. She turned the radio sitting on top of the refrigerator to a classical music station and tackled her previously dampened bundle of shirts. A few hours later, she was surprised when Karissa Kelley knocked lightly on the back door.

"I hope you don't mind," Karissa said almost apologetically. "But Mark suggested I come and see Amy. I was at her house, but I guess she isn't home."

"You don't have to explain, Kassy," Linda said. "I think this is a wonderful idea. Amy's sleeping now, but when she wakes up I'm sure she'd be very happy to see you. Can you stay?"

"That's why she didn't answer the front door bell. She must really be tired. I'd love to stay for a bit if that's okay."

"Well, come on in," Linda offered, "and I'll get you a cup of tea while you wait."

"I thought I heard voices over here," Amy said from Linda's open doorway a little while later. "Karissa, how nice to see you." Without waiting for an invitation, Amy joined the two friends.

"I see you've decided to join the productive part of society," Linda teased. "How about some tea?"

After a few pleasantries and several cups of tea, Amy noticed how comfortable Linda and Karissa were with each other. She found it enjoyable to listen to their chatter about the baby Karissa was expecting within a few weeks, prospective names, and the advantages of breast or bottle-feeding. It felt good for Amy to think of something other than her parents, her father's files, and the unanswered questions about her sister, Anna.

"I suppose you heard about Michael—I mean, what happened to him and all," Kassy said finally.

"I did. I'm sorry."

"So am I, finally."

"Pardon me?" Amy asked, glancing from Linda's face back to Karissa's.

"It took me a while, but I finally found the strength to forgive him. You probably also heard that—well, he wasn't very—"

"He was abusive," Linda said. "It's okay, Kassy." Turning to Amy, Linda explained. "The night Michael was killed he had beaten Karissa—"

"He'd been drinking with his friends and . . . well, it's all in the past now. It's over. It's so strange that even through Michael's death God gave me a whole brand-new life."

"You mean Katie?"

"You know about Katie?" Kassy asked.

"Amy met Mark a few weeks back," Linda explained. "Anyone who knows Mark Andrews knows about Katie."

"I suppose you've seen a picture of her, then," Kassy said, smiling.

"Within minutes," Amy laughed. "She's a darling. I'm sorry you didn't bring her with you. I would really love to see her."

"Well, if you want to see Katie, you look at a picture of her. If you want to experience her, you have to be with her in person. I didn't know if you were up to the Katie experience just yet." Kassy laughed, and Amy thought she hadn't heard such a lovely sound in a long time. "My mother's watching her this afternoon. Her house is so full of children all the time that Katie just fits right in."

"Karissa," Amy began quietly, "we didn't really know each other all that well in high school. But I have to tell you, even though you were one of the prettiest girls in the whole senior class, you are more beautiful than ever."

"Of course she's beautiful. She's pregnant!" Linda laughed.

"No," Amy shook her head. "It's more than that. In school you seemed so—I don't know. Sad. Everybody knew you were dating Michael Andrews, one of the most popular boys—and richest—in the whole town. But you seemed . . ." Amy let her sentence drop and searched for just the right words.

Karissa smiled at Amy and answered the question that was left hanging. "More than Michael, more than Katie—even more than Holden, Amy, Christ has made the difference in my life, in my heart. I have Jim Henry to thank for that."

"Jim?" Amy asked.

"Mark met Jim just a short while before Michael's accident. Mark asked him to share at Michael's funeral, and that's where I met him. Little by little he shared Christ with me."

"Now, Kassy," Linda interjected, "don't forget Mattie."

"I couldn't forget Mattie," Kassy said. "I lived next door to Mattie. She was a wonderful friend and neighbor. I even stayed with Jim and Linda for a short while."

"A few days—not long enough for me," Linda said.

"I want to know more," Amy said to Kassy.

"Well, there's nothing much more to tell. Jim just gave me a Scripture verse now and then, and I finally decided that I needed to make Jesus Christ my personal Savior. It really was very simple."

"But I thought you were—"

"I was raised in a Christian home, that's true. But even my parents were having some difficulties of their own. All my life I had been taught about Christ, but somehow I had never been introduced to Him—you know, for myself. And I've discovered that knowing *about* Him and *knowing* Him are two very different things."

"My father and mother held slightly different beliefs," Amy said. "We didn't go to church much. Mama's faith was so plain and basic. Daddy . . . well, he didn't like how Mama was treated by her family when she married him. It was Mama who taught me about Jesus. I don't think I ever heard my father say one way or another what he believed. But whenever Mama asked to go to church—you know, on Christmas or Easter—Daddy was always happy to take us. He was just so private about things like that. Mama was the one who did the praying in the family."

Linda seemed preoccupied with getting even the smallest wrinkle out of Jim's white shirt, but all the while she was silently praying that Kassy would be able to say something to help Amy realize her own spiritual need to know Christ on a personal level.

"Amy?" Kassy asked. "I don't mean to pry, but have you ever asked Christ into your heart?"

"Well, no . . . at least not that I ever remember. Mama always said that's where He lived. I just took it for granted."

Karissa moved, trying to get more comfortable. She rubbed her protruding stomach. "Oh my! The baby's awake," she laughed. "Look, if I hold real still, you can see him move."

"Him?" Linda asked. "You know it's a boy?"

"Not really," Kassy said. "But Katie never gave me fits like this. She was a quiet baby."

"Before she was born," Linda said to Amy. "But not anymore."

Kassy laughed. "Maybe this one will be active before, and quiet and calm afterward. I'm hoping so anyway."

"I wonder if that's why God has seemed so distant," Amy said quietly.

"What?" Kassy asked.

"It's just that I've tried to pray like Mama taught me. But since she died, God has seemed so far away. I almost felt as if I buried Him when we buried her."

"Oh, Amy," Kassy said, "it doesn't have to be like that. He can be personal and real and—tell her, Linda."

"You're doing just fine," Linda said, encouraging her friend to continue.

"You know," Amy said, her eyes filling with the tears that still came with very little provocation, "in the last few days I've been saying to God that I needed His help. I don't know whether you know it or not, but my parents have left me with a tremendous load of responsibility, and I need so much wisdom. I just don't have it. I can't do this by myself."

"You don't have to," Kassy said. "God wants to help you. Not only with this—not just here and now—but forever, and always. He wants to be your friend, Amy, just like He wanted to be mine."

"But how—I mean, I don't know how."

"It's so simple, Amy. You just ask Him."

"You mean, just ask Him?"

"Just ask Him."

"Now?"

"Why not?" Linda unplugged the iron to let it cool and came to sit alongside Amy, slipping her arm around her shoulders. Kassy shot Linda a look of gratitude and was more than willing to have Linda take over. Linda glanced at Kassy and sensed her relief. "Kassy, why don't you lead us in prayer?"

Understanding the importance of the moment, Kassy swallowed hard and bowed her head. "Dear heavenly Father," she began slowly, "thank you for being close to us and wanting to have us come close to you. Amy would like to meet you and have you be in her life on a personal basis. Please answer her prayer. Amen."

Large tears ran down Amy's cheeks and fell into her lap. Linda slightly tightened her arm around Amy's shoulders.

"You'll need to say your own prayer now, Amy," she urged softly.

"Okay," Amy whispered. "Dear Lord, I want you to come into my life, into my heart. I want to know you like Linda and Karissa do. Amen."

For a long moment, the three sat in silence at the kitchen table. It was Amy who finally spoke. "Is that it?"

"That's it," Linda said. Her broad smile and bright eyes underscored both the simplicity and the importance of Amy's prayer.

"Now what?" Amy asked.

"Now, everything is different," Karissa said. "It may not feel like it right now. But you'll see, just like it happened for me, everything in your whole life has just changed."

"Changed? But how?"

"For one thing, you're part of our family now," Kassy said. "You know I came from a big family. There are six kids in my family. But that was nothing compared to the family I came into when I accepted Christ."

"You mean, if I come to your church—right?" Amy asked.

"Even if you don't," Linda quickly joined in. "Going to church doesn't make you any more or any less a part of God's family. Your own mother is proof of that."

"Oh, Linda," Amy asked excitedly, "my mother knew God like this, didn't she?"

"I know she did," Linda said. "She told me about it more than once. How she managed to stay so close to the Lord all these years without being involved with other Christians is a mystery to me. She had something almost like a gift, you might say. The ability to—I don't know—serve in solitude."

Amy laughed. "I can't believe how you must think we lived. My mother wasn't lonely. She had friends in from time to time. She just liked to have it quiet. You came to see her on a regular basis, didn't you?"

Linda nodded.

"And, Mattie, didn't she come by once or twice a week?"

Again Linda nodded.

"That's all she needed. Really, she didn't have great social needs. She and my father were not only married, they were best friends. They had each other. I was afraid of what his death would do to her, but even then she never complained about being lonely. Not once."

Kassy glanced at the clock on the radio on the refrigerator. "Listen, I have to go. Mom will have her hands full with kids after school, and Katie is sure to be up from her nap by now." She struggled to her feet and crossed the room, pausing at the back door. "Amy, I wish you'd come to our church. I hate to think of you being all alone—especially now. Please, will you think about it?"

"I will come, Kassy. I'm not sure when, but very soon," Amy promised.

Linda began winding the cord around the base of the now-cool iron. She folded up the ironing board and replaced it on its hook on the back porch.

"Linda," Amy said tentatively, "I've come to a conclusion. I need to take a break from all this. I've been going through my father's files day and night now for four weeks. I guess I don't have to tell you how overwhelming this all is to me. But I need a day or two doing something different—thinking about something else."

"Got any ideas?"

Before Amy could answer, a car in Amy's driveway interrupted their conversation.

"It's our lawyer, Mr. Carlson," Amy said, glancing out the back door. "Come with me. I'd like you to meet him."

Linda followed close behind Amy, and introductions were made. After they were inside the house, Amy urged Herbert Carlson to discuss anything he needed to freely in front of Linda.

"I've been approached to see if you're willing to part with the downtown properties," Mr. Carlson said. "As you know, there are several who want you to sell so the project can go forward."

"I don't understand," Amy said. "How am I holding things up?"

Herbert Carlson quickly explained to Amy how important the several adjoining downtown properties her father owned were to the future of the proposed shopping mall.

"But we have tenants in those properties," Amy said. "What would this do to them? How would a shopping mall affect their businesses?"

"You sound just like your father," Mr. Carlson said, smiling. "I was hoping this would be your reaction. If it would be all right, Amy, I'd like to go back to the interested parties and tell them you haven't made your decision yet."

"Well, there's nothing else to tell them. I haven't. I can't make a decision because I don't know what's at stake or even what's being offered. I need some time to think this through."

"If I might make a suggestion?" Mr. Carlson asked.

"Of course." Amy was glad for his direction and advice.

"Talk to your tenants, Amy. They need to hear from you— to see you. You know your father's death came as quite a shock to them. They hoped your mother wouldn't sell just yet. In fact, they were hoping she wouldn't do anything at all until you finished college. But now, unfortunately, that's all changed."

"Are you in contact with the tenants, Mr. Carlson?"

The lawyer nodded.

"Then," Amy said, "tell them for me that I'm not going to make any hasty decisions. And I won't make any decisions at all concerning the property until I've been in contact with them personally—myself."

The smile that spread across his soft, wrinkled face showed Herbert Carlson's relief. "I'll be on my way then, Amy. I'm sorry I popped in on you like this without an appointment, but I felt it was imperative that we speak about this matter. There are many more issues we need to discuss whenever you're up to it."

"Anything pressing? I mean, is there something urgent I need to know about?"

"No. Nothing urgent. I've taken care of most of Morningside's immediate needs. I've used the liberty you gave me just before your mother's funeral. Things are settled there for the moment. Something out there always needs attention, it seems."

"I'm thinking of driving out there one of these days, Mr. Carlson. Do you think that would be all right?" Amy asked.

"I think that would be wonderful. They'd be more than happy to see you."

"Do you think I should call first?"

"You could, I suppose. But then, your father often just went out unannounced. I'm sure you'd be very welcome anytime." Herbert Carlson paused with his hand on the front door knob. "You know, Amy," he said, "I would like to know what you plan to do about some of the donor pledges that your father made to different organizations and projects. Do you have any questions about those?"

"Not right now," Amy said. "Just tell those who need to know that I'm reviewing everything at the moment. I really don't see any need to make any changes in my father's plans. At least not so far."

"You know, your father considered his financial blessings something he—"

"Somewhat of a trust," Amy finished the lawyer's sentence for him. "And," she said, "so do I."

"Mr. Carlson," Linda asked before the man could get out the door, "can you tell Amy who the interested parties are? Who asked you to speak to her about the sale of the downtown properties?"

"Well, there's no reason not to, I suppose. It's the Jennings firm. They have a great deal of interest in this project, you know. Young Marshall has a lot to lose if this deal doesn't go through. He's made some pretty hefty promises. Some are even questioning whether or not he can deliver on those promises. But then, Amy, he's your fiancé. I'm sure you know how important this is to him. I must admit, though, I am a bit puzzled as to why he didn't approach you himself."

"We—well, I—have broken our engagement, Mr. Carlson. Didn't Marshall tell you?"

"No, he didn't mention it to me. Perhaps he thought you did. I wondered why he hadn't spoken to you about this himself. Now I see. I'll be more careful from now on, Amy. I thought he was speaking for you, then couldn't figure out why he thought it necessary that I—" Herbert Carlson's face creased with a frown. "How many people know about this?"

"I haven't any idea," Amy said. "It's no secret. I told Jim and Linda. I think Mark Andrews knows."

"Amy, I know this is probably not the best time, but the planning commission is meeting next week. Would you mind attending that meeting? I'll arrange for someone to pick you up if you'd like. Maybe the young pastor would like to sit in on that meeting too. You know the new church building is causing quite a bit of interest. He'd be encouraged if he could hear the remarks I've heard."

"Jim is already planning to attend. Something about permits being granted," Linda offered.

"I'd be happy to attend, Mr. Carlson," Amy said. "Just let me know when and where."

Eleven

Waking early on Saturday morning, Amy was aware of a difference. She felt she had direction and purpose, maybe for the first time in her life. It was a short-term purpose—she knew that—but a welcome one. With the planning commission meeting just three days away, she had lots of homework to do. Earlier she had decided to leave the file marked *Proposed Summerwind Shopping Mall* in her father's office unread—at least for the time being. She wanted to ask her downtown tenants some questions and didn't want to be influenced by her father's remarks or the file's contents just yet. She would begin with Mr. Mattson's tailor shop. He was expecting her a little before nine. Then she would stop at Sternhagen's Bakery and end up at Brown's Camera and Film Shop. Fern's Beauty Parlor would have to wait until later. Amy knew that by the time she was finished with the other three, Fern's would be filled with the Saturday regulars. She'd call Fern at home later tonight.

Amy was determined that by the end of the day she would know how these four long-standing tenants felt about the prospect of the downtown shopping mall and its possible impact on their businesses.

Driving toward the small, quaint downtown area, Amy realized how good it felt to be out. For too long she had stayed too close to home. The thought of not going anywhere beyond her father's office and his papers suddenly felt confining. She was glad she had a purpose—almost a mission that took her out of the house.

"I don't really have a business that would do well in a shopping mall," Mr. Mattson said when she approached the subject. "I've built a good business for myself and have a regular clientele. The only reason I'd like to see the mall here is because I'd like to shop there myself. But for my business?

Well, maybe it's time for me to retire anyway. I've been doing this for nearly forty years already. Twenty-five right here in this little store. When your daddy bought this building, well, nothing could have made me happier. He was such a good man, Miss Weaver. We all miss him."

"Have you thought of relocating?" Amy asked the small, stooped figure of a man.

"Relocating? No, I'm too old. I don't see how I could relocate. Where would I go? I've depended on word of mouth for my trade. Advertising isn't built into my budget. How would my customers find me? No, when it's time, I'll close the shop. But you can't let my problems stand in the way of a good business decision. You know, your daddy always said the mall would come one day. Sooner or later, he used to say, we'll not be able to hold back progress any longer."

"When did he say that, Mr. Mattson?" Amy asked.

"He's been saying that for five years, I'd guess. We had this conversation just before his unfortunate death. He didn't want it to take me by surprise. He was a kind man. Smart too. He tried to get me to relocate many times. Said he'd even help pay for it. Said he'd try to get me a good deal on a small shop somewhere nearby. He even offered to pay for my advertisement—you know—so's my customers could find me."

Amy discovered her father had prepared Mrs. Sternhagen as well. "He told me I should open a sandwich shop. Use my homemade bread and pies to pull 'em in. I was thinking I'd like to add soup to the menu. Keep it simple, you know. I've often thought it would be nice to have a lunch counter in here. But just never got around to it. I thought about what it might be like to go into the mall and be able to serve coffee to my morning regulars along with my doughnuts and sticky buns. Then the lunch crowd. My husband thinks I'm crazy, but my daughter said she'd like to come help me now that the grandkids are all in school. There is one thing that bothers me, though." The large woman lowered her voice. "Maybe it's something you could help me with."

"What's that?" Amy asked. "I'll do anything I can. After all, you've sent home how many cookies? I think I might be in your debt forever."

"Well, if your property here is the key to the whole thing, might you be in a better position to dicker for decent rent in that mall?"

"I might be at that," Amy said. "I'll see what I can do. But, Mrs. Sternhagen, what would you do in the meantime? I mean, if I sell this building, and you have to close for a while, what will you do?"

"I might be able to find a temporary location nearby. And, my husband's got that new Winnebago—you know—one of those newfangled motor coaches. He's been pestering me to take a long vacation. This might be the perfect time. Besides, I figure that if that development company wants this mall so bad, they'd not only pay top dollar for the real estate, but might be willing to compensate the business owners to boot. What do you think?"

"I think, Mrs. Sternhagen, I'd like to have you be my agent," Amy laughed. "No wonder your business is such a success."

"Hi, Brownie," Amy called to the friendly shopkeeper as she entered the next store. "Got a minute?"

Once she was settled in the small shop office and repair room, Amy got right to the point and asked Mr. Brown about his views on the shopping mall.

"I'm resigned to it, but that's all. I'm afraid it will change the flavor of Summerwind. It's not something you can try out and if it doesn't work here, move it over there and try something else. It will change our town; that's for sure."

"But how will it affect your business?"

"Total disruption is my guess. I'd have to relocate entirely. One move is all I'm going to make. None of this temporary stuff for me. I think the best thing for me to do is to find a location and make the move. I can see the writing on the wall, Miss Amy. I know it's coming. You can't stop it—and I'm not sure you should if you could. Your father even suggested I find a location across the street or as near to the mall as I could get. You know, for the traffic. People are going to come to that mall, that's one thing for sure. You want me to start looking for another place?"

"Not yet, Brownie. Not yet. I'm not here to tell you it's time for that. I just wanted to know what you thought. You know we're sitting on the last piece of real estate they need for that project to happen. I just want to make the right decision, that's all."

"I thought you already did," Brown said. "I heard that young man of yours had already—"

"No, you heard wrong. I've not made my decision yet. I wanted to talk to you first. Do you think you could come to a meeting at my house with the other tenants on Monday night?"

"Sure, what for?"

"You know, others may have only the town to think about. But we've got our businesses here, and our families to think of as well. This is a decision we need to face together. You've been our tenant for how many years now? Fifteen?"

"Goin' on seventeen," Brown said.

"Well, this decision affects us all, and we need to face it together. Will you tell the others? I'll call Fern tonight. But you and the others, come to my house then, Monday night, seven-thirty."

"You got a good head on your shoulders, Miss Amy," Brown said.

"Thank you, Brownie," Amy replied. "But I'm inexperienced. I'll need your help and advice. Can I count on that?"

"Yes, ma'am, you sure can." Brown walked the young woman out of the back room and to the front door of the shop. "You know, Miss Amy, your papa would be mighty proud of you for taking this route through this situation. If you weren't so pretty, you'd be just like him."

Leaving the camera shop, Amy found a phone booth and dialed Linda's number and persuaded her to meet behind the library for a picnic lunch.

Sitting beside the bubbling fountain in the little park area behind the library, Amy waited for Linda and let each conversation of the morning replay through her mind. She was pretty sure of what she wanted to do with the downtown property, but just how to go about it was the challenge, the same challenge she knew her father faced as well. Tomorrow morning, she decided, while the little downtown area was silent, while the merchants were either sleeping in or going to church, Amy would again walk downtown, bringing her father's file on the downtown mall with her. And, here, she would read his notes and ideas. Yes, here in this very place.

"Hi," Linda said quietly so as not to startle her friend. "I could see you were in deep thought."

"I've a lot to think about," Amy said.

"I love this little spot," Linda said, looking around at the tasteful tropical landscape. "You don't know this, but this is where Jim and I came to sit and listen when we were trying to decide whether or not to come to River Place Community Church."

"No, I didn't know that."

"We came over here one Sunday afternoon after Jim had preached for the small little group meeting in the Grange Hall outside of town. I think there were only about fifteen or twenty people there that morning. It was really scary. We sat right here and listened to the bubbling fountain; the water lilies were in bloom that day. We both felt God's presence here. Strange, isn't it? Here, right outside the library, God spoke His peace and love to us in a very special way."

"Now, *I* have to tell *you* something," Amy said. Her voice dropped to a hoarse whisper. "My father donated this garden. He often sat out here on an old park bench while my mother was inside looking for books or meeting with the librarian to discuss some author or another. He thought this spot had promise as kind of a place to meditate and think."

"Or hear God," Linda added.

"Do you remember that Kassy said my life was changed the other day when I asked Christ into my heart?"

"I remember," Linda said. Smiling, she squinted against the noonday sun. "Has your life changed?"

"I think it has," Amy said. "I really think it has. I've been talking to the tenants of my father's buildings. They're the ones who will be uprooted by the mall. I wanted to know how they felt about it all."

"And?"

"And, they've been thinking along the lines of what they would do. Each of them is so different. They are really nice people. I've invited them over to my house on Monday night. Do you think you and Jim could come?"

"I'll check with Jim, I don't think we have anything

planned. What's the purpose of the meeting?"

"I want them to hear each other. I don't think they've talked about this much to each other. I want them to see that they are not alone. I also want to get their ideas about what I should do. They knew my father; they've worked downtown. I'm sure they've also talked to their customers about this new mall. I want to hear it all. They are all successful business owners. I think I should listen to them for advice."

"Why not ask Mark Andrews, too? I think he'd enjoy hearing from the merchants in a more relaxed setting than a planning commission meeting."

"Good idea," Amy said. "I'll call him."

"Have you been out to Morningside yet?"

"No. I intended to go, but then this came up. I think this has to come first. So many people are involved."

"Have you heard from Marshall?"

"No, not yet."

"Think you will?"

"Probably. He's been pretty silent. You know, he almost looked like he was afraid of Mark that day. I was surprised. He always seemed so confident—even forceful with me. I was surprised when he didn't stand up to Mark. Oh, don't get me wrong—I was also grateful that he didn't. I just can't figure him out. If he needed this property, why didn't he just come right out and say so? Why did he think he had to manipulate me to get it?"

"Maybe he was after more than just the property," Linda said.

"You think?"

"I don't know, he could have just told you about the mall plans and maybe you would have sold the property. What would he have gotten—a fee of some sort?"

"Probably," Amy said.

"Why settle for a fee when he could marry a beautiful girl and get the whole thing at the same time?" Linda asked.

"Then you think he was just after my money?"

"Not just he, and not just the money—you're a beautiful young woman, Amy. I'm sure he saw you as an asset not only to his business, but to his personal life, too."

"What do you mean, 'not just he'?" Amy asked.

"I mean his mother, that's what."

"Oh, yeah, Adele. Well, I don't want to be anybody's asset," Amy said softly.

"Do you know what you do want?" Linda asked.

Amy ran her slender finger through the rippling water at the base of the fountain. "I want to marry a Christian. You know, someone who knows Christ like Jim does. Someone who in twenty years will be like Mark Andrews."

"Aha," Linda said. Her broad grin made Amy smile in response. "So here we have our first prayer request."

"What?"

"She wants a Christian husband, Lord," Linda said gazing up into the puffy white clouds floating overhead. "Someone who will be as wonderful as Mark Andrews in twenty years."

"Maybe that's asking too much," Amy said.

"For God?"

"No, for me."

"Oh, pooh. God gave me Jim, didn't He?"

"Yeah, well—"

"Don't underestimate God or yourself, Amy Weaver. And besides, if God needs any help, He knows I'd love to give Him a hand on this one."

Amy laughed and threw her head back, tossing her long hair behind her shoulders and down her back.

"It's so good to see you laugh," Linda said reaching for Amy's hand.

"Listen, Linda Henry," Amy said in mock seriousness. "I didn't invite you down here to plan my life and marriage. I wanted to ask your opinion about something entirely different."

"Okay, I'm short on money, but long on opinions."

"I'd like to redecorate the house. My mother had it the way she liked it for all these years, and I think she'd approve if I changed it to suit me."

"You know, you may be right about that." Linda clasped her hands together. "Then you're going to stay. I was afraid you might want to move. What about school? Didn't she want you to finish school, too?"

"Yeah, well. It's too late to finish this semester anyway. Since

I'd have to wait at least until the second term I might as well change things while I'm making up my mind about what to do. Besides, I'd like to have it done before Christmas. I can't think of what Christmas will be like without my parents. This was to be my first Christmas without my father. I had no idea I'd have neither of them this year." Amy paused, then returned to the original purpose for their picnic meeting. "I'm not exactly sure what I want to do, yet. I've never done this before. I thought perhaps I could persuade you to help me pick colors, maybe even new carpet. I don't know. I just want to change things."

"Do you have any basic ideas of what you'd like?"

"You'll not believe this, I'm sure. But I'd like to make my room into a den. And horrors of horrors, I think I'd like to bring the TV in there." Amy laughed out loud again.

"Amy! Are you sure?"

"You're thinking about Mama, aren't you?"

"Well, I know how she felt about such things."

"After Daddy died she told me I could bring his set into my room if I wanted. I didn't think it was necessary. After all, I was in school. Now I realize she may have wanted me to bring it in for her. I'm not sure, but I think she went outside and watched it with Daddy some after I went away to school."

For the next hour Amy and Linda sat in the warm November sunshine, laughing and tossing around ideas and color schemes for Amy's project.

———

Marshall caught sight of her shiny blond hair before he realized who was sitting with Linda Henry. The sight of her made him catch his breath. Funny, he'd never noticed how her hair sparkled in the sun like that before. Watching her from a distance, he felt a sharp stab of loneliness and regret. He could hear her voice, but not make out her words. Once or twice he caught the sound of her melodious laughter. She stood and he noticed how gracefully she moved and how animated her hands became when she talked to Linda. He knew he was looking at the same girl, but either he was seeing her differently, or she was different—very different. Marshall Jennings decided he'd call her again. This time for entirely different reasons.

Twelve

Fortified with information gleaned from her father's notes, encouraged by the positive support of her friends, and motivated by her determination to represent her tenants in a responsible manner, Amy stepped slowly to the podium in the city council chambers. She smoothed the slim skirt of her navy blue woolen crepe suit. To keep her hands from revealing how nervous she was, she placed them palm side down on her notes.

She glanced at Jim Henry, who sat motionless. Only the confident expression in his eyes told her he believed she was doing the right thing. Looking past Jim at Mark Andrews, she caught his slight grin and the briefest wink of encouragement.

"I want to begin by thanking the ladies and gentlemen of the Summerwind planning commission for giving me this opportunity to speak on the issue of the proposed shopping mall, which involves many of us, but certainly affects many more. As you know, my father owned what has become a key piece of this entire puzzle, and that piece has now been placed in my hands. I refer, of course, to the property along Main Street." Amy paused momentarily and glanced at her notes.

"I appreciate the fact that you have heard Marshall Jennings speak in my behalf at previous meetings," Amy said.

On the other side of the room, Marshall shifted in his chair, dreading what he and the others attending the meeting would hear next.

"Mr. Jennings has been at somewhat of a disadvantage, however, and I owe him both my gratitude and my apologies. It is no longer fair to him, or to me, to have him speak representing my interests. It is time I spoke for myself. As you know, with the recent loss of my parents, I have had much to deal with personally, but I am ready now to move ahead on the issue of the proposed shopping mall. Please don't misunderstand . . ." Amy took another well-placed pause for emphasis. "I'm not quite ready to move ahead with the mall—just the issues the proposed mall project raises."

Marshall watched the beautiful young woman with interest, a detail not overlooked by Linda Henry.

"Summerwind is our home. It's my home." Amy's confidence grew with every word she spoke. "I was born here. I went to school and grew up here. The decisions made in this room not only affect the town as we have always known it, but for those of us who call Summerwind home, these decisions affect our lives and the lives of our children."

Jim and Linda smiled at each other and Jim took Linda's hand in his own, then turned his attention back to Amy.

"I have several questions that I'd like to pose to this commission. Questions that while difficult to answer, must be answered for me to make a rational and responsible decision concerning my involvement and support of the proposed shopping mall."

Marshall shifted in his chair and, after glancing around the room at the faces staring in admiration for Amy's courage, turned his full focus back on Amy.

"For example," she said, sliding one page of notes behind another, "does this project represent true commerce, or is it an attempt at commercialism? Is it good for our entire community or only for the personal gain of a few? I've been told it will create new jobs. But does it do so at the expense of old, established businesses? Will we look to our own citizens for the talent needed in the areas of contracting, construction, and landscape? Or will we seek and depend on the word and work of outsiders and strangers?"

"Looks like we may have lost John Weaver, but we haven't lost his influence or balanced opinions," one commissioner whispered to another.

"And," Amy continued, "is there really an advantage of new construction rather than renovation or restoration of what we already have? My father strongly believed that we are to look to the past for learning from our experience and mistakes, all the while looking to the future for our hope. He passed that belief on to me. Have we done that in this matter? Have we sought the insight of those in neighboring small cities who have faced the same decision we wrestle with tonight? I'm afraid I haven't come with the decision you have expected or maybe even wanted. But until I have some answers to my questions, I cannot make the decision you need. It is not my intention to be difficult, but only responsible—to my hometown, to my tenants, of course, and also to my father. But more than that, I want to be responsible to my future children. I cannot make this decision for me without considering them. Thank you."

A hush fell over the crowded room as Amy quietly gathered her notes and turned from the podium.

"Thank you, Miss Weaver," the chairman of the committee said just as spontaneous, enthusiastic applause burst from the crowd.

After a few moments, the sound of the chairman's gavel called the meeting to order. "Well, friends," the chairman said, "I think Miss Weaver has a right to have her questions answered. What about it?"

"Mr. Chairman . . ." One of the council members sitting toward the end of the long semicircular table impatiently signaled for attention. "We've been over this now for the last two years, and considering all the time and effort many of our citizens have made, I move we approve the plans for the proposed shopping mall."

"Second," came the supporting vote from another committee member.

"Let me see if I can get this right," the chairman said. "We have a motion that we proceed with the plans and necessary permits, is that right?" The motioner nodded. "And we have a second. The motion on the floor is now open for discussion."

"Mr. Chairman!" Mark Andrews rose from his seat and approached the same podium Amy had just left.

"The chair recognizes Mr. Mark Andrews."

"I move for the previous motion to be declared out of order, sir."

"On what grounds, Mr. Andrews?"

"On the grounds that until all the property in question is sold and in escrow, there can be no permits granted, nor can the blueprints or anything else be approved. The city simply doesn't have the authority to overrule the property rights of the titled owner. Unless, of course, you plan on condemning Miss Weaver's property?"

"Well then, Andrews," the irritated committee member shouted. "Then talk some sense into that young woman's head, will you? You stand to lose as much on this deal as anyone!"

"What do I stand to lose, sir? I have only invested the time and personal interest it has required to present my contractor's bid. If we don't move ahead with this project right now, or if we never do—we've come to a decision, haven't we? I certainly have no money invested in this project except the small amount referred to in my bid, which is always a speculative amount for a contractor."

Jim sat very still and watched the argumentative council member thump a note pad with the end of his pen.

"Are you going to tell me, Mr. Chairman," the committee member who seconded the motion said, "that a young woman barely out of her teens can come in here and with a bat of her baby blue eyes and a few noble, even idealistic comments block this entire project?"

"No, sir," the chairman said with a distinct twinkle in his eyes. "I'm not going to tell you that."

Amy felt the color flood her cheeks.

"I'm telling you that an articulate and intelligent young citizen of our community can block this project with her power as a property owner. She's got the 'deed to the ranch,' boys," he said, maintaining a friendly tone in his voice. "We might as well set our minds to answering her questions and resolving the issues she has raised here tonight. For now, I table the motion," he said, bringing his gavel down with a sharp sound of final authority. "Miss Weaver," the chairman continued, "I want to congratulate you on bringing this committee to its knees. We've been riding a pretty high horse for a mighty long time. It's time we got to the business at hand—the careful planning of our community. By the way, are you free for lunch sometime next week? I'm sure by, oh, say, Wednesday of next week some of our committee members here might have the answers to at least some of your questions. Would it be all right if my office called you and arranged that lunch?"

Amy glanced at Mark Andrews, who nodded with a smile.

"That would be fine," Amy said, hoping Mark would be willing to attend as well.

"And now," the committee chairman announced, tapping his gavel once again for order. "Next agenda item. River Place Community Church. Blueprint approval, building permits, requested variances, and let's see, is that it?"

Jim Henry approached the podium to stand beside Mark. "Yes, sir," Jim said.

"Let's see, there was just one question. Oh yes. Is your eventual plan to also have a nursery school or some sort of children's facility or program?"

"Eventually, yes, Mr. Chairman."

"Then we unanimously approve the plans as you have presented them with this one condition. That at our first meeting in January, before you begin construction, you come back to this committee with a letter of blueprint approval from the licensing boards involved with that facility. Can you do that by then?"

"I think so, sir. I don't see why not."

"Fine. Any questions for the young minister here? Good," the chairman said without waiting for a response. "Meeting adjourned."

At once the entire room buzzed with conversation and congratulations for Amy. Marshall watched from a distance as the people swarmed around the star attraction of the evening. Eventually he made his way toward her.

"Can I give you a lift home?" he asked.

"No, thanks," she said. "But you can buy me a hamburger."

"Jake's?"

"Meet you there."

"We can go in my car," he said, moving to take her arm.

"I don't think so. I have mine. I'd rather meet you there."

"Okay," Marshall said, lifting his hands slightly in a gesture of surrender. "See you at Jake's."

"Amy," Linda said, coming to stand beside her friend. "You sure you want to do this?"

"Oh yes. I'm very sure. This meeting may be over, but my agenda still has an item or two on it."

"You want us to tag along?" Jim offered.

"No thanks. This is something I need to do by myself."

"Listen," Linda said, shrugging and leaning toward her husband, "if you want to stop in afterward. Please—"

"Don't worry about me," Amy laughed. "And don't wait up, either. This conversation is long overdue."

———

"So what do you want?" Marshall said as Amy slipped into the booth and faced him across the table.

"I think I'd like a hamburger, loaded with everything," she said with a smile. "I'm famished. And a Coke—no, make it a chocolate milk shake."

"That's not what I meant. What do you want from me?"

"Like I said . . ." Amy folded her hands on the table in front of her. "Answers."

The waitress interrupted their conversation while she took their order, then a few friends stopped by to offer Amy their condolences and to welcome her home.

"Look," Amy said after she had swallowed the last bite of her sandwich. "I think I have this all figured out. Why don't I just give you my version, and you just tell me whether I'm right or not."

"Okay," Marshall said, looking somewhat uncertain. "Shoot."

"The way I see it, you first approached me because you thought you could influence my dad by being involved with me. Then, when he died, you saw the opportunity of a lifetime. Something much more effective and profitable than influencing him—controlling me—and of course his money, not to mention the handsome fee you'd pocket in addition to controlling the proceeds from the sale of the downtown location. How convenient it would be—not just to be near his money, but to be married to it."

"Amy," Marshall said, looking down. "I don't know what to say."

"There is nothing *to* say, Marsh." Amy sipped her milkshake and then began to dab the straw up and down in its icy cold thickness. "I've been trying to decide whether I'm more disappointed in you or in me."

"I know why you'd be disappointed in me, but why would you be disappointed in yourself?" Marshall asked.

"I consider myself a relatively intelligent person. I'm disappointed because I didn't see through you. You know, I actually thought you loved me—that you found me attractive and wanted to marry me for all the right reasons. I can't believe I was so blind."

"Amy, you make me sound so coldhearted and calculating."

"No, Marsh, I'm embarrassed to admit I don't know you that well. All I know is what you presented to me. Do you realize I don't even know your favorite color or your political party preference?"

"You—I mean we—"

"I believed every word you said, Marsh. At least at first. You said all the right things, and you said them in all the right ways. My gosh, you even knew how to make sure they were said in the right places. The grounds at the country club, the summer symphonies under the stars. It took me a long time to realize that you hadn't once said you loved me. You just always acted like you did, and the mood was always right and everything was just so perfect. So I told myself that it didn't matter that you never said the words. I even told myself that the reason you wanted to get married right away was because you were concerned about me and wanted to take care of me. So, I thought all I had to do was convince you I could take care of myself. That once you saw I wasn't in such distress as you thought, you'd understand and see for yourself that I couldn't rush into marriage with everything else I was dealing with."

Amy paused, and an uncomfortable silence hung between them. "You know," she continued in a much softer tone, "I even thought that you didn't want me to finish school because you wanted to be with me. All that time I thought I was having to choose between my education and you. I kept thinking it would eventually dawn on you that this was important to me and that because I was important to you, you'd somehow come to understand. I had no idea it wasn't me at all—it was you—you were rushing against the clock. Fighting against the very day I would begin to think for myself."

"Weren't you thinking for yourself by staying in school?"

"I'm still sorting that out, Marshall. I haven't told anyone else this, but I'm finally ready to admit I was in school for my mother's sake. Mine too, probably. But certainly because it was her dream as much or even more than mine. You wanted me to drop out—she begged me to finish. Between the two of you, how was I supposed to know what *I* wanted?"

"And how about now? Do you know what you want now?"

"I'm working on it," Amy said with a deep sigh. "But it scares me sometimes. I don't have to tell you my father left quite an estate for me to manage. I just pray I'm ready for it."

"I'd say by what I saw tonight you're more than ready. Say, ever think about going into politics?"

"Absolutely not," she said emphatically.

"Why not? You'd be perfect. Sort of an iron fist in a velvet glove."

"Is that how you see me?"

"That's not a fair question," Marshall said, again dropping his gaze to avoid her eyes.

"Can I get you anything else?" the waitress asked.

"Will a five get us the table for the rest of the evening?" Marshall grinned at the uniformed young woman.

"A ten will get you a *do not disturb* sign and an unlimited supply of Cokes, coffee, or whatever your little hearts desire," she countered.

"Just privacy, please," Marshall said, slipping a folded bill into her waiting palm.

"I can do better than that," she cooed, shoving the money into her pocket. "How about invisibility?"

Marshall watched her walk away, then turned his attention back to Amy. "Will you hear my side of the story?"

"First, tell me. Am I wrong?"

"Not entirely." Marshall paused as a slight wince crossed Amy's striking features. "We're being honest, okay? My father learned about you at some meeting or another. He said that if he couldn't convince your father to sell the property for the mall deal to go through, perhaps it wouldn't hurt if I—well, you know, got to know you."

"Why do I think I don't want to hear this?"

"But I wasn't interested—at first anyway. Then I met you at some function—I can't even remember what it was now."

"The unveiling of the cornerstone memorial," Amy said.

"Yeah, I guess it was. Anyway," Marshall continued, "my father poked me in the ribs as you walked away with your dad. 'Not bad, eh?' he said. I had no idea you were beautiful. I thought with all I'd heard about your brains and being class valedictorian and all, you'd be ugly. You know, with thick glasses out to here."

Amy felt her skin flush at Marshall's compliment.

"I took a renewed interest in my—"

"Assignment," Amy said, finishing the sentence for him.

"Amy," he said soberly. "Part of my pressuring you to get married was because I needed to wrap up this deal—still do, by the way. But another part of me was afraid that at any moment you'd find out the truth and—well, you'd do just exactly what you did. You'd give me the gate without delay or ceremony. I handled the whole thing wrong, Amy."

"I'm not a *thing* to be handled, Marsh."

"I know that. See? Even now I'm not doing well, am I?"

"Not very," she said.

"Amy," he began. "Could we begin again? I don't mean take the ring back this very moment. But is there a chance we could start over—from the beginning?"

"No," she said without hesitation.

"Why not?"

"We've got a definite conflict of interest, Marshall. Until I get this mall issue settled once and for all, there's not much else I can think of. Please, don't ask me."

"After this blows over?"

"It's not going to blow over. You know that."

"What then? When it's resolved?"

"That's a better word. I've got to know I'm making the right decisions."

"Decisions? Plural? You have more than one decision to make?"

"It's not as simple as just selling the property, Marshall. If it was, I'd do it in a minute. I have my tenants to consider.

What's right for them. Did you know that Mr. Mattson thinks he could be forced into an early retirement because of this? He's not ready for that. Retirement would kill him."

"And the others?"

"Do you really care?"

"Of course, I care."

"Well, Mrs. Sternhagen might be interested in moving into the new mall. She's got some ideas of expanding and branching out. If, that is, the right arrangements can be made."

"What arrangements?"

"And, Mr. Brown"—Amy ignored the question—"he's not that opposed to the whole idea either. It's just that . . ." Thinking better of revealing all the details to Marshall Jennings, she let her sentence die unfinished. "And then there's Fern. Is a beauty shop really a mall business? What about her? She's been in this location for years. What would happen to her? Would offending half the gossips in town—who, I might add, are married to some of the most influential men in the city—benefit the mall? Isn't word of mouth considered one of the most powerful forms of advertising?"

"Okay, Amy, what is it you want?"

"Are you ready to hear it?"

"Let me have it, straight. I might as well get this over with."

"I want to see a fully underwritten relocation plan acceptable to both Mr. Mattson and Fern. I want the backers for the mall project to provide temporary locations at the same rent they are paying now for those displaced by the project who will sign leases for mall spaces before construction begins. And I want a five-year discounted leasing fee and a set percentage that their lease can't go over at the end of that five years. And—"

"You mean there's more?" Marshall looked distressed.

"I understand that a mall space is leased just as space, am I correct?"

"That's right."

"Then I want you to find low-interest financing for businesses that will be relocated because of the building. If someone moves because they want to, that's one thing. But if building the mall forces them to move, we should be willing to help as much as possible."

"Does anyone else know about all this?"

"Of course!" Amy smiled triumphantly.

"I was afraid of that," he said with a measure of defeat in his voice.

"Do you want the property or not?"

"It's not a matter of want, Amy. You know that."

"Then what's the problem?"

"Where, in heaven's name, do you think we can come up with the funding for such a plan as you propose? You know, Miss Weaver, you're holding the mall for ransom with these demands."

"You mean you can't think of one place that this money could come from? Oh, Marshall, you disappoint me. How many—besides you, that is—are skimming double fees, right off the top of this whole deal? How many of you tycoon types are making money without risking one thing? Your offices are located off the premises. Your businesses will not be disturbed. You'll not be forced into an early retirement. All you have at stake here is your future. And, of course, your business reputation as well as your father's. All you need is everyone's cooperation. And you'll get it, too—eventually. If you play your cards right."

"Do you plan to present this next week when you lunch with the *boys* from city hall?"

"Me? I'm not sure that's the best idea you've ever had, Marshall. Think about it—"

"You can't be serious," he said, the truth slowly sinking in. "I can't believe you think I'd—"

"You'd be perfect. You're so persuasive. Besides, you're the big talker who said I was about to agree to this sale at any moment. I'm prepared to sign papers to this effect. You can have them in your hand when you join us for lunch."

"You're really putting a lot of pressure on me, Amy."

"You know, Daddy used to say something. Just a private phrase, you know, like families make up. He used to say 'Nox, nix, nouse.' "

"And what does that mean, pray tell?"

"It means turn about is fair play—or in other words, what goes around comes around."

"You mean, if you can't take it you shouldn't dish it out?"

"Yeah, that's pretty close—or even paint or get off the ladder. Or how about if you can't stand the heat, you better get out of the kitchen, or—"

"Stop, will you? I get the point. You've really painted me into a corner here, Amy."

"Don't look now, my friend, but you're the one holding the brush. You did this all by yourself."

"You know, Amy Weaver," Marshall said, meeting her sparkling blue eyes with his, "you're not only beautiful, you're brilliant." He slid his hand across the table toward her, hoping she'd respond in some way he could interpret as encouragement.

Amy slid gracefully toward the edge of the vinyl upholstered booth. Standing up, she said, "I'm sure you won't mind picking up the tab."

"Can I call you on Friday?"

"I'll see you at lunch next week. You've got a lot of work to do by then." Amy turned to walk away, then paused and faced him again. "There is one thing you could do for me, though," she teased.

"Name it."

"Tell your mother to quit calling me. I have nothing to say to her."

"Okay, then how about Sunday?" he called to her retreating figure. She didn't answer. "Movie, Saturday night?" he raised his voice a little louder as she moved farther away and closer to the door.

"Don't look now, mister," the waitress observed, watching Amy leave the hamburger shop, "but you just got the cold shoulder."

"Those lovely shoulders are anything but cold," Marshall said. "Believe me, I may have thought that once, but I won't make that mistake again."

Thirteen

Amy was both taken off guard by and immediately grateful for Linda's invitation to spend Thanksgiving with a few of the families from their growing church. With all the excitement surrounding the sense of advocacy she felt growing within her, she had pushed away the thought that this would be the first Thanksgiving not only without her father, but also without her mother. Less than six weeks had passed since her mother's death, and Amy Weaver's life had changed completely.

The day was different for Amy than any other holiday she had ever spent. Busy, happy people gathered to enjoy one another's company, to share their common faith and friendship. Dinner was spread out over long folding tables covered with a variety of tablecloths. The church-rented school-gymnasium-turned-dining room echoed with cheerful conversation punctuated with hearty laughter and the squeals of playful children. She was more than a little surprised to meet Karissa's parents, as well as a classmate or two from Summerwind High School who were now attending Jim and Linda's church.

"Well, when are you going out to Morningside?" Linda asked Amy as they dried dishes together after the huge family-style potluck dinner.

"Soon," Amy answered, "very soon. In fact, I'm planning on going tomorrow. Want to come along?"

"I'd love to, but I can't. I promised Mattie I'd help her make fruitcakes for our Christmas baskets. I was almost hoping you'd come and give us a hand. Kassy will be there, and her mother, Kate. It's becoming a tradition."

"I'm sorry, Linda. I'd love to," Amy said, tempted to change her plans. "But I really must get this over with. I also want to see if they need anything at the home—and figure out what I have to do before Christmas. I know my father always made sure they had a nice Christmas."

"Why not drop by Mattie's house afterward? You won't be out there all day, will you?"

"Out where?" Jim asked, popping his head through the doorway of the institutional-sized kitchen.

"Amy's going out to Morningside tomorrow," Linda said.

"Let us know what you find out, okay?" Jim directed his question to Amy.

"I'll let you both know, whatever I find out, whatever it is."

———

Early the next morning, Amy reviewed the Morningside file from her father's office and made note of a few items she needed to follow up on. Did the kitchen wiring scheduled to be installed just before his sudden death ever get done? Did the plumber install the new laundry tubs in the service room? She knew Chet Ramsey or Mr. Carlson probably knew the answers to her questions, but she wanted to have a legitimate excuse for arriving at Morningside unannounced. How many residents live there? Where did they come from? Do they have families? Amy's mind was filled with these questions and many more. Most of all, what about Anna Weaver? She picked up the snapshots again and examined them closely, searching for family resemblance. Hair and eye coloring were hard to tell in the photos. And was that the Weaver dimple? Or perhaps just a smudge on the pudgy chin of the Anna Weaver in the picture?

Impatient, Amy managed to wait until a little past nine before she headed the family car toward the small outlying community of Morningside and specifically to the location of what was known to her as simply The Home.

She hadn't driven out this way for more than two years. She tried to recall the last time. Perhaps it was when she and her mother came through Morningside on their way to buy cherries grown at Mile High, the small orchard-filled valley located partway up the side of the mountain exactly at the 5,280-foot elevation. Or was it to pick peaches or plums in one of the lower valley orchards? Amy's vision blurred as her mind filled with the memories of the delightful outings shared with her mother. Shaking her head, she glanced at the file on the seat beside her. Her carefully sketched instructions to her destination were clipped to the outside of the folder. Straightening her shoulders, she tossed her head, reclaiming her determination to get the answers she desperately wanted.

Carefully, she guided the car down the tree-lined street toward the intersection of Olive and Quartz. *Trees and rocks,* she said to herself. *Tree streets go north and south, and rock streets run east and west.* Anticipating the next corner, she turned on the left turn signal. Her attention was drawn to several children playing happily in a generous stream of water running along the curb. It wasn't unusual for the irrigation water to be running this time of year, but the cool November day, even in this tropical climate, meant the water would be icy cold. She shivered involuntarily at the thought of little bare feet in the frigid water.

Only after turning the corner did she take note of people milling around and the fire engines parked beyond hastily erected barricades in the street ahead. Firemen walked and worked unhurried, obviously returning their gear to their truck and emptying their hoses, to the delight of the children playing down the street. Knowing she was in the right neighborhood, Amy pulled over, stopped the car, and got out. The acrid odor of charred wood and hot tar filled her nose.

"Can I help you, lady?" a tired fireman asked as she pushed her way through the silent, stunned crowd of people.

"I'm looking for this address," she said, showing him a slip of paper. "It's got to be right around here somewhere."

"Not anymore," the man commented. "It was right over there," he said, nodding toward the burned-out ruins of a large wood-framed structure.

"What happened?" she said. Fear gripped her insides. She fought against the awful burned smell and tried to push the stark reality of the scene away.

"Had a fire, that's what happened," he said. "Big one, too. Too far along by the time we got here to do much good."

"This can't be!" Amy cried aloud. "This can't be!"

"Now take it easy, young lady," the fireman dropped the

thick, now-empty canvas hose on the ground and came to stand beside her. "You live around here someplace?"

"No, it's just that I was coming to see if—"

"You know the people that were in that house?"

"There were people in there?" Amy felt terror insidiously squeeze her throat until she could hardly breathe.

"Yeah, about six or so. Did you know someone in there? Relatives, or something?"

"What happened to the people? Are they all right? Are they injured? Have they been taken to the hospital?" Amy fought hysteria.

"Lady," the fireman said while motioning to his captain, "maybe you'd better sit down." He tried to lead Amy to the side of the fire truck.

"I don't want to sit down. I want some answers," she cried. "Where are the residents of the house?"

"Ma'am? I'm Victor Medina. I'm the captain in charge here. Who are you?"

"I'm Amy Weaver. I live in Summerwind."

"John Weaver's daughter?"

"Yes. Did you know my father?"

"Sure did, miss. He was a favorite around these parts. No wonder you're upset. He had a lot of interest in this place. We helped him a time or two raise a few needed dollars for the kids here."

"What happened?"

"We're not sure yet. The investigator over there is trying to determine that right now. Looks like it was set. We're just not sure if it was intentional or accidental. We'll find out, though. Sampson there, he's a good man."

"Set? You think someone would—"

"We're not sure yet, miss. But you can bet we'll find out."

"Hey, Cap!" one of the grimy men called. "We're ready to roll!"

"Go on, then. I'm right behind you." He turned his attention back to Amy. "We're done here. We were too late. The call didn't come in right away. A neighbor smelled smoke and came to investigate, then had to run home and call from there."

"Captain," Amy said, "was anyone hurt?"

"Afraid so, miss. The woman, or caretaker, whatever you call her, kept trying to get back in. One of her charges was unaccounted for. The docs had to tranquilize her before she would let them take her to the hospital. She had some pretty nasty burns on her face and hands. She was really upset."

"Did you find the person she was looking for?"

"We found him later. It was too late. Our guess is that he died very early into the blaze. His body was found in the hot spot—where the fire started. May have even started it himself."

"And the others? Were there others?"

"Mostly shaken up, I think. They were all taken to the hospital in Rolling Green."

"Why not Summerwind Community?"

"Rolling Green's closer. Besides, if they're seriously injured, they'll be transferred." He looked at Amy. "You're going there, aren't you?"

"Yes, of course I am."

"That's good. I didn't know what to do, who to call. I would have tried to reach you after I got back to the station. I know John would've wanted to be called right away. I assumed somebody from his family would want to know."

Amy drove as quickly as she could to the hospital in Rolling Green, a small town just a few miles farther down the highway. She followed the big hospital signs to the small medical facility and decided to call Jim and Linda before she did anything else.

Finally reaching Linda at Mattie's, Amy quickly reported the incident and the sad news of the death of one of the residents.

"No, I don't know anything more," Amy said. "I don't even know who I'm looking for. But that shouldn't be too hard. This is a very small hospital. I'm sure they don't get many emergencies here, let alone fire victims."

"Amy, are you all right? Do you want me to try and reach Jim, or maybe Mark?"

"No," Amy said into the receiver. "I'm not sure about anything yet, or if I'll even be here much longer. I'll call when I know."

———

"Treated the lot of them," the nurse in the small emergency room told her. "They were all very lucky. That plucky little old woman got them all out."

"Not all," Amy said. "Do you know where she is now? Can I see her?"

"Released," said the curt nurse. "Left, oh, I'd say half an hour ago."

"Where'd they go? The house was completely destroyed. Where would they go?"

"I don't know that. Someone from the county was asking questions. Maybe he would know. All those poor little—yeah, I'd call the county if I were you. They're the ones who support them, you know. Their families don't want them; that's for sure."

Amy returned to the pay phone near the entrance. After a few calls to the social services offices with no answer, Amy finally realized it was a holiday weekend. She'd get no information before Monday morning. Walking back to her car, she thought she could still smell the fire. Slipping behind the wheel, she put her head on the steering wheel and waited until her head stopped throbbing and her tears dried.

"Now what?" she said aloud. "What in the world do I do now? Dear Lord, those poor people. Where will they go; where will they stay? How can I find them?"

———

"Miss Weaver?" A tall, good-looking young man stood on the front porch of Amy's house several hours later.

"Yes," she said. "May I help you?"

"I'm Owen Sampson with the county investigation division." He opened his badge for Amy to see. "I'm the investigator in charge of the Morningside fire. I'd like to ask you a few questions, if I may."

"Certainly," Amy said, stepping aside for him to enter. "I'm not sure I can help you, but—"

"You came out to the fire scene. Did you just happen to come or was there—I mean, did you know about the fire?"

"No, I had no idea. I was just coming to . . ." She paused. She couldn't expect a total stranger to understand about finding the photographs in her father's file. "I was on some unfinished business for my father."

"I see. Is he here? May I speak with him?"

"No, I'm afraid he passed away a few months ago."

"Oh, I'm sorry, miss. I didn't know."

Amy felt warmed by the gentle tone in his voice, but immediately awkward when she realized her instant attraction to this total stranger.

"I understand your father owned Morningside Home," Mr. Sampson continued. "Is that right?"

"Not that I know of," Amy said. "I've not found any indication of that in my father's papers."

"This is my day for misinformation, I guess. Captain Medina said your father was—"

"My father was a benefactor of the Morningside Home, Mr. Sampson. He donated materials, labor, and I'm not sure what else, but I'm positive he didn't own it. I would have found those papers, I'm sure."

"Well, then, miss. I'm sorry to have troubled you. I guess you'll . . ." He hesitated, then turned to go out the door.

"I'll what?" For some reason she couldn't quite explain, she didn't want him to leave just yet.

"Nothing. I'll be on my way. Thanks for your time."

"Mr. Sampson," Amy said before he could reach the front door. "When did you arrive at the fire?"

He turned back around at her question, his hand resting on the door handle. "I got the call almost immediately. Captain Medina put out a call as soon as they suspected . . ." He left his sentence unfinished.

"Suspected?"

"It's a fire of suspicious origin, Miss Weaver. I'm always called as soon as possible. I can tell—you know, get a better feel for things if I can get there while the fire is still burning."

"And?"

"And it looks like it started under the front porch. Right where the body was found."

Amy felt the color drain from her face and closed her eyes momentarily against the pain. *Too much death*, she thought.

"It's a fatality fire, Miss Weaver."

She knew the investigator had softened his voice for her sake.

"A male victim," he went on quietly. "We just don't know if it was an accidental fire or a deliberate one."

"Deliberate? Somebody deliberately . . . I can't believe that anyone would set fire to a house with—"

"I didn't say deliberately set fire to the house. I've got my hunches, however, that the fire may have been deliberately set."

"But I don't understand," Amy said.

"You see, miss," Owen explained, leaning against the door-frame, "someone may have meant to put a match to something—a stack of paper, a note, or letter—even a firecracker—but with no intention whatsoever of setting fire to a house. But when a fire flares up, it can catch a person off guard, unprepared."

"Is that what happened?"

"That's my best guess at the moment. It's what I'll go on, unless I turn up evidence to the contrary. I know the fire started under the porch where the body was. The fire burned the longest there, I can tell by the—well, by the way the burned wood looks. Fire leaves tracks, you could say. Trails that can be traced to the origin. And fire burns up before it burns out. I've seen fires where the flames shot upward then fanned out, burning the ceiling, and then moved upstairs without even touching outside walls." He smiled at Amy, then suddenly looked at his watch. "But I'm taking too much of your time," he said, reaching once again for the door handle.

"No, wait," she said almost too quickly. "Now I have a question or two. Did you see any of the residents when you got there? I mean, had they been taken away yet?"

"No, the woman, I'm not sure what you'd call her, the housemother or caretaker, she was nearly hysterical. The medical people were trying to calm her down just as I arrived.

She kept saying one of her boys was missing and thought he must be inside. I thought we'd lose her when Captain Vic had to tell her the bad news."

"But did you see any young women with her? One of the residents, I mean. Wait, I have a picture." Amy picked up the file lying next to her keys and purse on the dining room table. "Here," she said, retrieving a photo from the file, "did you see this person?"

Mr. Sampson studied the picture of the childlike woman clutching a rag doll. "Can't say that I did. When did you say this was taken?" he asked. He turned the photo over, hoping a date might be written on the back. "Anna Weaver. A relative of yours?"

"I'm not sure," Amy said quietly.

"You're not sure?" he asked, puzzled.

"It's hard to explain, Mr. Sampson," she went on. "I was trying to find out who this is. That's why I went out there. It's hard to explain." Amy swallowed hard and tried not to notice the friendly sparkle in his eye and the slight dimple in his chin that appeared now and then as he talked.

"You said that already," he said.

"It's a family matter," she said abruptly. Suddenly she wanted to end the conversation or at least change the subject.

"I see. I didn't mean to pry. Sounds to me like you've got your own investigation going on, Miss Weaver."

"If you find out where she's been taken—if you hear anything that would help me find her—would you let me know? I feel sort of responsible for her."

"I'll keep my eyes and ears open," Owen said. "And I'll let you know if I do. Can I call you—if I hear anything, that is?"

"I'd appreciate that," she said politely, returning his smile. "I really would."

"Could I have your number, then?"

"Oh, of course," she said. Opening her purse, Amy fumbled around until she found one of her father's business cards. Taking it from her hand, Owen inadvertently brushed the tips of her fingers. She hoped the slight, almost imperceptible tremble escaped his notice and wondered if it was because of the trauma of the fire or because she felt almost clumsy in his disarming presence.

"Are you John?" he asked. His smile broadened to reveal his slightly crooked front teeth.

"No, of course not. I'm Amy."

"Who's John?"

"My father. It's the same number," she said. Owen Sampson hadn't been in her house fifteen minutes, and she was already hoping he'd find a reason to return.

"Amy Weaver," Owen said and wrote her name on the card, then turned it over. "Looking for Anna Weaver," he spoke as he wrote the notation. "I don't want to forget my excuse to call you again. I hope I have news for you soon, Amy Weaver," he said.

"Me too," she answered, then quickly added, "I hope you have some news about Anna soon."

Amy quietly shut the door and watched through the lace curtains stretched tight across the small leaded window as Owen walked toward the street. She noticed how the late afternoon sunlight caught his light brown crown of curls, teasing them with golden red highlights. His abrupt turn and friendly wave caught her off guard, and she felt her cheeks burn with shyness. The fact that in the middle of everything else going on in her life she felt drawn to a perfect stranger was embarrassing. That she could even feel, much less show, interest in a man—any man—was unthinkable at a time like this. Even a man as attractive as Owen Sampson.

———

"Hey, Owen!" Jim's voice called from the next yard. "Owen Sampson! What are you doing in this neck of the woods?"

"Hey, Jim. Fancy running into you like this. Just checking a few facts on a case with Miss Weaver, next door."

"No kidding? What case is that?"

"There was a fire out in Morningside earlier today. Thought she might have some details I could use."

"A fire? Serious?"

"Afraid so. Residential fire. Claimed a life. She was there." Owen nodded toward Amy's house. "She seemed pretty upset by it all. Just came to do my homework. You know her?"

"Sure do. Nice girl."

"Yeah, I noticed," Owen said before quickly changing the subject. "Say, we haven't seen you around the chessboard lately. Given up the game? What's the matter—Paddy Mc-Carron got you whipped?"

"No, at least not for good. Been pretty busy. We'll be starting the construction on our new church soon. Lots of legwork to do before even a shovelful of dirt can be turned."

"That church of yours is growing lickety-split, according to my brother-in-law."

"Don's a good man," Jim said. "Promised to run a Saturday crew once we get the foundation poured." Jim wasn't about to let Owen go without more information. "So tell me about that fire."

"Nothing much to tell. Have to investigate because of the fatality. Because the residents are wards of the state and the home was state licensed, we have to make doubly sure there were no safety code violations, that's all. It's a pretty open and shut deal, if you ask me. Looks like the poor guy was playing with matches—you know, the same old story. Maybe even trying to smoke. Who knows? If the state wants more, I'll have to look further. They may be satisfied with what I've got already. The house was old, and the dry timber went up like a torch. He really didn't have a chance. Looked to me like the place was crammed with newspapers and comic books under there. That stuff goes up fast."

Jim and Owen exchanged a few more pleasantries, and when Owen left, Jim went in the house to find Linda. He was sure she would want to go next door and talk to Amy.

Fourteen

Amy was frustrated. In the few hours since the fire, she had tried unsuccessfully to contact someone from the county. She had no choice but to wait until Monday to find out where the residents of Morningside Home had been taken. She tried to recall the information she had been given earlier in the day. *Someone from the county came and they were released.* And what was it that Captain Medina said? *If they can't handle them at Rolling Green, they'll be transferred.* But to where? Even Owen Sampson's visit to her home hadn't given her the answers she wanted.

If the county offices were closed for the holiday weekend, how did the hospital get someone to come pick them up? *Where in the world?* she thought. *Who could possibly know?* "Mr. Carlson," she said aloud. "Why didn't I think of him sooner?"

Hope surged within her and she rushed toward the phone, only to be interrupted by its sudden ring.

"Hello?" she said impatiently.

"Amy?" Marshall asked. "You all right? You sound a little—"

"Oh, Marshall," she said briskly, "I can't talk to you now. Please, I have to make a phone call."

"Okay," he said hesitantly. "I'll call you later, then."

"No, Marsh, there's no point." The last person in the world she wanted to talk to was Marshall Jennings.

"Then, tomorrow. I do need to see you as soon as possible," he said.

"Marshall, please."

"I'll call you tomorrow," he said, then hung up the phone.

"Great," Amy muttered toward the receiver in her hand. "That's all I need."

"Mr. Carlson is out of town for the weekend," his secretary said after Amy dialed his office number. "I'm just here to do a little catch-up work. Is there anything I can do for you?"

"I'm trying to find the name of the woman who lives at Morningside Home. Do you think Mr. Carlson has that on file?" Amy asked.

"He probably does. But I'm not sure I should—"

"Listen," Amy pleaded. "There's been a fire. I was out there this morning and the whole place is destroyed. No one knows where she is, or can tell me how the other residents are. One of the young men died out there today. I must find her. Please, can't you just look and see if her name—"

"Miss Weaver," the woman's voice softened with sympathy. "This is awful. Listen, are you at home? Can I call you back? Let me look through the files and see what I can find."

"Thank you," Amy said more calmly. "I'll be right here, waiting."

"What's going on?" Jim asked as soon as Amy answered his knock at her back door. "I saw Owen Sampson, and he told me about the fire. I was going to tell Linda, but I don't know where she is. Have you seen her? Does she know yet?"

"She's probably still at Mattie's," Amy said. "I talked to her earlier. She knows. I was supposed to call her back when I found out anything, but I haven't." Amy's frustration and fear surfaced, and she sank into a kitchen chair and buried her face in her arms on the table.

Jim paced the kitchen floor. A weeping woman was always awkward for him, and Linda always knew exactly what to do. Greatly relieved when he heard his own back door slam next door, he picked up the phone and dialed his own number.

Linda's presence in the room a few minutes later calmed both her husband and her friend. "Amy," Linda soothed, "what can we do? How can we help you?"

"I don't know," Amy sobbed. "I'm so afraid. They were injured enough to take to the hospital, but now it's as if they vanished into thin air." For the next few minutes Amy blurted out the whole story of how she had come upon the scene, of driving to the hospital in Rolling Green. "That's when I called you," she said, meeting Linda's eyes with her own. "It's like everything is working against me. All I want to do is find out if those people are okay and if Anna Weaver is in those photographs or up there in the cemetery. Is that so bad?"

"No, honey," Linda said reassuringly. "Of course not."

"Amy," Jim said quietly. "I think we need to pray about this, don't you?" He slid into a seat opposite her at the table and reached across and took her hand as Linda pulled a chair closer and slipped her arm around Amy's shoulder.

"Dear Lord," Jim began, then poured out the whole situation to God while Amy cried quietly. "And that, Father," Jim concluded, "is all we know. We ask your divine protection on those injured and affected by this unfortunate fire. And we ask your guidance and help for Amy as she searches for the answers she needs. In your name we pray. Amen."

With a little coaxing, Linda persuaded Amy to eat some soup and once again promised to stay with her while she rested and to wake her if Mr. Carlson's secretary called. Jim excused himself and went to his own house to try to reach Owen Sampson. If he had only known the extent of Amy's pain earlier, he could have pressed Owen for more information while he had the chance.

"Owen," Jim said after several unsuccessful attempts, "it's Jim Henry. I've been trying to get through to you for over an hour. Do you have any more information on that fire? Our neighbor, Amy Weaver, has a personal interest in the residents and hasn't been able to locate any of them. Is there any chance—"

"That's what I've been working on," Owen said. "I picked up a few more details. I'm waiting for a call back right now. In fact, I thought that this might be that call. I went back to the fire scene, and I think I might have some information for Amy. Where are you? Can I get back to you?"

"I'll be at Amy's," Jim said.

"I have the number," Owen said. "I'll call you there."

———

When Owen Sampson rang the doorbell at Amy's an hour later, it was Jim who opened the door.

"I think I have some information," he said, grinning

broadly at Jim. "And I think it might be good news."

"Great," Jim said enthusiastically. "Mr. Carlson's secretary gave us the name of Agatha Jones, but that's all we know."

"Yeah, I got that name too. She's a foster mother. Sort of a guardian for several mentally retarded adults. She's had most of them with her since they were children. She's the only mother a couple of them have ever known. Morningside was a licensed foster home—a specialized licensed foster home. Mrs. Jones has been managing on her own since her husband died several years ago. Seems one of the men had a fascination with fire. She's been trying to get him relocated for some time, but finding just the right facility has been difficult. Seems she didn't want him in an institution, but it really was her only option. Now, it seems, her hesitancy cost him his life, and her and the others their home."

"I'd better get Amy," Linda said when she heard Owen's story. "She'd never forgive us if we didn't wake her."

Owen carefully repeated to Amy the information he had given Jim a few minutes earlier and then continued. "She's at County General," he said. "In the burn unit. Seems she tried to pull the man out before the fire department got there. Only the heat was too intense and she—well, she's burned on her face, chest, and hands. Rolling Green didn't even see her; they rerouted the ambulance and she was taken straight to County."

"And the others?" Amy asked, almost afraid to hear. "Do you know where Anna is?"

"A temporary home, I guess. One was hospitalized—more hysteria than injury. She's in the psychiatric ward at County. Right upstairs from Agatha Jones."

"How'd you find all this out?" Jim asked.

"Got connections here and there. A few friends in the police department who knew where to call and how to ask the right questions. Our own firemen have been asking questions in the neighborhood all afternoon. I just put the pieces together." Owen paused, then produced a small plastic bag he had kept tucked inside his jacket. "And then there's this," he said, reaching his hand inside the bag and retrieving its contents.

Amy reached for the familiar-looking rag doll with one hand and covered her mouth with the other. Her eyes immediately filled with tears as she clutched the doll to her breast.

"What's this?" Jim asked.

Amy just shook her head, unable to speak.

Owen walked to the dining room table and picked up the picture Amy had shown him earlier. "Just as I thought," he said quietly, looking at the picture, then passing it to Jim and Linda.

"Can I go to the hospital?" Amy asked. "Do you think they'd let me in? Please, can we just go over there and try?"

"They'll not let you in with that filthy thing," Owen said, pointing to the dirty and smudged doll.

"But if I find Anna, she'll want it," Amy protested. "Wait a minute!" she said suddenly and disappeared into her old bedroom. Emerging a few minutes later, Amy held out a cleaner version of the same doll. "Is this better?"

"Much," Owen smiled.

Clutching the doll, Amy walked with Linda, Jim, and Owen through the glass doors of County General's emergency room. Owen stepped forward and showed his identification badge to the young woman sitting behind a sliding glass window and asked a few questions, then turned back to the small waiting group of friends.

"The burn unit is upstairs," Owen informed them. "We probably won't be able to see her, but we can go up and at least talk to the nurse."

"And the others?" Amy asked.

"She just came on at three," Owen explained, "and she doesn't have that information yet. Come on," he said, leading the way to the elevator.

Once inside the elevator, Amy wrapped her arms around the doll and took a deep breath.

"Nervous?" Linda asked.

"A little," Amy replied. "I can't believe this has happened. I just . . ." Her sentence died when the elevator came to a stop and the door opened onto a crowded, bustling hospital corridor.

"Welcome to the world of medicine at County General," Owen said as they got off the elevator. Winding his way through people and personnel, he led the small troupe to the nurse's station and asked for the nurse in charge of Agatha Jones.

"Are you her family?" the brusque nurse asked.

"No," Owen explained, once again producing his identification. "I'm in charge of investigating the fire. These are her friends."

"Sorry, only family," the nurse said without emotion.

"She doesn't have any family," Amy blurted out. "We're all she has."

"I see," the nurse replied. "Well, then. Come with me. Only one of you can go in. You, Mr. Investigator, will have to wait. She's in no shape to answer any of your questions tonight. Who will it be, then?"

"Me," Amy said without hesitation and stepped forward to follow the nurse, who was already leading the way to Agatha's room.

"Don't even think of taking that thing in there," the nurse said, pointing to the doll. "Mrs. Jones is at great risk for infection as it is." Pausing at a doorway, she handed Amy an oversized covering and cotton booties. "Here, put this on," she said, "and slip those over your shoes. Then wash your hands over there."

While Amy washed and dried her hands, the nurse slipped a large, elastic-edged cap over Amy's long hair and tucked it up underneath, then turned to scrub and gown herself. "Put those on," she said, nodding toward a box of rubber gloves. Amy obediently stretched the gloves over her hands and followed the nurse behind the curtain drawn around the bed.

"Aggie," the nurse said gently.

Amy couldn't help but notice the sudden change in the woman's demeanor when she approached the bedside of her patient. "Aggie, dear, can you hear me?"

Amy looked toward the bandage-protected upper body and face of Agatha Jones. Her gauze-swathed hands lay motionless beside her on the sterile white sheets. She fought hard to hold back her tears.

"Aggie, you have a friend here who wants to see you," the nurse said to her injured patient. "Come closer," she whispered, motioning to Amy. "What's your name?"

"Amy Weaver," Amy said softly. "John Weaver's daughter."

Both Amy and the attending nurse waited for Aggie's response. Only a low moan came from the white bandages.

"That's right, Aggie. Your friend Amy is here to see you." The nurse checked the line of tubing fastened to Aggie's arm. "She's a little sleepy right now," the nurse explained. "We're trying to keep her as quiet as possible. She's been pretty upset—understandable under the circumstances."

"Aggie," Amy whispered, bending lower toward the limp, wounded woman. "I came as soon as I could find you. I was there today. I came to see you this morning. I . . . I'm sorry I didn't come sooner."

"S'all right," Aggie managed to mutter. "Where's my children?"

"What?" Amy asked, unable to understand the words coming from between Aggie's swollen lips.

"She's been asking about her children," the nurse said.

"I'm trying to find out right now. I'll find them, Aggie. I promise. Then I'll come back and tell you everything, okay?"

"Good," Aggie mumbled, "thank you."

"She needs to rest," the nurse said, nodding toward the door.

Amy stepped closer and looked into Aggie's drugged eyes. "I'll be back, I promise. I'll find the others. I'll see you soon."

Aggie took a deep breath, and Amy could see the pain shoot across her face. Then Aggie closed her eyes, and Amy watched as her breathing became more even and relaxed.

"I think your coming has put her mind at ease. She's been fitful—almost hard to handle ever since she came in this morning. When I came on at three, the day nurses said she'd been almost hysterical at times. That's why we gave her a sedative."

"How badly is she hurt?"

"Her burns are not that bad. We can help keep the pain

down with medication. We'll fight against infection for the next few days. But I'd say she'll have few scars if any, but quite a bit of tenderness—that new skin underneath and all. She could have been much worse. The bandages make it look a lot worse than it really is. In a few days when we take them away, we'll know more about permanent damage."

Amy glanced over her shoulder for one last look at the helpless figure lying in the room before rejoining the others.

"You know, one of the others was taken upstairs," the nurse said as Amy shed the scrub gown and protective shoe coverings. "I heard she had to be restrained and finally sedated."

"Really? Upstairs?"

"Yes, sixth floor. You know, the psych ward." The nurse's words were said with a clinical detachment.

"Do you know her name?"

"I have no idea," the nurse said. "You could check with the admissions office downstairs. They might be able to tell you. Although if you don't have a name—"

"I have a name," Amy said with sudden resolution.

Amy walked quickly to the area where Linda, Jim, and Owen waited. "Come on," she said, grabbing the rag doll from the seat beside Linda. "I think Anna's here."

In the elevator, Owen offered to try to get the information once they reached the admissions office. "It's after visiting hours—they might be more willing to give it to me," he said. "A badge works wonders."

"She's here," he said after a few moments at the admissions office.

"Anna?" Amy's voice refused to come out in anything above a whisper.

"It's Anna," he said. "Ready?"

Amy nodded and Linda quickly came to stand at her elbow. "You want us to go with you?"

"Of course," Amy said.

———

"I'm sorry, miss. It's long past visiting hours, and she's had a very traumatic day." Amy inwardly screamed at the nurse's cool professional manner, but managed to retain her composure.

"But I just learned she was here," Amy said. "I've been looking for her all day. Ever since the fire."

"And who are you?" the nurse asked politely, though somewhat detached.

"I'm . . ." Amy paused for a moment, then straightened her shoulders and tossed her head back confidently. "I'm Amy Weaver."

"Oh," the nurse replied with surprise. "I don't have any family information down here at all."

"Her name is Anna Weaver, right?" Amy asked.

"It is," the nurse answered.

"Is this the Anna Weaver you have here?" Owen asked, coming to stand beside Amy and producing the photo Amy had shown him earlier.

"Yes, I believe it is."

"This is Amy Weaver," Owen said. "And we're not sure who this is," he said, producing the doll. "But we know she's probably wondering what happened to it."

"She sits and cries, rocks back and forth, and says, 'baby, baby, mama, mama.' We've given her a light sedative, nothing very heavy. Just enough to calm her down a bit. I'm sure she'll be glad to see you."

Amy didn't have the courage to tell the nurse that Anna wouldn't know her, that she probably didn't even know she existed. But she wanted to see Anna so desperately she kept the information to herself and hoped that Owen and the others would do the same.

"I'm violating hospital policy here," the nurse explained. "But, come on, just you. The others will have to wait out here."

Linda nodded her encouragement.

"Here," Owen said and handed Amy the picture. "You might want this."

Amy slipped the photograph into her pocket and followed the nurse through a series of locked doors and finally into Anna's darkened room.

"She's over there." The nurse motioned toward the corner

of the room. "She wouldn't eat any supper and she refuses to get into the bed."

"I want to go home," Anna whimpered from her squatted position in the corner.

"Hello, Anna," Amy said softly to the plump, pitiful young woman. "I brought someone who's been looking for you." Amy squatted down and held out the rag doll. "She's been crying all day without you."

Anna's big eyes searched Amy's face without recognition. "I want my mama," Anna whined. "I want baby."

"Here's baby," Amy said, continuing to hold the limp doll toward Anna. "Here's your baby."

Anna dropped her eyes away from Amy's gaze and shrugged her shoulders, tilting her head shyly.

"Go ahead, Anna," Amy urged. "Here's baby. She's a little dirty. She fell into the water. A nice man pulled her out and brought her to me so I could give her back to you. Isn't this your baby?"

Anna glanced out of the corner of her eyes at the rag doll in Amy's outstretched hands. A smile tugged at the corner of her mouth.

"I want to go home," Anna said, sticking a finger deep into her mouth. "I want my mama."

"Baby's been hurt, Anna," Amy said. "She has to stay in the hospital. You can't leave her here all by herself, can you? She wants you to stay with her. She needs you to take care of her. See how hurt she is?" Amy touched the dirty spots on the doll's legs and arms.

Anna continued to chew on her fingers, but looked with more interest at the doll Amy held. Looking briefly at Amy, then turning her face toward the wall, Anna held out her hand toward the doll in Amy's hand. Amy pressed the soft cloth body into the curve of Anna's arm, which quickly closed around the beloved toy. Anna buried her face in the shaggy yarn hair. "I want Mama," she whined softly.

"Mama's downstairs," Amy whispered gently. "She's in her room. She—well, she got hurt today. And the nurses are fixing her up. She's right downstairs."

"I want to go—"

"No, honey. Not tonight," Amy said. "You have dolly here to take care of. She fell down today and needs to stay in the hospital. If you take care of baby, I'll go tell Mama you're safe. I'll take care of Mama, okay? I'll tell her you're right here with baby dolly here so she won't worry about you."

Amy glanced up into the face of the smiling nurse, who had been watching the entire scene with fascination. Without saying a word, she gestured toward the bed and raised her eyebrows, indicating that perhaps Amy could persuade Anna to get into the bed.

"Anna, sweetheart," Amy said to the huddled figure on the floor. "Baby needs to go to bed. She got so cold coming over here. Can you see if you can get her to go to bed? Will you sleep with her so she won't be afraid? She's never been away from home before." Amy took a deep breath. "Can you do that, honey? Can you get your baby to go to bed?"

Amy stood and held out her hand as Anna struggled to her feet and kept as close to the wall as possible. Remembering the photo, Amy said, "Anna, I have something else for you." She pulled the picture from her pocket. "Here, honey, bring baby to bed and I'll give this to you. It's special. I promise, I'll give it to you when you bring baby to bed."

Suspiciously, Anna walked slowly toward Amy's outstretched hand. Amy noticed her slight shuffle. Anna kept the fingers of one hand in her mouth and tightly gripped the doll in her other hand.

"That's a girl," Amy said. "Bring baby to bed."

"We need to restrain her," the nurse whispered to Amy.

"In a minute," Amy said. "Let me see if I can get closer to her, okay?"

"I'd be a fool to argue with you. We haven't even been able to get her out of that corner."

"Look, Anna," Amy said, coming close enough to touch the child-woman. "Look here, do you know who this is?" Amy held out the picture. "Is this Anna and her baby?"

Anna looked at the picture in Amy's hand and nodded.

"Would you like to have this?"

Anna nodded again.

"When you get baby into bed, I'll give you the picture, okay?"

Without taking her eyes from the promised photo, Anna Weaver obediently climbed into bed, holding her dolly in a tight, possessive grip. After she was in bed, Amy gave her the picture.

"Anna, sweetheart. Can you wear the special pajamas the nurse has for you?" Amy asked.

Anna shook her head in refusal.

"But, Anna,"—Amy took a deep breath and wondered how she would persuade Anna to accept the bed restraint—"baby might fall out of bed. If you put this on and put baby right here inside with you, she'll be safe. We don't have a baby bed for her. You don't want her to fall out, now do you?"

Anna shook her head. "What's your name?" Anna asked between the fingers in her mouth.

"Amy."

"My name's Anna."

"I know," Amy said softly. "Can I sit with you, Anna?"

Anna nodded, and Amy sat close enough to put her arm around Anna's shoulders.

"Who's this?" Amy asked, pointing to the smiling face in the photograph.

"That's me," Anna said.

"And who's this?" Amy said, pointing to the doll.

"Baby. That's my baby."

"Are you hungry, Anna? Would you like something to eat?" Anna shook her head.

"Are you tired? Baby's tired, aren't you, baby?" Amy said, addressing the question to the doll clutched tightly in Anna's arm. "Anna, would you like me to bring you another picture?" Anna nodded.

"Then tomorrow, I'll come back and bring you another picture. But you have to promise me you'll take care of baby. Okay?" Anna nodded and Amy continued. "Here, darling," she said, taking the restraining harness from the nurse's hand. "Put on your special pajamas, tuck baby right in here so she won't fall, and then you go to sleep. I'll be back before you know it. And I'll bring you another picture. That's a good girl,"

Amy said as Anna obediently held out her arms and Amy slipped on the restraint. "That's my good Anna."

"What's your name?" Anna repeated the question.

"Amy."

"Are you my friend?" the innocent child-woman asked.

"Yes, honey, I'm your friend."

Sitting on the bed, Amy soothed Anna's forehead and finally kissed her lightly as Anna fell asleep almost immediately with baby doll securely tucked inside the required hospital restraint. Amy stood to one side as the nurse quickly fastened the restraint to the bed and pulled up the side rails as well. Silently, they slipped from the room.

"Are you just a friend?" the nurse said in a hushed tone as they walked down the hallway and back through the locked doors. "I thought you were her sister."

"I'm not sure there's a difference," Amy said thoughtfully. "Not in our case, anyway."

Amy walked wearily toward the threesome waiting for her near the elevator. *Now what? Where do I go from here?* The question struggled to surface in her mind. *Who knows?* her inner dialogue continued. "I'm too tired to think about this right now," she said aloud to no one in particular. "I just want to go home and go to bed."

Fifteen

Finally alone in the dark house, Amy discovered that as bone tired as she was, sleep would not come. In the dark she reached for her robe and found her slippers. Wrapping herself in the quilt off her bed, she went into the living room and sat in her mother's favorite chair by the window.

Slowly, she began to mentally organize the loose threads of her life. There was so much to think about, so many lives involved.

The meeting with the city leaders to discuss the conditions of the sale of her downtown property was only days away. She really didn't want to block the project, nor did she want to call attention to herself or flex any selfish muscles. It was the long-standing businesses, the livelihood of her tenants, and the responsibility she knew her father would expect her to take in their behalf that motivated her. Marshall Jennings would grandstand the issues if at all possible. He was building a business reputation for himself in Summerwind, and he'd use anything or anyone to accomplish his goals. *So, let him*, she said to herself. *As long as they are taken care of and treated well, I don't care who gets the credit.* He'd be calling before long, she knew that. Furthermore, she knew she'd have to be ready and strong enough to keep her head. Marshall wasn't especially bright, in Amy's opinion, but he was clever. *Owen, on the other hand, is very intelligent.* Amy pushed thoughts of Owen Sampson from her mind. *I can't think about him right now*, she scolded herself. *There's too much else to think about.*

"There's Morningside," she said aloud into the darkness.

Clutching the quilt tightly around her, she pulled her knees up and rested her feet on the edge of the soft cushion. Closing her eyes, she saw Anna's wide-eyed and trusting face.

Who is Anna Weaver? The question burned not only in her mind, but in her heart. *Where did this person come from? And who is Baby Anna? Do I have a right to know? After all these years, was it better to leave it alone? Was Adele Jennings right all along?*

"Oh, Mama," Amy sighed, "I wish you could tell me all about this. Tell me what to do."

Amy walked to her mother's bedroom and stood beside the large bed as she had so many nights as a child. Bad dreams, upset stomachs, and earaches had brought her here then—unanswered questions, heartache, and loneliness brought her here now.

Dropping the quilt from her own bed on the floor, Amy pulled back the covers and slipped between the sheets. Burying her face in her mother's pillow, she pulled her father's pillow within the circle of her arms. Silently, her tears slipping onto the carefully ironed pillowcases, Amy Weaver cried herself to sleep.

———

"I have news," Owen said in an early morning phone call. "There was a message waiting for me when I got back to the station house late last night. The other Morningside residents have been taken to temporary homes."

"Are they together?" Amy asked. Massaging her temple and forehead, she tried to rub the weariness away. Even with a headache, she liked the sound of his voice.

"No, I'm afraid not," he said. "It's pretty hard to place them together. Most places that can care for them are already overcrowded. The two boys are together, and the other girl is alone. They hope to take Anna to be with the other girl as soon as she can be released from the hospital."

"She's only there because she was hysterical at being separated from Aggie," Amy said.

"I gathered that much last night," Owen responded.

"I'll be going back to see Aggie this morning before I go up to see Anna. I want to check on her progress myself."

"Want some company?"

Amy hesitated, afraid to admit that she liked the idea of Owen's company.

"I don't have anything else to do today," Owen said. "Besides, it wouldn't hurt to see if Anna can give us any further information on the fire."

"I'm not sure they'll let you see her," Amy said, remembering how frightened Anna was of even the nurses.

"That's all right, you can ask her everything I need to know. I'd really like to drive you over."

"Thank you. That would be nice. I wasn't looking forward to going alone."

Owen said he'd be by in forty-five minutes, giving Amy time to shower and dress. "I haven't had breakfast yet. Why not stop at Bob's on the way?" Owen suggested.

Amy wondered why she agreed, but once she was sitting across from Owen sipping the rich, strong restaurant coffee, she was glad she did. She told herself she was grateful only for his company, certainly not because she had an interest in him otherwise. Not noticing his strong, handsome features took a nearly impossible level of inner discipline. *It's just because I'm going through so much right now,* she lied to herself. *I'm just grateful for his help—and nothing more.*

"I have a confession to make," he said.

"Oh?" Amy's stomach tightened slightly.

"I told you something, that if I was totally honest . . ." Owen stammered. "I have to admit it bordered on untruth. I have all the information I need to file my report. In fact, my report is already in. I really don't expect Anna to be able to shed any more light on the case, but . . ."

He really didn't have to finish his sentence. Amy felt her neck burn and knew that a deep pink color would soon flood her cheeks.

"The truth is . . ." he hesitated, "it was a good excuse to see you again."

"Oh," she said simply. Her heart pounded in her chest. She tried to casually sip her coffee, keeping her eyes away from looking into the warmth of the hazel brown of his.

"Did I need an excuse?" he asked. His wide smile, ever so slightly to one side, made the dimple in his chin appear again.

"Owen, I . . ."

"Are you involved with someone, Amy?" he asked. Amy liked the way he was up front and direct. "If you are, just say so and I'll back away."

"I'm not," she said. "Not really."

"No?"

"Well, I mean, I was and in some respects still am. But not like that."

"Like that?"

"I recently broke off—well, I was engaged."

"Recently?"

"Yeah," she said.

"Well, is this my lucky day or not?" Owen teased.

"You're embarrassing me," she complained quietly, catching the honey-colored glimmer in his eye.

"I'd never do that, Miss Weaver. Not on purpose anyway. And I won't rush you either. Need some time?"

"Maybe," she said. "I'd appreciate that."

"A week or two enough?" He was smiling again. Amy willed her stomach to remain calm.

"I guess . . ." She knew her answer sounded vague, but didn't try to correct it.

———

At the hospital an hour later, Amy approached the nurse on duty. "How is Aggie Jones?"

"She had a fairly good night, considering. I understand you came by last night. The night nurse said it really helped put her mind at ease. Go ahead and gown; we're still being cautious. Maybe even overly cautious. But even though her burns aren't that serious, an infection could be. She'll be glad to see you. She's talking a lot more this morning. We're not sedating her as much as we did last night."

"Aggie?" Amy said, coming close to the still-bandaged woman. "Hello." Amy smiled at the eyes that opened to her greeting.

"Amy Weaver?" Aggie asked hoarsely.

"Good morning," Amy said. "How are you feeling?"

"Sore," Aggie said. "Then you are John's daughter."

"Yes."

"I'm glad you're here," Aggie said, then licked her sore, cracked lips.

"Are you thirsty? Can I get you some water?" Amy reached for the glass on the bedside stand. "Here," she said, holding the straw to Aggie's parched mouth.

"Thanks," Aggie said after taking a couple of sips. "Have you seen Anna?"

"Yes. I saw her last night. I'm going up after I see you. I wanted to see you first."

"Is she all right?"

"I don't know how she is this morning. I took her her doll last night and then stayed with her until she went to sleep."

"John gave her that doll," Aggie said quietly. "I thought it was gone—everything's gone, isn't it?"

"But you're alive, Aggie, and the others are all safe. I know where they are."

"Are they okay?"

"As far as I can tell, they are safe."

"Thank God! But Jimmy," Aggie started to cry. "Poor Jimmy."

"They're notifying his family, I imagine," Amy said.

"It won't matter," Aggie said. "They never bother about him. Most of them don't. They don't know what to do. These little children need special attention, Amy. They're like children who never grow up—except in size. Jimmy was only about three or four years old in his mind, but he had the strength of a man. I couldn't handle him anymore."

"How long did he live with you?"

"Since he was eight or nine. His parents brought him one day, and they never looked back. It was the saddest thing to see. Mary's parents, though, they come by. And once in a while they take her home with them. They're always good about remembering her birthday, and she is with them almost every Christmas. Ernest is alone, though. We're all the family he has. Beau's family don't contact me directly. But they send gifts with the social worker. And Anna, well, she had your father. He was always wonderful to all the children but was especially partial to Anna."

"Why was that, Aggie?" Amy said, leaning closer.

"It's a long story, I'm afraid," Aggie said, motioning toward the glass for more water.

After taking another few sips, Aggie started coughing. Instinctively, Amy slipped her arm under the woman for support and reached for the call button. By the time the nurse arrived, Aggie was spitting up dark, oily phlegm.

"Well, well," the nurse said cheerfully. "Getting some of that grimy smoke out of there, I see."

Amy gently began massaging the back of Aggie's shoulders. "Just relax, Aggie. Don't force it. It'll come when it's ready. That's right," she coaxed. Aggie relaxed against her gentle touch. "That's good."

"Well, miss, I see you're no stranger to hospitals," the nurse said with an inquiring tone.

"I'm a third-year nursing student—or at least I was."

"You didn't drop out, I hope," the nurse said more forcefully. "There's a shortage of good nurses. I bet you'd be a good one."

"For the time being, anyway," Amy said. "I haven't decided about next year."

"You know, County General has just opened a two-year program for licensed practical nurses—LPNs—if you're interested. Seems they'll be doing all the patient care before long and the RNs will be relegated to paperwork and supervisory positions. It's not my idea of nursing, but it seems to be the coming thing nowadays." As Amy held her gently, the nurse straightened Aggie's pillows. "There, my pet," the nurse said affectionately. "Better now?"

"Thank you," Aggie said. "I'm just so tired."

"Listen, Aggie," Amy said, "I'll go on up and check on Anna, okay? We've got plenty of time to talk later—when you're a bit more rested. And once you get those bandages off, we'll have a nice long visit. How's that?"

"Tell Anna I love her. Tell her everything's going to be all right." Aggie's eyes filled with tears.

"I will, Aggie. I will. And don't you forget that yourself," Amy said. "Everything *is* going to be all right."

Owen was waiting for Amy when she came out of the burn unit. Silently, they walked together to the elevator. He didn't want to press her into talking. He just knew he liked being with her. He'd be happy to sit all morning out in the hallway waiting for her. Without question, this young woman was someone he guessed could hold his interest all morning, all year, maybe even his entire lifetime.

"You okay?" he asked simply as the elevator doors closed them in alone in the center of the busy hospital.

"Yes, thanks," she replied.

"You ready for Anna?"

"I hope so," she said.

"You'll do fine," he reassured. Knowing her less than twenty-four hours, he already guessed there wasn't much she couldn't handle. His conversation with Jim and Linda Henry the previous night had confirmed his first impressions that Amy Weaver was a young woman of strength and character. A woman worth knowing. Owen Sampson had dated many women and had been teased often about being such an eligible bachelor. Even his twenty-seven-year-old sister, two years his junior, was married with two kids and another one on the way. His parents, in their mid-fifties, said God was keeping him for someone more special than even he could imagine. He smiled at Amy as they stepped from the elevator and wondered what they'd think of Amy. *And,* he thought, *what in the world would she think of them?*

"Good morning, Anna. Remember me?" Amy said with a gentle smile playing on her lips. "How'd you sleep? How's baby this morning?"

"What's your name?" Anna asked, staring at her hands. She sat near the bed, with the restraints Amy had convinced her to wear last night now attached to the chair.

"My name's Amy. I came last night, remember?"

"Uh-huh," Anna said quietly, nodding her head.

"I saw your mama downstairs."

"I want my mama." Anna started to cry.

"Very soon," Amy promised. "She's kind of hurt now. She got hurt at the fire yesterday. Do you remember the fire?"

Anna nodded.

"Do you know how it happened?"

Anna tilted her head to one side and frowned.

"You can tell me, Anna. Don't be afraid, okay? Nobody's going to hurt you. Do you know how the fire started, sweetheart?"

"Jimmy did it."

"Did you see him do it, darling?"

"He didn't let me go in there. His funny books were under there."

"Under where?"

"Under the porch. I wanted to see them too, but he said I couldn't. He never let me see them."

"Where'd he get the funny books, honey?"

"I don't know," Anna said, shrugging her shoulders. She stole a quick glance into Amy's eyes, then quickly looked away.

"I brought you something," Amy said, reaching into the front pocket on her purse. "You want a surprise?"

Anna shrugged, but the smile tugging at her mouth said it was exactly what she wanted.

"I brought you a picture," Amy said, "just like I promised. See?" Amy held out another snapshot from her father's file.

Anna looked at the picture but didn't take it from Amy's hand.

"Do you know who this is?" Amy pointed to Aggie's image.

"That's my mama," Anna said.

"And who's this?" Amy pointed to Anna's own smiling face.

"That's me," she said.

"And who's that?" Amy asked, pointing to her own father's familiar profile standing to one side almost out of the picture completely.

"That's my daddy," Anna said sadly.

Amy's heart almost stopped for a moment before it began beating hard and fast. "Is that your daddy?" she asked, trying to keep her voice calm and soothing.

"Uh-huh," Anna said, nodding vigorously.

"Where's your daddy, Anna?"

"In heaven with Jesus," the child-woman said. "Mama says he likes it there. She says he isn't coming back anymore."

"That's right, sweetheart," Amy whispered. "He's in heaven."

"Do you know my daddy?"

"Uh-huh." Amy nodded, then added quietly, "He was my daddy too."

Anna looked at Amy with a wide-open expression of total trust. "Oh," she said with total, innocent acceptance.

"Listen, Anna." Amy rummaged through her purse for a pad and pencil. "Can we write your mama a note? Do you think she'd like that?"

"I can write my name," Anna said, taking the writing materials from Amy's hand.

For the next few minutes Anna and Amy worked together making a handwritten get-well message for Aggie. Once the project was finished to the satisfaction of both, Amy promised to take it to Aggie.

"And a present," Anna said. Her eyes twinkled and she clasped her hands at her breast.

"Let's see," Amy said joining into the game. "What shall it be?"

Suddenly Anna grabbed Amy's hand and planted a damp kiss firmly in the palm. Then she ceremoniously closed Amy's fingers and patted her kiss-filled fist. "Now don't lose it, okay?"

"I won't, Anna, I promise." Amy could barely contain her emotions. "I have to go now, okay?"

"Will you come back?"

"Yes, sweetheart, I promise." Her fist tightly closed around Anna's kiss-present, Amy barely made it into the hallway before the tears poured down her cheeks. Her emotions threatened to explode within her chest, and she pressed her fist to her mouth. How would she ever explain to anyone the little kiss-present game her father had taught her—and obviously had taught Anna as well? How many times had she been the courier for her father sending her mother such a tender gift?

Had Anna also carried the same gift to Aggie? Such a thought terrified her, but as much as she tried to push it away, it wouldn't be put out of her mind.

Owen stood as soon as he heard her footsteps approaching the locked door of the psych ward. Without warning, she burst into audible sobs the moment she stepped through the doorway. Instinctively, Owen opened his arms and gently pulled Amy into his protective embrace.

When her sobs finally subsided, Owen gently guided her to a seat nearby. He chose to ignore the inquisitive glances and even several open stares of others in the waiting area. Opening her purse, he found a tissue and tenderly began wiping her tears.

"Can you talk about it?" he asked when she seemed to be more composed. Amy shook her head. "Do you want to go?" he asked. She nodded, and Owen helped her to her feet and slipped his arm around her waist for support.

After they were on the highway between County Hospital and Summerwind, he asked, "Do you want to go home?"

"No," she said barely above a hoarse whisper. "I want to go to the cemetery."

"Do you want to go alone?" he asked, hoping she'd let him go with her.

"No," she said. "I don't. Do you mind? I'd—" Her voice broke and she became silent.

"I'll take you," he said.

"Thank you," she replied. For the twenty-minute ride to the Summerwind Cemetery, only Amy's quiet, involuntary, sighlike sobs broke the silence.

Sixteen

"I'll wait here," Owen said as he pulled the car to the curb.

"Yes, thank you," Amy said.

Owen watched as Amy walked across the well-groomed lawn dotted with the flat, rectangular granite markers. The thick elm trees provided cooling shade even in the middle of the day. The tall, pencil-shaped cypress trees lined the gracefully curved walkways, and majestic thin palms towered above, swaying gently in the chilly late November breeze.

Glancing away from the parklike surroundings, Owen noticed how tightly Amy kept her arms about her middle and wished she had worn a jacket instead of a lightweight cardigan sweater. He thought he saw her shiver against the light wind and wished she'd come back to the car. Glancing in the backseat, he saw his college letter sweater rolled and tossed in a heap. Without further thought, he grabbed the sweater and decided to take it to Amy.

"This is my father, Owen," she said as he came close enough to hear. "John Weaver."

Owen wanted to take away the loneliness that cast dark shadows across her blue eyes. He gently covered her shoulders with his heavy sweater.

"And this is my mother, Charlotte Weaver."

Amy turned away and began walking toward what appeared to be the manager's office and maintenance building. Owen didn't move until she paused and turned slightly toward him. Needing no further invitation, he fell into step beside her. Several hundred feet down the path she turned and stepped carefully toward another grave. Owen followed close behind.

"And this is my sister," Amy said, staring at the headstone.

Baby Anna. Owen read the inscription silently. He looked

into Amy's eyes and saw her pain and confusion.

"At least I think this is my sister," she said barely above a whisper.

"Then who is—?" he asked, gesturing toward the distant County General Hospital.

"I have no idea," she said. "I have no idea whatsoever."

"And why isn't she buried over there, with your parents?" Owen felt immediately sorry he had expressed his own confusion. "I'm sorry, Amy, this isn't any of my business. I didn't mean to intrude."

Amy turned to face him. "Don't be sorry. You're not intruding. I haven't the slightest idea why she isn't buried over there. Perhaps these places weren't available when Mama came to buy Daddy's—" Her voice broke and Owen saw the tears spill down her face. "There are so many unanswered questions," she said softly. "So many things I just don't know or understand."

Owen wanted to take this beautiful young woman in his arms and surround her with comfort and protection. *It's too soon. Don't rush this*, he reminded himself firmly.

———

"Amy," Owen said as he walked her to her front door a little later, "could I help you find out what this is all about? Would you mind if I asked around a little? Maybe I can come up with something, maybe not. But I'd really like to help."

"But don't you have your work? Aren't you too busy for this?"

"No," Owen said. "I'm not that busy. I'd really like to help. I think I know how to ask questions and get accurate and helpful answers. It's what I do for a living, you know."

"I just don't want to impose," Amy said. "I don't want to be any bother."

"It's no bother, really."

Turning to put her key in the lock, Amy almost tripped over a bouquet of flowers placed at the door by one of the city florists.

Owen held the lovely arrangement and watched as she read the card attached. *Missing you, Marshall.* Her short intake of breath and the frown that briefly crossed her forehead didn't escape Owen's notice.

"Something wrong?" he asked.

"No, not really," she answered as she unlocked the door. She paused before going in. "Thank you, Owen," she said. "For going with me today. I appreciated not being alone out there."

"You're welcome. Anytime," he said, still holding the flowers. "I can call you, then? When I have some information?"

"Yes," Amy said. "You can call me." As she turned her head slightly, a long blond strand of hair fell forward over her shoulder. "Even if you don't have any information. I mean," she quickly added, "even dead ends tell us something, don't they?"

"They certainly do," he responded. "Then I'll talk to you later."

"Later," she agreed.

"Amy," he said as she moved to enter the house. "Your flowers." He shoved the bouquet slightly toward her.

"I don't want them," she said simply, tucking the sender's card back between the blossoms.

"Then I'll—" Owen stepped backward, smiling. "I'll just take care of them."

"Thank you again," Amy said as she quietly shut the door.

Back in his car, Owen balanced the bright bouquet on the seat beside him and waited until he turned the corner before he reached for the sender's card. "Too bad, Marshall," he said aloud, "whoever you are."

———

On Sunday morning, Amy decided at the last minute to go to church. The experience was a heartwarming one as members of the small, nontraditional congregation made her feel welcome. Pleasantly surprised to see Owen slip in and sit on the opposite side of the room, she quickly looked away when he smiled at her. Something in his glance made her pulse quicken. As nice as it was, she felt guilty at the same time. After all, church wasn't a place for flirtations. Suddenly, she wondered if her mother would approve of Owen Sampson, then willed her thoughts to return to Jim Henry's remarks as he prepared his congregation for worship.

Politely refusing an invitation to dinner at the Kelleys' with Jim and Linda, Amy decided to have a quiet day at home with Princess. She wished her father's television set were in the house but resisted the thought of going out to his office. She retrieved the Sunday paper from the front porch and settled down on the sofa with a cup of tea and the comics, the contented family pet curled up at her feet. Soon the quietness bored her, and disturbingly, her thoughts kept wandering to Owen. She wished she had gone with Jim and Linda. Glancing at the clock, she realized that a long, uneventful afternoon stretching out in front of her was not how she wanted to spend the day.

"I wish I hadn't told him to give me some time," she confided to Princess. "After all, I'm not recovering from my breakup with Marsh in the usual sort of way, don't you agree?"

Princess wagged her tail.

"Listen to me, will you?" she scolded. "I'm acting like a high school girl."

Then, taking a deep breath, she decided time was exactly what she needed. After all, too much had happened to her in a few short weeks. Right after her father's death, she had rushed into an engagement with Marshall, a mistake she was determined not to repeat. "Not with Owen, not with anyone," she whispered into the silent room.

"Come on, doggie," she said in a moment of determination. "We can make better use of the afternoon than this."

Changing into her jeans and an old sweater, she walked resolutely toward the garage. Stacked full of magazines, Charlotte's quilting frame, canning jars, and old furniture, the garage hadn't housed the family automobile for years. She swung open the double doors and cringed as the iron hinges squeaked from rust.

"Hey, what's going on over there?" Linda called from the other side of the fence that separated their yards. Unable to see much through the thick oleander bushes hedging both sides of the chain link fence, Linda peered through a small opening in the foliage.

"Come on over and see for yourself," Amy called back good-naturedly. "But you better be prepared—don't wear that," she said, pointing to Linda's tailored white-and-navy linen suit. "Get your work clothes on and come give me a hand."

"Sounds good to me," Linda answered. "I don't have anything better to do. Jim's meeting with the church board all afternoon anyway. Have you had lunch?"

"Not yet," Amy said. "I thought I'd better get started out here first."

"Oh sure. Then you wouldn't eat until suppertime. Come on over. Kassy sent home a meatloaf sandwich for you. She thought you might not take the time to eat right. Let's sit awhile before we tackle whatever it is you've got going over there. We'll be fortified and ready for the long haul."

By late afternoon the two young women had managed to haul a half-dozen boxes of old magazines out into the driveway as well as an old wringer washing machine. "It's probably still in good working order," Amy observed. "Mama didn't believe in throwing anything out."

"No kidding," Linda quipped.

Amy's wrought-iron baby crib was stacked to one side of the driveway with Charlotte's quilting frame and some curtain stretchers. Some pants stretchers and an old ironing board were put alongside the washing machine awaiting a pickup from the Salvation Army or the Goodwill. Amy was undecided about the treadle Singer sewing machine and, since the oak cabinet was too heavy to move easily, decided to deal with it later.

"What about this daybed?" Linda asked as she pointed to the wooden and metal piece covered with a dusty canvas in the corner.

"I don't know. Mama always kept it for company. But we didn't really have all that much company. It's kind of charming, don't you think?"

They pulled it out into the driveway for a closer inspection. Linda noted that with the right cover and a few large pillows, it could be quite useful in a TV room or on a back sitting porch or sun-room.

"Good idea," Amy said. "I'll take it inside when I make my room into the TV room."

"Then what will you do with the twin beds? Put them out in the garage?" Linda teased.

"No, I won't," Amy retorted. It felt good to do something physically challenging for a change, and Linda's lighthearted company kept Amy's spirits up as well. "I'll either put them in the front bedroom or I'll keep my mother's big bed and get rid of them. Do you know anyone who could use them? Maybe I could give them to someone who really needs them."

"What about Agatha Jones? I bet she could use some furniture."

Amy's heart skipped a beat at Linda's suggestion, and she dropped her end of the daybed mattress, nearly knocking Linda off balance. "What a wonderful idea! I bet with just a little effort we could find all kinds of people who would like to donate furniture and household goods to help replace what she lost. And I know just the person who would help us," Amy said, running toward the house to call Owen, with Princess excitedly running right behind her.

"Wait a minute, Amy!" Linda yelled after her. "Amy! Finish *this* project before you start another one, will you?"

Amy rummaged through the files on the dining room table for Owen's business card. "I only want his advice," she said to herself, ignoring her own inner signals. Then she quickly dialed his number from the phone in the kitchen. Disappointed when he didn't answer after the sixth ring, she slowly replaced the receiver in its cradle. The knock at her front door spread a smile across her face.

Opening the door, she found Marshall Jennings waiting for her to answer his knock.

"Oh, Marshall," she said, not even trying to hide her disappointment.

"Well, I'm happy to know seeing me pleases you so much," he said in an irritated tone.

"I didn't know you were coming."

"I wanted to surprise you," he said. "May I come in?"

"I'm sort of busy right now," she said, glancing at her dirty work clothes, then at his crisply pressed navy slacks and pull-over V-necked sweater. "I'm cleaning the garage. I can see you're not ready to help me do that."

"No, that I'm not. Can't it wait? I was hoping you'd be in the mood to go for a drive. We've still a lot of things to talk over. I just wanted to—"

"Wait a minute, Marsh," Amy warned, holding up both hands as if to keep him from coming any closer. "We don't have anything to discuss. We broke our engagement. We didn't get a divorce. There's no property settlement or children involved here."

"*You* broke the engagement—I didn't."

"That's all it takes," she said impatiently. Of all things, Amy didn't want Marshall around today—not today. Today she was beginning to see a purpose and have plans beyond her pain, something that would take her out of her own grief and give her a reason for getting up in the morning besides her father's papers and files. "Please, Marshall, this isn't a good day."

"Amy," he said, stepping closer and catching her hands in his to pull her near, "I miss you."

"So you said."

"Oh, then you got my flowers," he remarked, looking around the room. "Where are they?"

"I didn't keep them. I don't want flowers from you."

"Amy, look, I've done some pretty stupid things where you're concerned. Can't you let me try to make things right?"

"You had six months to do that. Why now? Why didn't you—"

"You're not making this any easier for me," he said, bringing his face near enough for Amy to feel his breath as he spoke. "Amy, love, I need you. Can't you see what this is doing to me?"

"No," she said, breaking free of his clasp. "No. You don't seem to understand my position here—I said it's over and it's over. Can it be more simple than that?"

"Can't we at least try to be friends?" he asked in a more conciliatory tone. "Can't you at least allow me that?"

"Marshall Jennings," Amy laughed, "if we could be friends, we'd probably still be engaged. I don't think you know how to be friends. All you know is how to move in when it best suits you and take advantage of any situation you see might be able to work in your favor. No, I don't think I want that kind of friend."

"I heard about the fire," Marshall said, determined not to give up.

"Oh?"

"It's in the morning paper."

"It is? I read the paper this morning—I didn't see it."

"Did you read the regional section?"

"Come to think of it," Amy said, picking up the scattered newspaper from the floor near the couch, "I only read the comics."

Quickly searching through the thick sections, Amy was pleased to find the story occupying a prominent place on the front page of the regional section. Slowly lowering herself to sit on the couch, she scanned the text.

"This is great," she said softly.

"I don't understand," Marshall said, coming to sit beside her.

"Another story next week should get us all the help we need," Amy replied. "I'll contact the feature editor and see if we can get a human interest story on Aggie. Then I'll contact the Morningside Fire Department and see if we can get them to help us with a fund raiser or even a donation spot for household goods, furniture, and perhaps even nonperishable food."

"Amy, you're carrying this a little far, if you ask me."

"I didn't."

"Yes, you are."

"I didn't ask you," she said without taking her eyes from the pictures in the newspaper.

"Listen to reason, will you? We've already got a shopping mall project that's on hold because you want to babysit the tenants in your building. Can't you take care of one thing at a time? Come on, what is most pressing? The downtown project or a houseful of displaced, feeble-minded people? Where are your priorities? Take care of your charity cases after the business issues are settled, will you?"

"I'd like you to go now." Amy struggled to control her temper.

"Amy, listen to me." Marshall's voice was edged with panic. "I've got a business reputation hanging in the balance here, and all you can think of is an old out-of-date tailor, a middle-aged woman who makes cookies, and this group of idiots who should be in an institution somewhere. You can't be everyone's social worker. I need you to have your head on straight right now. Let the do-gooders raise the money and food if necessary. You've got the entire city's economic future hanging in the balance because of your stupid—"

"I said, you should leave now," Amy repeated, raising her voice slightly. "Don't say any more, Marshall—I mean it." She held up her hand to stop him.

"How can I make you understand?" Marshall said, stepping tentatively toward the front door. "Can't you see how important this is?"

"Now *you* listen to me, Marshall Jennings," Amy said firmly. Standing to her feet, she closed the distance between them. With both hands firmly placed on her hips, she threw her long hair behind her back with a determined toss of her head. Tilting her face upward to look directly into Marshall's, she continued. "Those people have been living near poverty on whatever the state provides. If it hadn't been for my father's generosity and the commitment of Agatha Jones, those dear, simple people would have been sent to some cold, impersonal state facility and forgotten by now. Can you imagine how miserable they would be? No. Of course not. Not you. You live up the hill in your fancy house with a swimming pool and gas barbecue. Now they have nothing. All Aggie owns is the land. My guess is that she was grossly underinsured. But what does that matter to you? You've got your fancy shopping mall to build. The likes of Aggie Jones and her family wouldn't even be welcome in that place, would they? No," she continued after pausing only long enough to catch her breath. "Of course not. Your upper-class friends would be uncomfortable if Aggie brought her family there, wouldn't they? So let's just put them in some institution and keep the doors closed and the gates locked so we don't have to be reminded that some are born less fortunate than others. That some people are born with big hearts and damaged brains. That some people, no matter how you try, can only be taught to love and sing little songs and play simple games."

Marshall turned on his heel and headed out the door.

"Go ahead and run away from all this, Marshall. But I won't. Not when I can do something to make a difference in their lives," Amy yelled after his retreating figure. "You go right ahead and carry on your father's business. And," she said, with even more determination in her voice, "let me do the same."

Without looking back, Marshall almost jumped into his car and sped away. Amy crossed the porch looking after him, unaware of Linda's presence behind her as she allowed some tears to spill down her cheeks.

"Well, Miss Weaver," Linda said in mock dismay, "I pray I never get on the bad side of you."

Turning toward her friend, Amy quickly wiped away her tears with the back of her dirty hand. Linda took one look at the dirt-streaked, smiling face and spun her friend around to see her reflection in the living room window. Together, the two women broke into gales of laughter.

"I didn't know it could happen like this," Amy said after washing her face and joining Linda in the kitchen for a bottle of cola.

"What couldn't happen like what?"

"Within two months, my whole life has turned completely around. It's kind of scary. I hardly even recognize myself."

"How's that?" Linda asked before touching her lips to an icy bottle of soda.

"I've always thought of what my father left as an inheritance. I've never assumed it came without responsibility. But he left me more than that. I don't know," she said, thoughtfully searching for the right word. "It's more than an inheritance, don't you see that?"

Linda waited for Amy to finish her thought.

"My parents taught me a way of life. To look at wealth as a

blessing to be shared—to meet needs where people are helpless to meet their own. I have been handed an awesome responsibility, Linda. I can't shake the thought—it's more than
an inheritance."

"What is it, then?" Linda asked.

"What do you call it? An inheritance would be something
I'd feel free to spend or invest according to my own desires.
This isn't like that at all. My father's money has never been
our security or even our standing in the community. It's been
a means—a way to support something much more. What do
you call it when you've been given a way of life to carry on? A
set of standards and a desire to helping others?"

"I know what I'd call it," Linda said quietly.

Amy's face brightened with anticipation. "Well, then?"

"I'd call it a legacy."

Seventeen

A legacy. The thought lingered with Amy. She liked the idea of having something not only to be responsible for, but to continue and eventually pass on to others. On Monday she decided to think about something other than the shopping mall, Anna Weaver, and Aggie. Her luncheon with the city leaders was set for Wednesday.

Glad for the diversion of the redecorating project, she needed to get the bedrooms ready for the painters, coming first thing Wednesday morning.

"But first," she told Princess, "I have to call Mr. Carlson. I want to ask him a question. Oh no," she teased, "I'm not going to tell you, or anybody else. It's a secret. Just this one call, I promise, then we'll go through the rest of Mama's things and get ready to move into her bedroom. How will that be?" Princess wagged her tail in approval.

Amy spent the rest of Monday and most of Tuesday folding and packing away Charlotte's simple wardrobe and preparing her father's clothes for donating to the Salvation Army. Amy was a little taken back by the lacy nightgowns carefully stored in Charlotte's bottom dresser drawer. "Why, Mama," Amy whispered teasingly to her mother's picture, "I'm shocked." Immediately sobering, she said softly, "And, I miss you so much."

On Wednesday, Amy gave the painters their instructions before meeting with Marshall a little earlier than the rest of the community leaders. He had insisted, and wanting to make sure she knew what to expect at the luncheon, she acquiesced.

"So," she asked once they were seated at the restaurant, "what's on your mind?"

"You," he said bluntly. "I can't seem to get you out of it these days."

"Oh, and you could before?"

"Amy, don't be like that. You've had your say and I know where you stand. But hear me out, will you, please?"

"I'm listening," she said, sipping a cup of coffee.

"I miss you," he began.

"That again."

"You said you'd hear me out."

"I thought I was going to hear something new."

"Amy Weaver, I'm asking you for the last time, will you please marry me?"

"No."

"Just like that?"

"Just like that." She smiled over the top of her cup. Nothing would spoil this day for her, nothing. "Next subject."

"I thought that if we were married," he said, ignoring her last remark, "I could take care of the business things like the shopping mall and the relocation of the tenants—after the sale of the building, of course. And you—well, you could devote your entire time to taking care of your charity work."

"My charity work?" Amy laughed. "My charity work?"

"You know, finding places for those—well, the people displaced by the fire. I was thinking that maybe you could involve other people, too. You know, not have such a heavy financial drain on your own resources."

"Meaning there would be more for the business end of things—the end you would be handling, right?" Amy carefully replaced the china cup in the saucer and slowly raised her eyes to meet Marshall's straight on. "How dumb do you think I am, Marshall?"

"I don't think you're dumb, Amy," he said, trying to soften his tone toward her and avoid a scene reminiscent of the one in her living room on Sunday. "I just don't think you're very experienced in business, that's all. I'm afraid you could get taken advantage of if you don't have the right man watching out for you."

"You think I need a *man* looking out for my interests? You don't think I'm capable of doing that myself?"

"It's not that, necessarily," he said. "But you're a woman, Amy. It's more fitting that you should be involved with your, well, benevolent causes and put your mind at ease by having someone—"

"I have someone," she interrupted, then wished she hadn't.

"You what?"

"I have a good lawyer," she quickly covered her inadvertent slip. "And I have Mr. Ramsey to advise me, too. I bet I could go to most any man on the city council and get some sound advice if I really needed it. And, besides, I know Mark Andrews. He seems like a pretty astute businessman, wouldn't you agree?"

"His business went under a short while ago. Didn't you know that?"

"Didn't stay there long, did it?" Amy asked, but made a mental note to ask Jim about it later. "As I hear it, he's in the front running for the contractor's job on the new mall. You did know that, didn't you?"

"I thought Jason Furman was—" Marshall dropped his remark midsentence.

"The guy from San Diego? I don't think I favor an out-of-towner doing this job. Do you?"

"I don't think that matters so much," Marshall said.

"It does to me," Amy said, lifting her cup to her lips again. "Marsh, listen to me. Please, will you listen? We—you and me—" she said, gesturing back and forth, "we are not—are you listening? We are not getting married. I don't want to marry you." Suddenly she felt almost sorry for him. "Look, the others will be here soon. You just make the proposals I suggested and when they're through patting you on the back for being such a wonderful *benevolent* man, we'll get the sale of my building underway and the city can have its shopping mall and I can go back to my *charity* work."

"They'll see through this. They are all going to know you're behind this. No one is going to believe that this came from me. I'll look like I'm being controlled from behind."

"Put your heart into it, Marsh. You do have a heart in there somewhere, don't you?"

"After all the work I've done to put this deal together, I probably won't make a red cent. I'll lose my shirt on this—and for what?"

"For the good of the community," she said. "You might not make a killing on this deal, but just imagine how well thought of you will be. Surely your spotless reputation is important to you, isn't it?"

"You're enjoying this, aren't you?" he asked through clenched teeth.

"Getting what I think is best for my tenants? You bet. At your expense? No, Marshall, not at all. But then that's not really my doing. You have only yourself to thank for this."

"Well, gentlemen," Marshall said after making his presentation, "that about sums it up. A relocation plan is all that stands between us and our new downtown shopping mall. What do you say? Any takers or do I stand alone in this?"

"I think the city could help a bit," the mayor said, thoughtfully. "We might be able to waive certain permit fees and so forth. I'll take it up with our legal department."

"And," another business owner and city councilman said, "I think I might be able to offer some help, too."

Suddenly the entire room was filled with optimistic enthusiasm and ideas. Before long it was obvious that the official meeting was over and that a forward-looking community spirit had been restored. Amy flashed Marshall a wide smile. "Well done," she said. "I knew you could do it."

"See?" he teased. "We would make a great team."

Amy ignored his remark. "If you'll excuse me," she said, standing up. Several men jumped to their feet. "Please, sit down. Finish your dessert. Mr. Carlson can keep me posted. He'll be drawing up the first draft of the plan, if that's all right with everyone here? Good," she said as they nodded their heads almost in unison. "Mr. Ramsey," she said, nodding toward her father's long-standing business associate and friend. "May I see you and Mr. Andrews for a moment before I leave?" Amy intended to ask them to check into what it would cost to repair or replace Aggie's house. Mr. Carlson was already checking into the insurance claim. "Don't worry, gentlemen," she said, with a slight smile. "We won't discuss the shopping mall anymore today." Then looking directly at Marshall Jennings she said, "I just need to speak to them about one of my *charity* projects."

————

Amy watched excitedly as her wallpaper selection transformed her mother's bedroom into an atmosphere of soft femininity perfectly coordinated with the gentle pastel colors of Charlotte's quilt. A ruffled eyelet bedskirt, matching throw pillows, and valences at the windows brought the new look together.

Before long, she had completely dislodged every belonging of her parents that she didn't want to keep or didn't think Aggie might be able to use. The Salvation Army truck was swinging by every few mornings, just to save her the inconvenience of making a phone call.

"Are you moving?" a neighbor asked one morning when she went out to get the paper.

"No, just making a few changes." But it was an understatement and Amy knew it.

She just couldn't explain how everything in her life could change so much so quickly. The holidays were just around the corner and she dreaded them. She had decided to face the challenge of her first Christmas without her parents by making sure that this Christmas was totally different than any she had experienced before. She would return to her holiday traditions in the future, but for now she refused to be trapped by grief and robbed of the Christmas spirit that her parents had so carefully instilled in her each year.

The Morningside Fire Department met Amy's idea with enthusiasm and began the campaign to furnish a rented house for Aggie and her "children" before the holidays. Mark and Chet Ramsey made preliminary plans to make the home as comfortable as possible, and Mr. Carlson's office filed the insurance claim for Aggie.

Every other day or so, Amy visited Aggie and Anna, who were both anxious to be together again. It was on one of these visits that Amy approached Aggie with her ideas.

"I've found a house," Amy said. "Now, it's not a very big house, but I think it will do nicely—at least for the time being. Mr. Ramsey has suggested certain adjustments to make it more livable. I've arranged to have you look at it, and if it meets your approval, we'll rent it until we can make more permanent arrangements."

"You can't be serious," Aggie said, but her eyes pleaded for it to be so.

"It's a few miles from where your house was, and the yard isn't as nice, of course. But it's fenced in the back and at least you can all be together again."

"All except for Mary," Aggie said. Her smile told Amy her news was bittersweet. "Her family has relocated to another part of the state, and they want Mary closer. She's already gone. So it's just the boys, Anna, and me."

"Oh, Aggie," Amy said, bending to put her arms around the gentle, love-filled woman.

"It's like losing one of my own," Aggie said between her tears. "Just like losing one of my own."

"I think we could have you in the house by Christmas," Amy said, trying to cheer her up. "You and the others have been separated far too long."

"Christmas? But that's only two weeks away. How could we possibly. . . ?

"Leave it to me," Amy said. "And the fire department."

"They told me you've been paying Anna's bill," Aggie said, wiping her tears. "She would have been sent to another home by now. But you knew that, didn't you?"

"I don't want her with anyone but you," Amy said. "You're her mama. Everyone can see that."

"They let her come down and stay with me awhile this afternoon. It was good for both of us."

"Aggie," Amy said gently and sat on the bed beside the nearly healed woman. "I want to know about Anna."

"Anna," Aggie said quietly, thoughtfully. "Anna was a throwaway child."

"I don't understand," Amy said.

"It was obvious from the beginning she was retarded.

Someone actually threw her in a garbage dump—out in the desert. An old man rummaging for scrap metal found her and turned her into the county. She came to me almost immediately. She was only a little bit of a thing. Dr. Morgan was assigned as her doctor. He took county cases from time to time. She was pitiful small. The old doc didn't think she'd make it a year—two at the most. But as little as she was, she was strong. Strong-willed, too—she was a real handful once she got up around five or so. Your daddy, he spoiled her something rotten."

"Mrs. Jones," Amy whispered, "how did my father get involved?" Amy nearly held her breath as Aggie gave her question some thought.

"I don't want to stir up old family skeletons, Amy. But seein' your folks are gone and you're the one left to take care of things—well, it's only right that you know. Your papa was heartbroken over his own little Anna. Doc Morgan had to almost drag him into my house to look at this little pitiful baby. I'll never forget the night he came. Your papa looked like he'd been up for heaven only knows how long. His whisker-covered face and those hollow eyes—he was a sight. I had lots of pity for that little throwaway baby, that's for sure. But it was nothin' compared to the sorrow I felt in my heart for that daddy of yours." Aggie shifted to a more comfortable position before continuing.

"It was right after his own baby died that Doc brought him, like I said. He stood him next to the baby basket I kept in the kitchen. 'Look there,' Doc shouted at your daddy. 'See that baby? She's goin' to have a terrible life. See that mouth? She might have to have an operation just so she can eat right. And then, when we can feed her, what kind of life do you think she'll have then? Who's going to love her? Who's going to take care of her? The state? Is she going to live all her life in some locked room somewhere out of sight and away from people so she won't be stared at?' Then the doc said something I'll never forget. 'Your own daughter, John Weaver,' he said, 'was much worse off than this little one. This one might walk, maybe even talk or learn to feed herself one day. But that little baby Anna up there in the cemetery would have lived all her life in diapers and sat day after day in a wheelchair. She'd always have had to be hand fed. And then who'd take care of her once you're gone? Charlotte? What about when she's gone?' "

Amy's eyes filled with tears at the thought of her father's agony.

" 'Death was a blessing,' he said to your papa. 'Anna Weaver is safe and whole in the arms of Jesus while this one is at the mercy of an unloving state.' But, you know, Amy," Aggie said, interrupting her story, "she wasn't really at the mercy of an unloving state. She was with me. He just said that trying to get through to your daddy. Worked too, because your father looked at that little baby lyin' there in the baby basket in my kitchen and finally asked if he could hold her. Once he picked her up, he burst into the most painful, mournful cryin' I ever heard in my entire life. He just sat there holding that poor little feeble-minded baby until I thought I'd have to rip her out of his arms just to feed her. 'What's her name?' your daddy asked. I told him she didn't have a name yet. No one knew where she came from and nobody cared to give her one. That's when he asked if we could call her after his own dead baby. That's when she became Anna."

Amy's tears gave way to the sorrow she felt for her father. Aggie's tender-skinned arms opened, and Amy slipped between them to find comfort in the arms of a most remarkable woman who had comforted many in her lifetime—many with pain too deep for everyday people to even imagine.

"He couldn't stay away after that," Aggie said. "He helped my husband fix most anything that broke down and if it couldn't be fixed, he got us new. He came and played with Anna at least once a week, clear up until the week before he died. When my husband died, your daddy decided he needed to be Anna's legal guardian. He had that lawyer of his draw up the papers and added his last name to hers. As far as I know," Aggie said softly, " he never told your mama."

"Mama knew," Amy said. "She and my father were too close. She would know something that was this close to his heart. Even if he didn't tell her, she'd know. I knew, in a way, too. We always called your house in Morningside "The Home." We prayed for all the people that lived there who didn't have as much as others. I just thought the people who lived there were poor or something. I had no idea they were—"

"People with special needs?" Aggie filled in the words Amy couldn't find.

"What are we going to do now?" Amy asked.

"Well, tell me more about this house I can rent. I must have some insurance money coming soon. I'm sure I can—"

"You'll need that money, Aggie."

"For what? It's all I've got. The state doesn't pay enough for me to—"

"You'll need it to rebuild."

"Rebuild? I'm afraid there isn't enough for that, Amy."

"Yes, there is," she said. "There's more than enough."

Eighteen

"Anyone sitting here?" Owen asked on Sunday morning as he slipped into the empty chair beside Amy and Linda. Amy's broad smile was all the invitation Owen needed.

"I figured since you didn't answer your phone this morning, you'd probably be here," he said in response to her unasked question. "It's been two weeks," he whispered. "Hope you don't mind."

All through the service, Amy tried to listen to Jim's sermon, but her mind seemed to stick on one of the verses from the morning's Scripture reading.

"*He setteth the solitary in families . . .*" Jim's voice seemed to resound with a special authority when he read the Scriptures this particular December Sunday. Amy had decided at the last minute to attend the Sunday services. She had felt a warmth and special welcome by the people here, and now this. . . . A tear found its way to the corner of her eye and escaped down her cheek before she realized she was crying.

"You okay?" Owen whispered.

Amy nodded, then reread the passage in the Bible that lay open on her lap. There it was, Psalm sixty-eight, verse six, right in plain sight. God does set the solitary, the alone, the forgotten in families. *Though she was tossed on the dump heap at birth, it was God who put Anna within a family*, she thought. *And it was God who didn't leave Mama alone, but sent Linda and Mattie to her so she wouldn't be alone after Daddy died.*

Now Amy felt, probably for the first time in her entire life, that she could be part of a family—a large family. The sense of belonging wrapped her in the love of His people; God's family was supposed to become hers. On this particular day, she felt as if she had come home—that even as an adult, God had adopted her and made her His very own child.

"What day is this?" she whispered to Linda, who silently pointed to the date on the top of the typewritten church bulletin. "Oh, my gosh," Amy breathed.

"What's the matter?" Linda asked softly.

"Nothing, it's okay," Amy responded. But her eyes were riveted on the date. *It's my birthday,* she said to herself. *I'm twenty-one years old and I forgot my own birthday.* She closed her eyes and let the presence of God fill her heart completely. *I forgot,* she prayed silently, *but you didn't, did you, heavenly Father?*

After the service Owen introduced Amy to his sister Judy and her husband, Don. "Well, congratulations, Amy," Don teased. "We've been trying to get him to come to River Place for several months. Looks like we didn't have the power of persuasion he needed."

Judy took Amy to chat with some of the other women and left the men to tease each other good-naturedly.

"Have you met any of the rest of the Sampson family?" Judy asked when they had a moment alone.

"No, I just met Owen the day after Thanksgiving."

"Well, you'll have to meet the rest of our rowdy bunch. But understand this," she said smiling, "we don't have the corner on insanity, even though it may appear so."

"Come on," Owen said after eavesdropping in on their conversation. "Don't scare her off already."

"Want to come over for dinner?" Judy said, punching her brother playfully in the stomach.

"I can't," he said. "I have another invitation—and so," he said, turning to Amy, "do you."

———————

That afternoon, Jim and Linda, Mark Andrews, Owen, and Amy gathered around Mattie Sloan's dining room table for a traditional roast beef Sunday dinner. Karissa and Holden said they might drop by for dessert after Katie's nap. Karissa, being so near her delivery date, insisted she wasn't up for an entire afternoon of activity and visiting.

"You might as well take it away, Mattie," Mark said, scooting his chair away from the table and rubbing his stomach. "I'll keep eating as long as there is one scrap left on that platter."

"You don't get enough home cooking," Jim teased. "We need to find you a good woman, Mark Andrews."

"I only know of one that I'd be interested in," Mark said seriously. "But she doesn't even know I'm alive. Alas, you're looking at a man whose heart bursts with unrequited love."

"No kidding?" asked Linda. "And pray tell, who is this stupid woman?"

"Mathilda Sloan," he announced, trying to grab the spry elderly woman's hand as she cleared the table.

"Keep your hands to yourself, Mark Andrews," Mattie said, slapping his wrist. "Now mind your manners and how you talk."

"I'm afraid she's a one-man woman," Jim said joining in the fun. "That old Ben spoiled her rotten, can't you tell? Why, she's completely ruined, that's quite obvious."

Amy looked across the table at Mark Andrews with interest. He wasn't that old—fifty, maybe fifty-five. Not as old as her father, but then her parents didn't have any children until they were in their early forties. Amy thought of the verse that had leapt out at her earlier in the service. Mark was a solitary man. She had noticed that about him before, but God had put him, too, right in the middle of this unusual family—a family bound together by their love for one another and for Christ rather than physical birth. *Is this something totally new, or is it just new to me?* she wondered.

"Amy," Mark said, startling her out of her own thoughts. "What's happening with the house in Morningside? Where are the people living now, and what's being done to help them?"

Owen encouraged Amy to speak up without saying a word. His broad smile and slight, almost imperceptible wink told her this was a golden opportunity to share her hopes, and perhaps even her dreams, with those she had come to care about so much in such a short time.

Amy eagerly shared the plans to rent a house temporarily and her desire to help Aggie rebuild. The Morningside Fire Department had already begun their part of the effort, collecting donated household goods and furnishings and opening a special account at the small local bank for the cash donations.

Mark and the others listened intently, captured not only by her plans, but Amy's persuasive presentation. It was as if she had the ability to plant within others the dreams and hopes of her own heart.

When she was finished, she looked down to her hands in her lap, embarrassed that she might have said too much. Mark's voice finally broke the silence and caused her to lift her gaze to meet his across the table.

"What you're describing sounds like a foundation to me, Amy. Have you spoken to anyone about this? Mr. Carlson? What does he say?"

"I've not said anything to anyone," she admitted. "I didn't think anyone would—"

"Would want to help?" Mark asked.

"Why not?" Linda asked her young friend.

"Well," Amy's voice faltered. "I just didn't give it any thought. I just thought I'd—"

"You have a very special gift," Mark said. "I saw it the first time when you gave your graduation address. I saw it again when you spoke to the planning commission. Then again when you met with the city fathers for lunch. Which, by the way, was a most impressive and innovative plan. I might add that no one was fooled into thinking it was Marshall Jennings' idea. In all the business dealings he's had around town, no one has ever seen a benevolent, human side to the man. But all that aside, I've just seen it again here today. You, young lady, have a unique way of making people want to watch out and care for each other. Without even trying, you make people see a vision and want to catch it for themselves."

Amy blushed and shifted uncomfortably in her chair.

"If you were to form a nonprofit organization of some sort— your lawyer can tell you whether a foundation or corporation would be best—I can think of more than a few service organizations that would want to get behind this. With you as the spokesman—or spokeswoman—there's no telling how far and how quickly that home in Morningside could be rebuilt and be better than before. John Weaver has set an example for all of us. He didn't go around tooting his own horn, but he sure can't object now if someone else does, can he?"

"You mean, you think I should tell—"

"Not in a boastful, bragging kind of way—of course not. You couldn't do that even if you tried. But to carry on his work? His vision? You bet. I think it is time you let others know what was close to your father's heart and how he lived his life for others. And, in a way, what you do in the next few months will make all the difference—whether what your father gave his life to will survive his death or not. In a way, you are the key to making sure his legacy lives on."

At Mark's words, Amy shot a knowing look at Linda.

"This is what we call confirmation, Amy," Linda said. "I think the Lord has already been talking to you, hasn't He?"

"I think so," Amy said quietly. "In fact, one of the verses in this morning's Scripture reading really stuck with me."

"No kidding?" Jim asked with a hint of surprise in his voice.

"It's that verse that says something about the solitary being placed in families," Amy said. "I can't get it out of my mind."

"Well, I'll be—" Jim said. "Mattie, get your Bible, will you?" Jim turned Mattie's well-worn leather volume to the passage. "You know, this reading had nothing to do with my sermon. I struggled with that all week. But I felt so impressed to read that passage early in the service and then move on to my sermon later. They're not even connected. I was hoping no one would notice."

"This is wonderful," Mattie said. "I always love it when the Lord speaks to His children. You know, just sitting here like this together, as His children and part of His family, I think He wants to do something very special." A special hush fell on the group around the table. Mattie Sloan had walked closely with the Lord for over forty years and when she said God was moving, speaking, and leading, no one even thought of questioning her.

"What's He want us to do?" Amy asked innocently.

"He wants us to pray," Mattie said, standing up and extending her hands to Mark and Owen seated on either side of her.

Immediately the others stood and joined hands. Mattie Sloan's dining room table became an altar of prayer that sunny December afternoon. First one then another offered short, simple prayers asking for God's blessing, direction, and wisdom and declared to Him and before each other that God had brought them together to give them this vision of ministry through Amy. They pledged to support her in any way they could and to be involved as the Lord led each one individually and as a group.

Owen Sampson remained silent during most of the afternoon's discussion and prayer time. But when it seemed as though the prayer time had come to an end, he simply said, "Lord Jesus, use me, too. I'm yours."

"Amy," Mark said as he turned to leave the house. "It sure would help if you were of age. When will you be twenty-one?"

"I'm already twenty-one," she said softly as color flooded her cheeks.

"You are?" Linda asked. "And when did that happen? Does this have anything to do with that 'oh, my gosh' I heard in church this morning?"

"What? Do we have a birthday girl here?" Mattie exclaimed, clapping her hands together for attention. "Okay, everyone—all together now! Happy Birthday to you," Mattie's voice rang out and everyone joined in.

Owen watched from the doorway to the kitchen. It wouldn't take much more than a casual observer to see that he enjoyed every minute just being in the same room with Amy Weaver.

Amy's life became a flurry of activity. Painters and wallpaper hangers had her own house in an upheaval. Her furniture was covered with drop cloths, and most of her floors were buried under canvas, plastic sheeting, or newspapers. Most mornings she gave a few instructions, took Princess out to her father's office to keep her out from underfoot, then spent her midmornings with Mr. Carlson, Mark Andrews, or Chet Ramsey as they carefully laid both legal and practical plans for reuniting the Morningside Home family by Christmas.

Linda had organized a crew of ladies from her Thursday morning Bible study who chattered happily as they lined kitchen cabinets and scrubbed the rented house spotlessly clean. The Morningside Fire Department delivered the donated household furniture, and new sheets were purchased for the beds, which were covered with the nearly new blankets collected by the youth group of the First Methodist Church just a few miles down the road.

Aggie longed to be a part of the activity and finally persuaded the doctor to release her a few days before the anticipated arrival of her "family." Only Anna was permitted to come before the others. Mattie came for several days to supervise the cooking, and by the time the others came "home," the used deep freeze was filled with food, and the pantry was loaded with jars of home-canned fruits and vegetables as well as store-bought canned goods. Early on the morning of the "homecoming," Else Sternhagen's delivery truck brought breads, cookies, and a huge cake decorated with an impressive hand-scrawled "Welcome Home."

Owen was as involved as possible, but his four-days-on and four-days-off schedule prevented him from being present when the family was actually reunited. Captain Medina came, however, representing the Morningside Fire Department, and Ernest and Beau were delighted to take turns wearing his captain's hat.

"I get off tomorrow morning at six. Can you meet me for breakfast?" Owen said one evening when he finally reached Amy by phone. "We've had a really quiet shift this week and I've been able to spend some time on the phone. I've got some news I think you'd be interested in."

"Bob's?" Amy asked.

"Perfect," he said. "Seven-thirty?"

Owen was already sitting in a booth when Amy arrived a few minutes past seven-thirty. "I must have been out of my mind agreeing to this early hour," she said with a smile.

"You've been really busy, haven't you?" he asked.

"I've been meeting myself coming and going. With Christmas only a few days away, I've still got a million things to do."

"How's your own house project coming?" he asked.

"Finished," she said. "I took on too much, to tell you the truth. But when the needs at Morningside became so apparent, what could I do? I haven't even had much time to enjoy the work done at home. Did you know I can actually park a car in my garage?"

"Is that new?"

"I've never seen one in there in my whole life."

"Silly savers, huh?"

"My parents? And how." Amy ordered coffee, juice, and scrambled eggs with an English muffin. "I even have a TV room now. But I haven't been able to watch one program since I brought the TV in the house from my father's office."

"You look really good, Amy," Owen said appreciatively.

"Thank you," she said. "And you don't look too bad for someone who's been working all night, either."

"I've been asleep most of the night," he said. "We do that if there are no calls, you know."

"Oh," she said simply. "Guess there would be no reason not to."

"Look who's following us," Owen said, nodding toward the coffee shop's entrance. "Jim and Linda. Shall we ask them to join us?"

"That would be nice," Amy said, then almost wished she hadn't.

After polite, friendly conversation and a hearty breakfast, Owen cleared his throat. "I've something to tell you," he said to Amy.

"Hey, we can take a hint," Jim said, reaching across the table and tugging on his wife's sleeve.

"No, wait," Owen said. "I think Amy might want you to hear this. It's about your sister, Anna."

Jim and Linda remained quiet as Owen told Amy of the information he was able to pick up by searching records and making inquiries.

"Anna was born at home," he said. "Not in the house where you live now, but in a small house near Weaver's Building Supply. The delivery didn't go well and the midwife waited too long to call for Dr. Morgan. It seems that somehow the baby didn't get enough oxygen during labor and by the time she was born she was badly brain damaged, then died within just a few hours. Your mother never saw her. She was so weak after the delivery they thought they would lose her too. It seems as though your father was distraught for days—heartbroken about the baby and worried out of his mind over his wife."

"How did you find this out?" Jim asked when Amy turned away.

"I kept asking questions. I talked to the old pharmacist— you know, the one who retired last year? He was new in town at that time and remembered Doc Morgan telling him all about it. The Morgans felt so sorry for your parents they offered to have the baby buried in their own plot. Your father didn't even attend the burial—he wouldn't leave your mother's side."

"Then that explains why your father's interest in Anna of Morningside Home was so strong. Do you think he never accepted his baby daughter's death?" Jim asked.

Amy shook her head. "Not at all. He sent flowers to her grave on the third of every month."

"All these years?" Owen asked.

Amy nodded. "He named Anna after his own baby daughter. Almost in memory of her."

"And he never told you?" Jim asked.

"No," Amy said. "Aggie told me. But I think he would've eventually. You see, he became Anna's legal guardian. He would have realized eventually that he would have to tell me about *her* at least. I think he just put it off too long. Who would have guessed he would pass away before my mother? She was the one whose health was fragile. Not my father. They were very private people, Jim. Anna was their first child. In a way, I think the second Anna gave him back some of what he lost with the first. Maybe it was so personal he couldn't share it with anyone—not even my mother."

"There's more," Owen said. "I discovered that your mother visited Baby Anna's grave several times a year."

"As far as I can tell, she never knew about the flowers. Now I wonder if my father knew about her visits."

"Wow," Linda said to Owen, "you have been busy asking questions, haven't you? How'd you get people to talk to you about this?"

"I told them I was representing Miss Amy Weaver. That's all I had to say. It seems that while Anna's death was a tragedy, nobody considered it a secret. They just respected your parents so much they simply didn't talk about it."

"Jim?" Amy said, after a long moment of thoughtful silence. "I asked you once about moving Anna's grave. Is that ever done? And is it an okay thing to do? I mean there's nothing in the Bible or anything about this, is there?"

"You know, Amy, what lies in those graves up there on the hillside are only physical shells." He reached for Amy's hand reassuringly. "It isn't going to matter to your parents, or even your sister, if you leave the grave as it is."

"But it wouldn't matter to them if I moved it, either."

"No, it wouldn't. But why would you want to?"

"It's for me," she said thoughtfully, tears welling in her eyes. "I keep thinking of that poor little baby Anna who was thrown on a trash heap and found by some stranger. I don't know . . . it's all so confusing to me. But—"

"But it's important to you," Owen said gently, "isn't it?"

"Yes," Amy said softly, "it is." Owen's sensitivity and understanding felt good. "It's as if when I put her by my parents it will turn a page for me."

"Then do it," Owen said. "Cemeteries aren't for the dead anyway. They're for the living. You're the one who's living, Amy. If you would find comfort in having Anna's grave next to your parents', then we'll support you. We really will, won't we?" He gave Jim and Linda a questioning look.

"Of course," Jim said. "But you'll have to work out the legalities with Mr. Carlson."

"Do you have to be right there when it happens?" Linda asked. "I mean, wouldn't that be hard on you to watch?"

"I don't want to watch. I just want it done."

"Then," Jim said, seeming relieved at Amy's decision, "why not make the arrangements with Mr. Carlson and the cemetery, and when it's ready, we can go with you and have a memorial. I must admit I've never heard of this before, but then there's lots of things in the course of ministry that I never heard of before."

"That would give me a chance to have a new grave marker made," Amy said. "Or have a new inscription put on the old one." She glanced around the table at her dearest friends. "You all mean so much to me," she said with emotion. "I can't tell you how much."

Owen Sampson's eyes sparkled with his own unshed tears as he looked away from Amy and avoided Linda's gaze as well.

"And we all love you, too," Linda said softly.

Nineteen

As wonderful as it was, the rented house was a bit crowded, and Amy knew it didn't feel like home. On more than one occasion, she sensed Aggie's grief and homesickness.

Fighting her own sorrow by keeping as busy as possible, Amy made Aggie's "family" her obsession during the few days before Christmas and threw herself into helping them have a special holiday.

With all of Aggie's belongings gone, Amy had all the excuse she needed to buy whatever she thought would make the woman's life easier and her home more comfortable. The first day she shopped, she filled her car with canisters, plants, some pretty doilies, a new clock for the hallway, an electric blanket, and fluffy towels, then headed toward Mattie's house for help with the wrapping. Another trip yielded books, new sweaters, and socks.

When Mattie suggested games, Amy immediately shopped for checkers, cards, puzzles, then added several board games, including Chutes and Ladders, Candyland, and Sorry. Just before the stores closed on Christmas Eve, she bought new aprons for Aggie, colorful hot pads for the kitchen, and a lacy tablecloth.

Owen stood on the sidelines, shaking his head at the whirlwind of activity Amy created. "It's probably good she has a diversion," he told Jim one night over a chess game. "She'll settle down once Christmas is over."

Christmas dinner at Aggie's included Mattie, Jim, and Linda. Owen was on duty, but planned to slip away for pie. Only Amy knew he'd be bringing a few more gifts from the men at the station. Sounds of delight filled the house as the gifts were opened. The aromas of a large, stuffed roasting turkey and hot mulled cider whetted everyone's appetites, and the sounds of Perry Como, Mitch Miller, and Alvin and the Chipmunks coming from the new portable stereo record player added to the day's festive mood. After a big dinner, Jim challenged one after another at checkers while Linda supervised a jigsaw puzzle project. More than once, Anna paused to look at the dazzling Christmas tree, staring for long moments at the glittering angel perched only inches from the ceiling. Amy fought and finally suppressed thoughts of how pleased her father would have been with this holiday. Aggie frequently wiped her eyes with the corner of her apron, declaring, "I can't believe all this."

"Aggie," Amy said on Christmas night after the others were in bed and the house was finally quiet, "I've been thinking. Now, I want you to hear me out before you say anything, okay?"

"What's in that pretty head of yours now?" the older woman wanted to know. "I get worried when you start having ideas."

"Are you going to hear me out, or am I going to go on home now?" Amy teased.

"I'll shut up and let you talk," Aggie said.

"Good." Amy reached for another piece of Christmas fudge. "Mr. Carlson told me you weren't insured adequately to rebuild your house quite like it was before. Is that right?"

"Well, you know George and I bought that house many years ago, and we added on now and then to make room for more children. Your daddy saw to it that we got a good price on materials and such. But after a while none of us ever looked at the insurance policy anymore. And now—well, prices have really gone up. I'm not sure what I'm going to do. But if I only keep the three I have now, well—"

"But what about later?" Amy hesitated. "Later, when you're gone?"

"I can't even think about that," Aggie said.

"But you do, don't you?"

"Yes, I do, Amy," the woman said thoughtfully. "Especially since the fire."

"I have too," Amy said. "And I know my father thought about it too. It's just that he died before he could come to any real solution. But I think I may have come up with a plan that might help relieve your mind."

Aggie looked over the edge of her glasses perched tentatively on her tender-skinned nose.

"I was wondering," Amy hesitated again. "Now, realize that I haven't talked to anyone else about this. If you think my idea has any merit at all, we'll need to talk to someone—but I want to do it together. Okay?"

"Amy Weaver, you're making me nervous. Get to the point, all right?"

"Okay," Amy said, taking a deep breath. "I'm just going to jump right in the middle here. Aggie, would you be willing to put up your property if I matched it in funds from my father's estate and built a home for mentally retarded adults? I'm not just talking about a home that belongs to you—that you open and take people in. I'm talking about a professional facility."

"You mean an institution?" Aggie's eyes opened wide and her voice rose with shock.

"Oh no," Amy said. "Certainly not. I'm talking about a home setting. But one that would belong to a foundation that Mr. Carlson would help us set up. Then I could go out and raise funds for it. You know, financial donations so we could hire a staff to help you and a place you could live for the rest of your life. A place where people like Anna, Beau, and Ernest wouldn't have to worry about leaving if something happened to you or to me. What I'm talking about, Aggie," Amy said, leaning close to the older woman, "is making sure your compassion and care for these dear people lives beyond your lifetime." Amy took her eyes from the face of the woman sitting opposite her and relaxed back against the sofa cushions. "In a way," she continued softly, "it would do the same for what my father believed in. I want to do this for him as much as anything else."

"I like the idea," Aggie said quietly. "I really do. But I don't have anything to lose. I have to use my money to rebuild a home for my children," she nodded toward the bedrooms. "But, you—you don't have to do this. All that money your papa left you. You could live pretty high and mighty on what he left you, right?"

"Aggie, you don't know the half of it." Amy sighed before continuing. "He left so much money I *have* to find something to do with it. I always knew he had money, but I had no idea he had so much. He found ways to put it to good use, and now that responsibility has been passed on to me. I think this would be one of the ways I could do that. Will you let me?"

"Can I give it some thought?" Aggie asked.

"Of course," Amy responded. "Take all the time you need."

But Agatha Jones didn't need much time, and before the middle of January, Amy and Aggie spent as much time as possible pouring over blueprints. Then they conferred with Mark Andrews, who was more than happy to get the job as the summer project for his students at the high school.

"Tell me more about this program of yours," Amy said during one of their meetings with Jim, Linda, and Agatha.

"It's a simple one, really," Mark said. "After Michael died, I realized how much I hadn't taught him. How I didn't take the time to let him experience what it was like to build something from the ground up—to go from nothing and see something finished. I began to wonder how many other boys could use what I neglected to give my own son. So, I applied for a teaching position at the high school and presented my ideas and it took off from there. I work with the students during the school year, teaching wood shop and basic carpentry part time. At first I would only take those students that we might say are in danger of slipping through the cracks. Many have no father at home, low income—not a very bright future. But then, after a year into the project, that all changed." Mark hesitated to continue.

"What he's trying not to say," Jim added, "is that the demand started outweighing the available space and now his class is more popular than auto shop. Everybody wants to be in Mark's class. The beauty of this program is that every summer he puts these students to work on a construction job. By the time they graduate from high school—and they do graduate, thanks to Mark—they've had at least one summer's work experience and can go out and get good jobs right out of high school."

"I think," Mark said, trying to turn the attention away from himself and back to the blueprints scattered across the table, "that if we can get the cement work in by the end of May, we should be ready to start the Monday after graduation in June. We'll be finished by September, when the boys have to go back to school. If not, we'll have to hire professionals to come in and finish the job."

"Why can't we do both?" Amy asked.

"What do you mean?" Mark thought he understood her question but wanted to make sure the others did as well.

"I'm just asking, but do you usually run this crew of students by yourself?"

"Usually," he said. "It's how I spend my summers."

"Sounds like an elementary school essay," Linda quipped.

"What if we hired several men to supervise the project? Wouldn't it go faster?"

"It would," Mark said. "But I usually just do it myself to keep the costs down. But I have to admit, I've not had my boys take on a project of this size before."

"Well," Amy said, "I make a motion we ask Mark to propose to us an estimated budget for hiring the men needed to make sure this project is finished by September."

"I second the motion," Jim said. "Can I do that if I chair the meeting?"

"Okay, I second the motion," Linda laughed. "Let's keep this legal."

"All in favor?"

"Aye," said the five in unison.

"Carried," Jim said, firmly patting his hand on the table.

"Aggie?" Amy asked, noticing the woman was quiet. "How are you doing with all this?"

"I can't believe it, that's all. A laundry room and a recreation room both?"

"And a craft center, and a walk-in pantry," Linda said, pointing to different rooms indicated by blue lines and words written in a draftsman's definitive handwriting.

"And your very own bathroom, Aggie," Amy said smiling. "Won't that be heaven?"

"You have no idea how much this all means to me," Agatha said. "And to the children."

Again, the five enthusiastic people bowed their heads together, pointing and talking about the places for a volleyball court, a vegetable garden, and even a greenhouse. Already strong community support for the foundation was growing, and Amy had begun to slip comfortably into the role of the spokesman for Aggie's house.

"We can't keep calling this my house," Agatha said firmly, "it just isn't right."

"But Aggie," Amy tried to protest, "this is your house."

"No, my house is gone. This is more than I ever dreamed. This is a miracle—come right up out of the ashes of my whole life. It's too big to be called my house. You can name the kitchen after me, if you want, but I think we need something more descriptive for the house. We can't keep calling it Morningside Home, either."

"Do you have any ideas, Aggie?" Linda asked.

"No, I was hoping one of you could think of something."

"You know," Jim said after a few moments of silence, "I've been thinking of a passage of Scripture that may very well be the answer we're looking for. It's here," he said, turning in his small pocket Bible, "in Isaiah, chapter sixty-one. Listen to this."

Very slowly, he began to read the words to the small, attentive group huddled around Agatha Jones' secondhand kitchen table: " 'The spirit of the Lord is upon me; because the Lord hath anointed me to preach good tidings unto the meek; he hath sent me to bind up the brokenhearted, to proclaim liberty to the captives, and the opening of the prison to them that are bound. To proclaim the acceptable year of the Lord, and the day of vengeance of our God; to comfort all that mourn; to appoint to them that mourn in Zion, to give them beauty for ashes, the oil of joy for mourning, the garment of praise for the spirit of heaviness; that they might be called the trees of righteousness, the planting of the Lord, that he might be glorified. And they shall build the old wastes, they shall raise up the former desolations, and they shall repair the waste cities, the desolations of many generations.' "

"That's what this is all about, isn't it?" Amy asked and

reached to take Agatha's hand in her own while Jim continued reading.

" 'And strangers shall stand and feed your flocks, and the sons of the alien shall be your plowmen and your vinedressers.' "

Agatha's tears began to flow freely and Linda handed her a tissue.

" 'But ye'—listen to this Aggie, this is for you—'But ye shall be named the Priests of the Lord: men shall call you the Ministers of our God; and ye shall eat the riches of the Gentiles, and in their glory shall ye boast yourselves. For your shame, ye shall have double; and for confusion they shall rejoice in their portion; therefore in their land they shall possess the double; everlasting joy shall be unto them. For I the Lord love judgment, I hate robbery for burnt offering; and I will direct their work in truth, and I will make an everlasting covenant with them. And their seed shall be known among the Gentiles, and their offspring among the people: that they are the seed that God has blessed. I will greatly rejoice in the Lord, my soul shall be joyful in my God; for he hath clothed me with the garments of salvation, he hath covered me with the robe of righteousness, as a bridegroom decketh himself with ornaments and as a bride adorneth herself with her jewels. For as the earth bringeth forth her bud, and as the garden causeth the things that are sown in it to spring forth; so the Lord God will cause righteousness and praise to spring forth before all the nations.' "

Jim laid his Bible open on the blueprints scattered before them and sat back in his chair thoughtfully.

"I think we have the answer, Aggie," Amy said softly. "Right here, in God's Word. Did you hear what I heard?"

"I'm not sure," Aggie said, searching the faces of the others. "Two things kind of stuck out to me—oh, it was all wonderful—the beauty from ashes and that part about possessing double. But, there were two things—"

"Here," Amy said, pushing Jim's Bible closer to her. "Show me."

"Right here," she said after scanning the text. "Look." Agatha pointed to a word for Amy's inspection.

"Yeah," Amy said. "I heard that too."

"It's kind of what we talked about on Christmas. An everlasting covenant—something that will last. And then there was this one too. 'I will be joyful in my God.' "

"How about Covenant House?" Linda said thoughtfully. "That has a nice sound to it, doesn't it?"

"Yes," Agatha said. "It really sounds nice."

"Aggie," Jim said quietly, "do you know God in a personal, joyful way?"

The older woman shook her head as her tears ran unchecked down her pink cheeks.

"Do you want to?" Jim asked.

Aggie nodded without hesitation. "Yes, Pastor Jim, I do. I really do."

Jim moved to sit alongside of Aggie and read a few other passages of Scripture to her, then led her into her own personal relationship with Jesus Christ.

"Welcome," Amy said afterward, smiling through her own tears, "to the family."

———

In the car on the way back from Morningside, Mark and Jim bantered back and forth about the end of the football season and the lull before baseball's spring training began.

"All that's left is basketball," said Jim woefully, knowing full well that basketball was one of Mark's favorite sports. The two men joked in the front seat while Amy and Linda remained quiet in the back.

"Heard from Owen Sampson lately?" Linda asked finally.

Amy turned her head quickly and faced Linda squarely. "He calls once in a while, why?"

"Oh, just wondered," Linda said with a smile. "How's the downtown project coming?" Linda asked, changing the subject.

"I'm not sure," Amy answered. "I've given most of my attention to Aggie's house."

"Covenant House," Linda corrected.

Amy smiled. "Sounds nice, doesn't it?"

"So, will you be hearing about the downtown issue soon?"

"I suppose," Amy said. "Mark probably knows more than I do."

Mark and Jim exchanged looks.

"You haven't told her?" Jim asked.

"Told me what?" Amy said curiously.

"Mark?" Jim prodded.

"How about stopping off for a cup of coffee?" Linda suggested. "It's not that late, is it?"

"I think that would be a good idea," Jim said. "Got any dessert?"

"Some of Mattie's lemon meringue pie, that's all."

"That's all?" Jim said. "Well, then that's settled."

———————

After Linda and Jim had cleaned the dishes away, Mark joined Amy in the Henry's comfortable living room.

"I get the feeling you have something to tell me," Amy said. "And why do I also get the feeling I'm not going to like it?"

Mark cleared his throat and jumped into the subject he dreaded, even though it had been decided long ago that he was to be the one to bring her up-to-date with the downtown project's progress.

"It's not going well, Amy," he said. "In fact, it's not going at all. At least for the time being."

"What happened?"

Mark poured out the detailed facts as clearly as he understood them. "You see," he said finally, "it boils down to the fact that without the financial backing the Jennings firm thought they had, the entire project is in jeopardy. Many—not just a few, mind you—tried to tell Marshall that his financial package wasn't as strong as he hoped it was, but he wouldn't listen. He somehow thought he had a backer that simply didn't come through. Some deadlines were missed when his silent partner didn't materialize."

"Does anybody know what happened? Or who this silent partner was?" Amy asked as Jim and Linda came back into the room.

"Amy," Jim said gently, "isn't it pretty obvious who that partner was supposed to be?"

"You can't mean me," Amy said with surprise.

"Who else could it be?" Mark asked.

"You mean he actually thought—but that can't be right. I never said I'd invest any money in the project. In fact I only agreed to sell my building so he—" She stopped short of completing her thought. "Did he think I would—"

"Honey," Mark said, taking her hand, "it's not clear what he thought. Who can know how he planned to get the money. But if you were married, wouldn't you have done anything to keep his business from going down the tubes?"

"Are you saying this is all my fault?"

"Of course not," Mark said firmly. "Don't even think that."

"This," Jim said joining in, "has nothing to do with you. This is one man's blind ambition, nothing more. He tried to use you. He thought he could. But that wasn't right, Amy. It wasn't right."

"Good things have come out of this, Amy," Mark said.

"Like what?" Her voice was filled with the hollow sound of doubt.

"The planning commission has met behind closed doors a couple of times lately and has decided to pursue other avenues. They have also decided to take your advice."

"My advice?"

"They are now checking into restoration instead of rebuilding. They are actually thinking about what would be good for our town, not just what would be new and exciting. We've got you to thank for that."

"But I thought you were all in favor of the new shopping mall. Why did you make a bid on the job if you weren't in agreement?"

"Sometimes you make a business judgment based on reality of the way things are—not on what you'd like them to be," Mark explained.

"So what happens now?" Amy asked.

"We sit tight. These decisions are not ones a community can hurry. You might want to have your tenants get together again and even some of the other downtown business owners. Have you ever thought of joining the downtown businessman's association?"

"But I'm not a businessman," Amy said firmly.

"Oh, but you are," Mark said. "Whether you like it or not. Now, you could send Mr. Carlson in your place, or even Mr. Ramsey. But I really think you'd make the most impact. They really don't know how to respond to a woman. It doesn't hurt to throw people off balance a little from time to time. Makes them think."

"But will they accept me?"

"Your father was a very respected man in this community, Amy. Out of that respect for him they will—at the beginning anyway. Once you're in, though, I'm afraid you're on your own. Could be tough—but I think you're up to the challenge. Why not at least give it a try?"

"I don't know . . ." she said.

"Listen, Amy," Jim said. "These are important people, connections that will benefit Covenant House and the library addition your father heavily pledged to support. You can't stay out of the center of attention like your mother did. You don't have the same options. Too much depends on it."

"Hey," Linda responded when Amy looked pleadingly at her friend. "Don't look at me. I get to hide behind Jim. You're left right out there, Amy. Sorry, girl, but that seems to be the way it is."

"But what do I have to do?"

"Probably not much more than just be out there. To keep your father's name and memory of what he stood for in front of people."

"All we're asking," Mark said, "is that you take the same position as anyone else who's been left a family business and reputation to uphold. I had to face the same thing with my father's business. It was easier for me, though. It was expected of me." He smiled. "You, on the other hand, are not at all what people expect."

Twenty

Everyone marveled at the ease with which Amy kept up with the busy pace of meeting with committees, speaking to women's groups, and keeping on top of the frustrations that come with a project as ambitious as Covenant House. On more than one occasion, Linda accompanied her as she visited children's hospitals, convalescent homes, and even a meeting with the school board, who were interested in the futuristic concept of educating the mentally impaired in the public school system. The year 1960 was the threshold to a new decade full of promise and progressive thinking. In the small, close community of Summerwind, Amy seemed to personify the hopes and dreams of a new generation of young adults ready to take the helm and steer their small city forward.

By early spring, Amy's life was filled with activity, busy from morning until night. Her bright, energetic smile was seen often in Summerwind's weekly newspaper, *The Breeze*. Amy Weaver had become a symbol of all that was good in Summerwind. A spokesman for the disadvantaged, a role model for children, and frequently the voice of the Summerwind Small Business Owner's Association. No one would have guessed that when the lights were finally out and she lay in the silent house in her mother's double bed, Amy Weaver, more times than not, cried herself to sleep.

Though her days were full and satisfying, carrying out her father's business, visiting Anna as often as she could and her own projects, her nights were unending bitter battles of grief and loneliness. Thoughts of Owen invaded her mind whenever she wasn't thinking about other things. She saw his face in her mind just before going to sleep and many times before she was fully awake. "I wish I knew how to handle these feelings," she admitted into the darkness of her room. "If only he'd say or do something or . . . " It was the time when she felt most deeply the loss of her mother. "Oh, Mama," she would cry into the softness of her pillow. "Mama, I wish you were here." Only when she prayed did she get relief from the tight, sorrowful knots of confusion that lay within her breast. "Dear God," she prayed, "please, help me."

Early mornings, she struggled to rid her mind of the cobwebs left behind by thoughts of Owen and the nightmares of trying unsuccessfully to reach her mother's outstretched hand or of her father trying to tell her something she couldn't quite hear or remember.

Only after two cups of coffee and reading several chapters from the Psalms aloud was she able to face another day of busy activity. Princess watched attentively as she read the Scriptures. "You're going to be the most biblically literate dog in town," Amy teased the friendly animal. "And, what do you think I ought to do about Owen Sampson, my little friend?"

Princess stood on her back feet and pawed the air as she pirouetted for Amy's approval.

"Oh, sure," Amy teased. "You'd call him, I suppose? As if he's just waiting for my call, no less? You have a lot to learn about men, Princess." She laughed and quickly scooped the small dog into her arms. "They don't think too much of pushy women—at least the good ones don't. And Owen, well now, in my opinion, he's not only one of the good ones—he's one of the best." She nuzzled the pet's soft fur. "I'll just have to be patient, I guess. He'll have to make the first move, that's for sure."

————

Owen Sampson waited patiently, watching Amy's busy life and the demands that seemed to press in on her. As much as he ached to be the central part of her life, he didn't want to add to her pressures. "One of these days, it will all settle down," he told himself. "She'll get her stride and make her adjustments. The time isn't right yet. Don't crowd her. She'll let you know somehow."

Waiting so long for the right woman made it easier and at

the same time more difficult to maintain what he considered a safe distance. After all, if she was the answer to his prayer, the reward of his waiting for God's perfect choice for him, it wouldn't do to rush her. Whenever possible he slipped in beside her at church. Soon they eased into an unspoken, unplanned routine of going to Jake's for burgers after the Wednesday evening service. The high school crowd usually thinned out by nine, and Owen made it a habit of putting two dollars worth of quarters in the juke box.

"I'd rather listen to Frank Sinatra, Joni James, and Eddie Fisher," he explained. "Somehow, I have a hard time talking with Little Richard screaming over my shoulder. Chubby Checker doesn't do much for me either."

Settled in a corner booth, Owen loved listening to Amy's updates on Covenant House.

"And Baby Anna," he said one Wednesday evening in March, "how are your plans coming for your sister?"

"The memorial is set for two weeks from this Sunday. April third comes on a Sunday, so I waited. It's her birthday. For all I know," Amy said seriously, "she's already been moved."

"Then you haven't been up there?" Owen asked. His stomach tightened protectively when he saw a small frown crease her forehead.

"No," Amy said. "No, I've been too busy. I still send flowers each month. But I don't send them just for Anna now. I ordered a family headstone. It should be in place by the time . . ." She let her voice trail off. "Could we change the subject?"

"Sure," Owen said. There wasn't much he wouldn't do for Amy Weaver. She looked up and his heart leaped.

"Good. Have you seen Karissa Kelley's baby boy?" Amy asked excitedly.

"Yeah, Holden's pretty proud, isn't he?"

"Jonathan," Amy said. "What a nice name. Have you seen Linda hold him?"

"Doesn't everyone hold him?"

"He does get passed around quite a bit, doesn't he?" Amy said with a smile.

Owen noticed her smile and was aware of how warm it made him feel. On more than one occasion he was afraid that her sorrow was permanent and would weigh her down forever.

"But you know," she continued, "when Linda holds him, she has a hard time giving him back. I think she wants a child of her own."

"Is there a problem?" Owen asked, all the while wishing they could talk about themselves instead of Jim and Linda. "I mean, I know it's probably a personal question, maybe even intrusive, but has she mentioned why they don't have any children?"

"No," Amy said. "All she says is that they're hoping to start their family very soon. I think it's her one and only personal wish. She spends so much time looking out for the good of others. Did you know Linda volunteers down at the nursery school a couple of mornings a week? She also supervises the nursery at church and gives herself completely to the new mother's ministry. But at her own heartfelt level, I think she would like nothing more than to have a family of her own. It's her dream."

"I know how she feels," Owen said. There was a faint tremor in his voice as though some emotion had touched him. He wasn't used to revealing his inner thoughts to anyone. But when he was with Amy, he desired to open his heart completely and without reservation. At that very moment, Owen Sampson knew he was tired of waiting. Nearly thirty years of age, and with Amy Weaver sitting across the table from him, he made up his mind. It was time she knew how he felt about her. "Amy," he said with deceptive calm, "I want to see more of you. I'm no longer satisfied with these little serendipities, as wonderful as they are. I don't want my relationship with you to be built on chance meetings, spontaneous moments grabbing burgers."

He watched her face intently as the shock of his confession registered first in her disarmingly clear blue eyes, then played at the corners of her mouth, tugging her soft lips into a nervous smile.

"Amy, do you know what I'm saying?" His voice was low and smooth, his intentions perfectly clear.

"Yes." Her voice seemed to come from a long way off.

"I'm saying," he said, reaching to take her hand in his own, "that I like you very much. I like who you are and what you are." He felt the smooth, delicate hand under his own and wanted to pull her into his arms. Instead, he traced the back of her hand with his thumb. "Amy Weaver," he whispered, afraid to look into her eyes, "I don't really know how to say this." He paused, searching his mind and heart for the right words to express his feelings.

"You don't have to say anything," she whispered.

"Oh, yes I do," he said. "I can't put it off any longer." How could he explain this indefinable feeling of rightness that filled his heart every time he was with her and the inescapable emptiness when he knew he wouldn't be seeing her again for days, maybe weeks? "Amy, I . . ." His voice faltered and an unaccustomed awkwardness threatened to squeeze his words off in his throat. Lifting his eyes to hers, he was surprised to find her watching him, her expression full of softness and her eyes shining.

"Go on," she said.

"Will you help me out here?"

"No."

"More coffee?" The waitress waved the hot, round container above their cups, then without waiting for an answer filled both to the brim. "We close in fifteen minutes, folks. Okay, okay!" she yelled over her shoulder to another customer. Without waiting for a response from Owen or Amy, she said almost under her breath, "Hang on to your britches, will you?" She walked briskly away.

"Shall we go?" Owen asked, reaching for the check.

"I'm not moving," she said, almost too quietly for anyone to hear.

"Pardon me?" he asked.

"I'm not moving until you finish what you started." She tossed her head slightly with the air of calm and confidence that Owen liked so much.

"Amy Weaver," he said, certain now that he was in love with her. "I'll not be forced into saying something like this hastily. They're about to close up this place and if you want to sit here all night by yourself, go right ahead. Be as stubborn as you want—but I will say this when I'm good and ready." He snatched the check from the table and crossed the room to pay the cashier. Glancing only once at the table, where she now sat alone watching his every move, Owen went out the door and waited.

Within a few minutes the door opened and he tried to calm his pulse as she walked toward him. When she reached his side, he took her hand in his and led her toward his car. Before he could open the door, she stopped him, gently placing her hand on his face.

"Owen," she said. He felt her looking beyond his eyes, deeply into his heart.

Owen slipped his arm around her waist and pulled her gently within the circle of his arms until her face was barely an inch from his. "Amy," he whispered. "I'm serious." His gaze traveled over her face and searched deeply into her eyes.

"I know," she said. His lips lightly brushed against hers as she spoke.

Raising his face from hers, he gently tightened his embrace and slowly pressed his lips against her forehead. Reluctantly, he released her and opened the car door. He checked his watch. Eleven-twenty, and he went on duty at midnight. He would be away from her for four days—it felt like an eternity.

———

"I've been invited to Sacramento," Amy told Owen over the phone when he called on Saturday. "The department of social welfare wants to know more about Covenant House. And, I've been asked to meet with some of the government wives and share our vision."

"When do you have to go?" he asked. Amy thought he sounded resigned.

"Tomorrow afternoon. There's a reception tomorrow evening. Then I'll meet with some of the social welfare people on Monday morning and speak at a luncheon at noon. I hope to catch an early evening flight back home. It's come up so suddenly."

"I was hoping to see you," he said, then quickly added, "but you'll be back Monday night, right? I'm off until Friday morning at six. Can I pick you up at the airport?"

"But I'll have my car, I don't know—"

"You let me worry about that, okay? I'll meet your plane."

"But I don't know which one I'll be on. There's one getting in at seven-thirty, another one at nine."

"I'll be there," he said. "Just you be on one of them, okay?"

"Okay," she said. "Owen," she faltered. Suddenly she was confronted with her own conflicting emotion. "I wish I wasn't going."

"I—" He hesitated, then said, "I'm glad you are. I think you're the perfect spokesman for Covenant House. Do you realize how much you could change the plight of mentally handicapped people, Amy? How many people's lives could be drastically changed if they were taken out of dark and depressing institutions and placed in warm, loving, family settings like Covenant House? This is an opportunity you can't afford to pass up, Amy. Who knows if you'd ever get another chance like this again?"

"Thank you," she said softly. Not wanting to keep anything from him she added, "I'm a little nervous."

"Only a little? I'd be petrified."

Amy wanted the conversation to go on and searched for things to say other than the deep, affectionate things she wanted to say, but was either too shy to voice or wanted to save for when they were together. "Owen," she said, finally breaking the silence. "I've been thinking about the other night at Jake's."

"And?"

"I really had a wonderful time," she said, her voice thickened with the warmth welling within her heart and chest.

"I did too," he said quietly. "I can't wait to see you again."

"Monday night."

"Seems so far away to me."

"Me too," she said. "I wish I didn't have to go." After they reluctantly ended their conversation, Amy leaned her forehead against the kitchen wall. The silence of the house was almost unbearable, and she decided she'd actually watch some TV in the small room that was once her bedroom. If she fell asleep there, she decided, no one would even know. Would it matter so much if she broke with convention and didn't sleep in a bed just this once?

Twenty-one

Descending the stairway from the plane, Amy looked quickly around, hoping to spot Owen. As she scanned the faces of waiting friends and family behind the chain link fence an odd twinge of disappointment filled her heart. Seeing Owen was the one thing she could think of that would help lift the heaviness centered in her chest.

"Miss Weaver. Miss Amy Weaver, please contact the information booth for a message. Miss Weaver."

Amy tightened her grip on her single small suitcase and headed for the center of the small airport.

"I'm Amy Weaver," she said to the navy blue uniformed woman behind the counter. "You paged me?"

"Oh yes, Miss Weaver," the woman said, handing her a handwritten note.

"Thank you," Amy mumbled, unfolding the paper and dreading the words she would find inside.

Sorry, had to work. Call you later—Owen.

A huge, painful knot twisted her insides. She stepped woodenly to the curb to catch the shuttle to the long-term lot where her car was parked. She was glad, at least, that she had caught the early flight and that she'd be home before it got too late. Safe in her own house, she would welcome the quietness. Not until then would she let herself reflect on her disastrous trip.

Parking her car near the garage, Amy went slowly toward the back porch and noticed the light over her sink was on. As she stepped inside, Princess jumped and greeted her excitedly. She realized the radio was playing softly from its familiar post atop the refrigerator and a note was propped against the sugar bowl on the kitchen table.

Welcome home, Linda's handwriting greeted her. *Princess*

216

has been fed, so don't let her try to talk you into feeding her again. Can't wait to hear all about your trip. Love, Linda.

Amy scooped Princess into her arms and buried her face in the dog's soft fur. Slipping out of her shoes, she padded barefoot into the bedroom and lay down fully clothed on the bed until Linda's soft knock at the screen door brought her back into the kitchen.

"Well," Linda said, her voice full of anticipation. "Tell me how it went up there with all the big mucky-mucks."

Amy turned toward the sink and busied herself rinsing and filling the tea kettle. As much as she wanted to confide in Linda, her feelings felt much too raw to discuss. She'd have to stick only to the events and avoid her own emotional responses if she were to relay the story accurately. Turning toward Linda, she tried to swallow the lump in her throat.

"Good heavens," Linda exclaimed. "You look as if you've had the wind knocked right out of you. What in the world happened?"

It didn't take Amy long to tell Linda that while some of those in high places were enthused about the concept of Covenant House, others who seemed so anxious to meet her at first were not really supportive at all. They saw it as a fanciful scheme of a rich girl to get some attention and make a place for herself socially in the community at the expense of those "poor helpless, mentally disadvantaged creatures."

One man came right out and asked her whether or not she had ever considered that a large group home was indeed a step backward toward more severe types of institutionalization and that the already overloaded social services department was having trouble placing adults now. If they licensed anything larger than Aggie's former residence, even as an experiment, and it turned out to be successful, there could very well be a public outcry for better and more up-to-date facilities than the state was ready or able to provide. " 'Funds, after all, are limited,' " Amy quoted, " 'and as generous as you might be able to be with Covenant House, I'm sure you can't see your way beyond just that one endeavor, am I right?' "

" 'My dear,' " Amy quoted one older woman as saying. " 'My dear Miss Weaver. It's not your motives we are questioning, it's your methods. Someone with high ideals such as yours could go far—with the right education, and of course, years of experience.' "

Linda came to the sink to stand beside her obviously distraught and exhausted friend.

"I came away with both my hands stinging from what I'd call an old-fashioned wrist slapping," Amy said. "I've been advised to put the money in my education—in my own future—rather than waste it on the future of people with such limited potential."

"Is that how you perceive Covenant House?" Linda asked. "As wasting money on people of limited potential? Is that how you view Anna?"

"No," Amy said almost angrily. "Of course not."

"How do you see it, then?"

"Linda, I'm too tired to think about this right now. I'm so confused. I thought this was such a wonderful idea before I went up there." Amy's head throbbed and her mind felt fuzzy.

"That was only yesterday, Amy. Just yesterday you knew without a doubt that Covenant House was a ministry, a wonderful act of compassion for those who could never in their entire lives have a place so nice to live in unless someone else provided it for them. Has that changed? You've become close to Anna . . . would she be more apt to be happy in something the state provides?"

"No," Amy said quietly. "I haven't changed my mind about any of those things." She wished the throbbing in her head would go away.

"Well, then," Linda said as if making an important point in a speech, "since the Covenant House project is an act of compassion for people we have come to love and care about—and certainly not a subversive act against the government or any of their precious politically motivated programs—what's the problem?"

"I don't know," Amy said. "Something is really bothering me. Something down so deep I . . . I can only feel it's there, but I can't tell you what it is. I just don't know how to describe it."

"Maybe the Lord is trying to tell you something," Linda said.

"Then why doesn't He just come right out and say it?" Amy shot back. "Does He always play these mind games?"

"No," Linda said sympathetically. "He's not playing games with you."

"I'm tired," Amy said, reaching for a glass of water and the aspirin bottle. "And I have a headache."

"You want me to go?"

"No," Amy said after swallowing two of the pills. "Where's Jim?"

"Church board meeting. We're about ready to have our ground breaking ceremony. Isn't it exciting?"

"Is Mark going to be the contractor on the new church?" Amy asked, glad to change the subject.

"I think so. We're really going to depend a lot on volunteer labor. Gerry Hill will be doing the electrical work. I'm not sure who's doing the plumbing just yet. But of course, Holden is already planning the landscape. As far as churches go, ours isn't going to be very big, but as far and Jim and I are concerned, it's gigantic." Linda glanced inside Amy's refrigerator. "You haven't much food in here."

"You hungry?"

"Aren't you?" Linda asked. "When did you eat last?"

"I don't know. I've been so busy and keyed up. I didn't eat much at noon. It was a luncheon with some of the state senators' wives. I was too nervous to eat."

"No wonder you have a headache. Wasn't Owen going to meet you at the airport?" Linda asked.

Amy shrugged and tried to keep her voice natural. "He had to work."

"Want to order a pizza? The new place downtown will deliver."

———

An hour later, with the remnants of their pizza still in its cardboard box between them, the two friends indulged, splitting another bottle of soda.

"Amy," Linda said, "I've been thinking about what that woman said to you earlier. Does there have to be a choice between your education and Covenant House? I mean," she hurriedly explained, "I know nothing of your finances, but do you think your father would have you give up your education for Aggie's family?"

"It's certainly not an either-or situation," Amy said. "My father left enough for both and also for me to live quite nicely, probably for the rest of my life."

"Wow," Linda said, whistling low. "I can't imagine."

"If that wasn't enough, he bought some stock that pays dividends regularly, set up a trust fund for a modest but steady income. Then there's his savings, a few bonds, and—"

"Stop!" Linda pretended to faint. "I can't stand anymore!"

"And," Amy continued, ignoring her friend's feigned emotional outburst, "let's not forget Weaver's Building Supply. That has turned a profit every year since it opened. Chet Ramsey is suggesting that it might be wise to consider selling it. He's wanting to retire before too long and a larger supply business in L.A. is interested if I want to sell out." Pausing only to take a sip of her soda, Amy said, "And, of course, there's the real estate. Downtown, uptown, and even out of town."

"Now you really must stop!" Linda exclaimed. "How can you manage all of this?"

"The same way my father did, I suppose. Carefully—very carefully."

"So back to my question—when will you go back to school?"

"I don't know," Amy said in a low, troubled voice. "I really don't know. It's all so confusing to me. Linda," she said, coming to sit opposite her friend at the table, "do you think it's possible that all these years I was interested in becoming a nurse because of my mother's illness? I can't help myself," she said without waiting for an answer, "but I've been almost—oh, I don't know, freed up somehow since my mother died. For some time, I've been discontented at school. I dreaded the classes and hated most of the subjects."

"Did you ever tell your mother this?"

"No. I couldn't. She was so excited about that scholarship. She wanted this for me in the worst way. But now I have different responsibilities to consider. It's the strangest thing. I always knew when I finished with school I'd probably come home and be with my mother. She certainly had no interest in Daddy's affairs. I knew that I'd have to manage things. How would a nursing degree help me with that? That's where Marshall came in, isn't it? But now, that's all changed. Just when I thought I was finally getting some clear direction—oh, I wish I knew what to do."

"Amy, listen to me," Linda insisted, her brown eyes exploring the depth of Amy's blue ones. "Never mind what happened in Sacramento. You have opportunities most people never even dream of. Doors are standing wide open in front of you. More than ever, it's going to be important that you know God's will for your life. What's He calling you to do? Where does He want you to fit into His kingdom? And," Linda added, her eyes sparkling with mischief, "where does Owen Sampson fit into this picture?"

"I wish I knew the answers to those questions. I really do."

————

At the station Owen filled out endless reports and evidence forms. He wanted to be finished by ten at the latest. He'd need to shower and change out of his smoke-filled clothes before he called Amy—if it wasn't too late already. No fire is ever routine, yet the seemingly unending details and paperwork can seem that way, especially if you want to be somewhere else.

Ignoring the rumbling in his empty stomach, Owen headed his small Plymouth Fury toward the south side of town and turned into the wide street where Amy lived next door to Jim and Linda Henry. He liked the young pastor and his wife and was grateful for their accessibility, especially when he didn't want to cause a ripple of gossip where Amy was concerned. *If Amy's light is on,* he said to himself, *I'll not go up to the door unless I can tell for sure if Jim and Linda are home. Then I'll see if Amy wants to get something to eat, or if she wants Jim and Linda to come over for a little while so we can all hear the details of her trip to Sacramento together.* He smiled in the darkness. How easy it was to plan his off hours around being with Amy Weaver.

Ten-fifteen, he noted on the clock in the dash. *I hope she's still up.*

Jim Henry pulled into his driveway just as Owen rounded the corner. *Perfect*, he said to himself. *Couldn't have planned that any better.*

"Hey, Owen," Jim said with friendly courtesy. "I was just thinking about you."

"You were?" Owen asked as he stepped away from his car. "How's that?"

"Heard about that packing house fire over in River Hills—you get called in on that one?"

"Afraid so. Just got off."

"Solve the mystery?"

"No mystery. Arson, plain and simple. Now it's just who and why. The police detectives will have to come up with those answers. My work is done; that's all I care about tonight."

Jim raised an eyebrow. "On your way to see Amy?"

"Not sure," Owen said thoughtfully. "I didn't call first. You and Linda up to coming over to her place for a little while? I'd like to hear about her trip."

"I think Linda's already there," Jim said, giving Owen a friendly slap on the back. "Come on, let's find out."

As the two men approached Amy's house, Princess did little more than offer a polite "woof."

"She's a big help," Linda said, greeting Jim. "As you can see, we're really protected here."

"Hi." Owen was speaking to both women, but he looked only at Amy, who merely smiled in return.

"Hey," Jim said enthusiastically, pointing at the box on the table. "Is that pizza?"

"It's cold," Amy said. "Let me heat it."

In a few minutes, the men had polished off the remains of Amy and Linda's dinner and Owen was picking at the crumbs hiding around the edges of the box.

"Well?" Jim said at last.

"Well, what?" Linda responded.

"Let's hear about that trip of yours," he said, tapping Amy lightly on the arm.

"Do I have to?" Amy asked. Her words were playful, but her meaning was clear. "I'm far too tired tonight."

"Quite a whirlwind trip, then," Jim commented, missing Linda's warning glance.

"You can't even begin to know," Linda said. "We can catch up on all this later, can't we?"

Owen leaned forward and lowered his voice. "Amy? You all right? Did you have any trouble?"

In spite of her weariness, she discovered she wanted nothing more than to pour out the entire story to Owen and Jim—yet fatigue and confusion held her back. "I can't get into this now. I want to tell you all about it, but first I need a good night's sleep."

"I'll call you first thing in the morning. I'm kind of bushed myself," Owen said, standing up. "Let's all get a good night's rest before we take on the state government."

In his car, Owen analyzed the brief meeting. Just seeing her should have been enough. He told himself over and over that's all he wanted tonight—just to see her. Still, the familiar faint shadow that robbed her blue eyes of their clear sparkle worried him. She might get a good night's sleep, but somehow Owen was certain he probably would not. Seventeen weeks ago he had never even heard Amy Weaver's name. But on November 27, 1959, Owen's life had changed. And, he knew, it changed forever.

Twenty-two

While Jim walked Owen to his car, Linda helped Amy clean up the kitchen. Silence fell between the two women. It was Linda who finally spoke.

"Owen's a nice guy, isn't he?"

"Um-hmm." Amy's matter-of-fact answer indicated she barely had heard Linda's question.

"He seems quite interested in you," Linda tried again.

"I know."

"Then the fact hasn't escaped you," Linda said.

"No, it hasn't."

"Well?" Linda asked.

"I'm too tired to think about this now," Amy said. "It's too confusing."

"I don't want to pressure you, Amy," Linda said, putting her arm around Amy's shoulder. "Whenever you're ready, I'm willing to listen, okay?"

"Okay," Amy said, turning to quickly embrace her friend.

As tired as she was, Amy had trouble getting to sleep. The dark house seemed emptier than ever and her loneliness more intense. Tossing on her bed, punching her pillows, Amy felt as though her heart were being squeezed by an unseen hand. Thoughts of her education, her future, and her present responsibilities were all tangled together. Even thoughts of Owen Sampson didn't seem to help untangle the mental and emotional mess within her. As grateful as she was for Linda's strength and friendship, she suddenly wished she had discussed her trip with Owen first.

Finally, she made her way to the TV room and watched mindlessly while Jack Paar cracked his jokes. During the late night movie, Amy pulled a quilt over herself and Princess curled up in her lap. She slept until three-thirty, when silence woke her. Noticing the station had gone off the air, she turned off the set. Stumbling into the front bedroom, she slipped into bed and as she had so many times before, let her tears fall unchecked onto her mother's bleached white pillowcases.

Early the next morning, Amy stumbled sleepily around the kitchen with Princess underfoot as usual. Finding only three eggs left in the carton, she decided to boil them and keep one for later. That's what Charlotte often did, saving the extra one for slicing on a salad or making an egg salad sandwich. Before she could get the coffeepot on or put the eggs on the stove to cook, the phone rang. She walked toward it, then changing her mind, turned slowly away. She glanced at the clock. It was not quite eight. *Owen*, she thought. Her deepening feelings for him only confused the painful issues stirring within her—decisions she couldn't even identify, much less articulate. *Maybe Owen Sampson represents an easy diversion*, she thought. *Can I really afford that right now?* She remained motionless until the phone stopped ringing.

———

Owen slowly replaced the receiver on its cradle. *Maybe she's still sleeping*, he thought, glancing at his watch. Eight o'clock. Remembering how tired she was last night, he scolded himself. *I'm probably calling too early.* Glancing around his small apartment, he looked for a project that would keep him busy for an hour or so. His simple surroundings were planned for efficiency—not comfort. He preferred to spend his off hours with his sister and her family rather than alone. He knew his brother-in-law would be off to work by now and that his nieces and nephews would soon be headed out the door to school. He could go to Judy's for a cup of coffee. She would probably make him some breakfast. But just as quickly as the thought crossed his mind, he dismissed it. *I want to be with Amy, not my sister*, he said to himself.

Yet he had to find something to do while he waited. He had washed and waxed his Plymouth at the station a few days before during a slow afternoon—it didn't need it again so soon.

His landlady kept the sidewalks swept and his laundry was current. Hunger finally turned his attention toward his small kitchenette. A half quart of milk was sour, and he had forgotten to put the bread in the refrigerator before he went on duty five days ago. The small patches of green mold prompted him to step on the pedal that opened the lid on the small round garbage container next to the refrigerator. "If you forget to put it in there," he said, nodding toward the refrigerator, "then you'll be throwing it in here." He ceremoniously gave the half loaf an overhand toss and landed it squarely in the paper sack lined container.

Grabbing a sweater, Owen left his tiny empty apartment and headed for Sternhagen's Bakery. He knew Else kept a pot of coffee perking in the back room. During his high school days, she always had a cup ready for him when he came back from making her deliveries. He'd see if he could work his way into her back room, confident the older woman could still be sweet-talked into feeding him. He'd call Amy again at nine.

———

At eight forty-five, after putting her few breakfast dishes in the sink and pouring another cup of coffee, once again Amy made her way out to her father's office with Princess tagging close behind.

"Let's get this over with, okay?" she asked the dog. "We're almost done. Let's just be disciplined and stick to it this time."

But when she opened the door she saw the large, inviting recliner chair in the corner. Walking slowly to the back of the chair, she gently touched the place where her father had so often leaned his head. She went around and sat down, letting the softness welcome her tired body. She slid the big chair easily into a reclining position as the foot rest came up under her legs. Pushing herself back as far as the chair would recline, she grabbed the hand-quilted lap robe her father always kept within easy reach. Covering herself, she motioned Princess to jump into her lap. Before long, both were sound asleep in the warmth of the late March sunshine streaming through the window.

"Amy!" At the sound of Linda's voice, Princess instantly

leapt from Amy's lap and barked, startling Amy from a deep, peaceful sleep.

"Out here," she called back, trying to shake her head and make herself wake up. "What time is it, anyway?" Amy asked as Linda came into the room.

"It's almost noon. I saw your car out in the drive and when you didn't answer your phone—"

"I must have dozed off."

"I guess you did. You still look tired. I'm sorry I woke you up."

"It's okay. I'm glad to see you. I didn't sleep well last night."

"Didn't you hear the phone?" Linda asked.

"It doesn't ring out here. My father didn't want to be disturbed when he worked. Mama just took messages for him in the house."

"You have a lot on your mind, don't you, Amy?"

"Yes. And I don't always like it. There's just so much to think about."

"How are you doing out here?" Linda asked, nodding her head toward the files and stacks of papers covering the top of John Weaver's desk.

"Almost done. I thought I'd finish up this morning. I'm down to Weaver's Building Supply, then Zeller's Lodge. Most of this is just filing. I've already been through almost all of it."

"I understand having files under Weaver's Building Supply, but Zeller's Lodge?"

"I don't know, I've not opened that one yet. The store takes one large section all its own. I'm pretty sure it's just copies of important papers that are also kept on file down at the store or at Mr. Carlson's office. My father was very careful about storing important records in two places. You know, just being cautious."

"Have you made any decisions about the store?" Linda asked. "I think many people wonder what you will do with it."

"No, not really. As long as Mr. Ramsey wants to work, I don't want to sell. He's thinking of retiring in a year or two. I've got some time. Mr. Carlson tells me the chain is still interested in buying me out. I don't know. I'll get to it in time."

"And what about you?" Linda asked. "How are you doing?"

"Me?" Amy asked. She stood slowly and walked to the window overlooking her mother's small fruit orchard. Confusion about Owen, Covenant House, and her future fogged together in her mind.

Amy was glad when Linda didn't rush or push her way into her private quietness. Momentarily lost in her own awareness of how much she needed the Lord's guidance, she suddenly spun around and spoke. "I don't know what to do," Amy admitted tearfully. "I really don't. Everywhere I turn I see so much responsibility. It's finally beginning to dawn on me—this—all this," she swung her arm in a sweeping gesture over her father's office. "All this isn't something I have to take care of for my father. He left it to me. *I* have to decide what to do. I can't just decide on what I think he would want me to do. He's gone." Amy's voice cracked and she covered her mouth with her hand. "He's gone, Linda." Her muffled words were spoken from a sad, broken heart.

Linda's expression told Amy that her friend's heart ached, too. "Yes, honey, he is."

"My father's gone and he's never coming back. He didn't tell me what to do when he died. He didn't leave me any instructions. He didn't tell me what to do about the shopping mall or the store or even the house. He didn't tell me when to change the oil in the car or if it needs new tires. I don't know how old the roof is or what to do if the furnace goes out. I'm alone, Linda. I'm all alone!"

Linda opened her arms and pulled Amy close while deep sobs shook her entire body. "Dear God," Linda prayed quietly. "Show us what to do. Help her, Lord."

Finally, when Amy's sobbing subsided, Linda pulled two chairs close to each other and Amy let herself be guided to sit in one of them. Taking a deep breath, Linda said, "I believe God heard our prayer, Amy. He's the only One who can help you—and He will. I know He will.

"Amy," she continued gently, "you're not alone. Yes, I know, it feels like it. But you have given your heart to Christ, remember? He's with you. It won't be the same; it'll never be the same for you ever again. Life is different now. You didn't ask for all this to happen to you, but it did. Yet, in spite of it all, in just a few short months you've made a difference in so many lives. Covenant House is becoming a reality because of you. The planning commission is considering renewal and restoration instead of destruction and rebuilding—all because of you."

"And Marshall Jennings is practically ruined because of me," Amy said between her tears. "Don't forget that."

"Marshall Jennings is practically ruined because of Marshall Jennings," Linda said, surprising Amy with the angry tone in her voice. "Don't you forget that."

"But there's just so much—so much I don't know what to do, I don't know which way to turn. It's all so confusing. I'm overwhelmed and I'm exhausted."

"Look," Linda offered. "Let's get these files put away. Tidy this place up a bit and get some order back into this room. You say these just have to be put away?" She asked, picking up a stack from a corner of the desk.

"Yes, but I can't ask you—"

"Oh, pooh," Linda said. "Maybe someday I'll need you to do my ironing. Come on now, help me out here. What about these papers?"

"Filing," Amy answered as she wiped her eyes with the sleeves of her sweatshirt.

"So, here," Linda said, looking at the entire section for Weaver's Building Supply. "Do you really have to go through these alone? Why not get Mr. Ramsey to come over and give you a guided tour through all these papers?"

"I could, I guess. It does make better sense than me trying to figure them out all by myself."

"That only leaves Zeller's Lodge. Isn't that the little motor lodge right outside of town?" Linda asked. "It's kind of a . . ." Amy knew the reputation of the small, dingy motel, but before Linda could retract her words, she grabbed the file from her hand.

"I might as well know what this is all about."

"Well," Linda made a move to take the file back, "not today. It can wait. I'm hungry. Let's make a sandwich, okay?"

"No," Amy insisted. Swinging the file out of Linda's reach, she accidentally threw the contents to the floor.

The two friends stood frozen as more than two dozen motel receipts scattered around and under the desk. *PAID*—stamped in large red letters across the top of each slip of paper—seemed to scream from the floor.

"Oh, my gosh," Linda said involuntarily.

Amy picked up one of the handwritten receipts and stared at it. "I think I need to call and find out what this is all about."

"Listen," Linda said, putting her hand firmly on the extension phone on the desk. "You don't have to know about this, do you? I mean, so there's some receipts from—"

"From a cheap little motel on the edge of town," Amy finished Linda's sentence. "I think this needs explanation. Don't you?" Fear and anger competed for space in Amy's pounding heart.

"But right this minute?" Linda asked. "I wish Jim was here—well, maybe not."

"Right this minute," Amy said, her voice clear and exact. "No matter what this turns out to be," she said, "it can't make anything worse, can it? And I don't want to spend another sleepless night wondering about this. When I find out, I can toss this file and be done with it. Now are you going to take your hand off the phone and let me make this call?"

"You want me to leave?"

"Don't you dare move!" Amy ordered. "No, I don't want you to leave. Stay right where you are, please," her voice softened.

"Right here," Linda said, pointing firmly toward her feet. "I'll not budge an inch."

Amy dialed the phone. Linda crossed her fingers behind her back, then moved across the room to pray instead. After a few moments, Amy reached someone.

"Hello, this is Amy Weaver calling. I've been doing my father's—yes, Weaver. John Weaver. He was my father. Like I said, I've been going through his papers and he has a file here with your—" Amy paused.

As Linda shifted her weight from one foot to the other, Amy motioned vigorously for her friend to come nearer. Once she was close, Amy grabbed her wrist as if she were afraid Linda might leave.

"He what?" Amy said, then listened.

Linda waited. "What's he saying? Why are you smiling like that?"

"I see, and how often did he—" Amy shut her eyes and felt fresh tears of relief begin to stream down her cheeks. "And what do you do now?"

"What's going on?" Linda whispered.

Amy waved her hand then put her finger to her lips to shush Linda. "I see. And where do they come from?" she said into the phone. "Listen, can I call you back? I'll get back to you as soon as I can."

Amy made a few more polite remarks and hung up the phone. "I should have known," she said softly.

"Are you going to tell me or am I going to have to choke it out of you?" Linda asked playfully.

"My father," Amy said wiping her eyes, "paid for people to stay there when they had no place else to go. He had an arrangement, they said. The police would pick up a hitchhiker or some other poor man down on his luck and take him there for a good night's sleep and a bath. They called my father a few times, but mostly they just sent him a bill and he paid it. They said he did this about once or twice a month. Finally they just kept a room and my father paid for it by the month."

"A good Samaritan," Linda said. "A real, genuine good Samaritan. Can you believe it?"

"Yes," Amy said. "I think I can." She laid her hand across her heart and took a deep breath, welcoming a light, almost giddy mood.

"Well, crisis over," Linda said. "Now I want to know about Owen Sampson."

"Later," Amy said playfully. "Right now I'm famished. Didn't you promise to make me a sandwich?"

Twenty-three

All during lunch, Amy managed to keep from talking to Linda about Owen Sampson. But as Linda cleared away the few dishes, she approached the subject directly.

"I don't know," Amy said finally. "I just don't know if this is a good time to get involved with anyone."

"Owen isn't just anyone," Linda lightly scolded. "He's really a wonderful man, Amy."

"But it's just so soon."

"Soon?"

"You know, after my mother's death. And Marsh." She certainly hadn't been a good judge of character where Marshall was concerned. How could she be sure she wouldn't make such a mistake again?

"Oh, come on, Amy," Linda said. "Owen isn't anything like Marshall and you know it."

True, all her instincts told her Owen Sampson was a wonderful man and that the deepening feelings she felt for him were quite different than what she had felt for Marshall Jennings. "I just don't know if I can trust my instincts. I got engaged to Marshall right after my father died and that was a mistake I never want to make again. I just don't trust my own judgment right now, where men are concerned."

Unfortunately, she didn't think to trust Linda and Jim's advice concerning Owen, either.

"I'm not going to force myself on anyone," Owen said to his sister Judy later that evening over dinner. "I've made my intentions as clear as I know how. I thought she might have felt the same way. I guess I was wrong. Perhaps it was just the moonlight."

232

"Come on, Owen," Judy said. "She's been through a lot lately. Give it another shot, will you?"

Owen leaned forward and placed his elbows on the table. "The ball's in her court, sis. I'm not a chaser. You know me well enough to know that by now."

"I think you're wrong, Owen," Judy said gently.

"This is too important, Judy," Owen said, unflinching under her penetrating gaze. "I don't think I'm wrong, but I care too much about Amy Weaver to let my own opinions stand in my way here. Tell me how you think I'm wrong."

Owen's sister paused before beginning her explanation. "I think," Judy said, still in her gentle, direct tone, "that you've waited a long, long time for someone like Amy to come along. We've seen you together at church and some of our social affairs. You are both so comfortable around each other—so natural. To tell you the truth, my brother, for someone who's always been so sure of himself—the confirmed bachelor—you now seem awkward when you're *not* with her. I think she could very well be the one, Owen. And I think you're giving up too easily. Are you sure it's not just your pride that's getting in the way here?"

"My pride?"

"Yes, your pride. What are you afraid of?"

"Well," Owen hesitated. "I certainly don't like the feeling I get when I know she's home and not answering the phone when I call."

"Is it *your* phone calls she's not answering—or is it that she's just not answering the phone right now? You know, people do have the right not to answer that darn thing if they don't want to. From what I understand, you might not be the only person calling her, you know."

"So what do you recommend? That I go storming over there and bang on her door until she sees me?" Owen's voice held a tinge of sarcasm that Judy chose to ignore.

"Is that what you want to do?" she asked, keeping her voice even and controlled.

Owen clenched his teeth. "Is that what I *should* do?" Owen searched his sister's face for an answer.

"What do you want to do?" she rephrased the question.

"What do you really want to do about Amy Weaver?"

"I want to go to her house and tell her—" Owen's voice broke, and when he spoke again, his tone was warm. "I want to go to her and tell her that I love her. That no matter what she's been through and how rough it's been, I want to be with her."

"Then?"

"Then what?"

"Then why don't you?" It was Don, Judy's husband, unable to keep out of the conversation any longer.

"You think I ought to?" Owen asked, his eyes wide as he looked at Don.

Don glanced between Judy and Owen, resting his eyes finally on those of his wife. "I know that when I fell in love with Judy nothing could have stopped me from telling her how I felt." Don turned his eyes back to meet Owen's. "You talk about the ball being in Amy's court. This is no game, Owen. If you love her the way I love your sister, this is far too important to stand on protocol. If I were you, and mind you I'm not—but if I were, I'd settle it in my own mind, and once that was done, I'd go over and knock on her front door and if she didn't answer, I'd go to the back door. If she still didn't answer, I'd sit right there until she came out." Don softened his tone. "She has the right to know how deeply you care for her, Owen. How else can she make her own decisions? She can't go on a hunch, now, can she?"

"I'll give this some thought," Owen said, standing to leave. "In fact, I'll make it a matter of serious prayer."

"That sounds good to me," Judy said. "We can't ask for more than that. Thank you for listening."

Before Owen left, he gave his sister a warm hug and shook the hand of his brother-in-law. "What would I do without you guys?"

"Die an old bachelor?" Judy quipped.

Once inside his car, Owen let his thoughts drift across town toward Amy's house. *What would she do if I just showed up on her doorstep?* he thought, then said aloud, "What would *I* do if I showed up on her doorstep?"

Owen Sampson hadn't had much experience pursuing

women. Since his early twenties, he had spent most of his time avoiding aggressive mothers, well-meaning aunts, and married friends' matchmaking wives. He held back from even giving friendly nods and smiles because he didn't want to be misunderstood as romantically interested. He hesitated accepting invitations from friends because of past awkward experiences of being unwittingly paired up with sometimes an equally unsuspecting, single woman. Blind dates he refused altogether. His family was sensitive to his feelings along these lines, and he knew they would never arrange anything or manipulate circumstances to force him into an embarrassing situation. Living on the defensive for most of his adult life, he felt inexperienced and unprepared for changing his approach. Only Amy Weaver had the power to bring him out of his self-imposed hermitage.

"Dear Lord," he said aloud while keeping an eye on traffic. "I've usually talked to you about other people—in fact almost always about other people. This is new for me, heavenly Father. I have to admit it's far easier to pray for missionaries and world events than it is to pray for myself. But, I'm in over my head—in fact, you might say I'm hopelessly in over my head. I can't reason this one through, God. I not only need your wisdom here, I need your help."

Owen navigated his car slowly down the street in front of Amy's house. Seeing the light on in her living room window, he thought momentarily about taking Don's advice immediately and boldly knocking on her front door. Instead, he pulled the car to the curb and turned off the headlights.

"Dear Father," he whispered into the darkness. "I've waited a long time for someone to come along like Amy. I don't want to mess this up. I don't want to run ahead of you—although I have to admit I'm tempted. Just help me to know what to do. Please, God, help me."

At that moment, Owen's heart raced as he saw her through the sheer lace curtains in her front room. She leaned toward the lamp on the table near the window, and he saw her shimmering hair fall forward like a soft halo of spun gold. He caught his breath. She was still up. *Should I go in?* he thought prayerfully. At that moment she turned off the lamp and the front of her house was immediately dark. "Guess not," Owen said aloud. He turned the key in the ignition and slowly pulled his car into the street and turned toward his own small, empty apartment. The solitude of his little place, so welcoming and safe before, seemed empty and cold now.

The next morning, Owen stared at the phone, trying to decide whether or not to call Amy. He picked up the phone but dialed Judy's number instead. When she didn't answer, Owen hung up the phone and his sense of aloneness intensified. He picked up the phone again and dialed, stopping short of the seven digits needed to connect him with Amy. He paused, then slowly replaced the receiver on its cradle. Impulsively, he decided to spend the day at the beach. *Wednesday*, he thought. *Last week I was counting the days until I could get off work—now I wish I could go back.* Without having to be told, Owen knew he was giving up too easily.

Grabbing his denim jacket and a large blanket, he headed toward his car. Without making the conscious decision, he once again drove in the direction of Amy's house. Pulling into her driveway was his way of making himself get out of the car and talk to her, even if only for a moment.

Amy answered the knock at her front door wearing a blue linen suit. Two layers of soft ivory ruffles caressed her neck and cascaded down the front. Owen noticed how the color of her suit accentuated the deep blue of her eyes and contrasted with her blond hair, which she had twisted up away from her slender face in a French roll.

"Hi," he said almost bashfully.

"Hi."

"I was just heading out to the beach. I was just wondering—well, probably not. I can see you have other plans. It's just that I thought it might be nice to—you know—go to the beach. There's not too many people out there this time of year. It's kind of quiet and—well, I can see you've got things to do. Maybe another time," Owen said. "I'm sorry, I should have called."

He wished he hadn't stopped by, but was glad to see her. Seeing her made him even more sure of his feelings for her. Last night, when he prayed, he almost had wondered if he was making too much of the situation. Seeing her this morning, he realized that he had, in fact, dramatically understated it. He turned to go, but was stopped by her voice, which held just a trace of laughter.

"Wait a minute," she said. "I haven't been answering the phone. I'm only going out to do a few errands. Nothing that can't wait until another time."

"You mean you don't have any appointments or anything?"

"Mr. Carlson is expecting me, but I'm just going in to sign some papers. It would only take a few minutes—ten at the most."

"But you're all dressed up," he said.

"I decided to try and look more professional—but really—the beach sounds like fun. I haven't been there in a long time. And," she added, her voice a little shaky, "I haven't had any *fun* for a very long time. Can you give me a few minutes to change?"

"Of course," he said, thinking he'd give her all morning if necessary. "Listen, I just have to gas up my car. How about if I come back in say . . ."

"Ten minutes," she said. "I'll only need ten minutes."

Watching her step back and close the door, Owen could barely conceal his delight. Who would have thought an impulse could have such positive results? "Calm down, Sampson," he scolded himself as he drove toward the gas station a few blocks away. "This is only a beach date—she hasn't accepted your marriage proposal." Suddenly the thought sent Owen's pulse racing. The very idea of having Amy be willing to change her plans and at the drop of a hat agree to spend the day with him was more than he could have ever hoped for.

Few words were spoken between them until after they left Herbert Carlson's office and were headed down the freeway toward the coast.

"I suppose I should have checked the weather before we left home," he said, pointing to the overcast sky.

"It doesn't matter," she said. "I don't care if it rains or not. It's just nice to get away and do something irresponsible."

"Is this irresponsible?"

"Well, impulsive, anyway."

"I hope this is okay—after all, I didn't give you much warning."

"I'm here," she said, smiling at him. "As you can see, it's obvious I didn't need much warning. If I remember right, you didn't have to do much talking to persuade me."

He glanced at her and without reservation returned her smile. "I'm glad you came. I was really headed out to spend the day alone. I used to go to the beach all the time by myself. Today it didn't seem like so much fun."

"I'm glad you asked me," she said.

"Me too."

Owen pulled the car into a nearly deserted parking lot overlooking the ocean. Low clouds hovered nearby, appearing to touch the water on the horizon. The water was dark and gray, accentuating the whiteness of the frothy breakers splashing rhythmically against the shore.

"I think we can find a path down to the water. Want to walk on the sand?" Owen asked.

Amy nodded, opened the door on her side of the car, and stepped out. "Did you bring an umbrella?" she asked as Owen got out behind her.

"I'm not sure," he said, walking to the back of the car and opening the trunk. "I didn't plan this very well, did I?"

"I think you did," she said. "I think it's perfect."

"No umbrella," he said, shutting the trunk lid. "What shall we do?"

"Maybe it won't rain."

"And if it does?"

"Well, then, we'll get wet, won't we?"

"Guess so." Owen took her hand and led her toward the boulders to find the path down to the water's edge. When they made it to the sand below, he didn't release her hand and she made no effort to free it. Silently, they walked along the firm, damp sand, leaving tracks for the tide to erase later.

The ocean breeze, the low clouds, and even the slight mist seemed to swirl around the young jean-clad couple without touching them or invading their thoughts. Unhurriedly, they made their way toward an unspecified destination. It was nearly a half-hour later when Owen paused, turned, and looked deeply into Amy Weaver's eyes before pulling her gently into his arms and tenderly, slowly, touching his lips to hers. Encircling her in his arms, Owen felt her snuggle her face into the crook of his neck. With one hand, he reached up and loosened the pins holding her hair until it tumbled freely down her back and moved gently, lightly at the whispered command of the wind.

Releasing her from his embrace, he stepped back at arm's length from her and caught her hand once again in his. For a moment, he studied her face intently.

"Amy . . ." His voice was thick and unsteady. "I love you."

For a long moment, Amy looked back at him. Owen didn't even feel awkward as she studied his face unhurriedly, feature by feature. He stared back in waiting silence, his sight of her blurred with emotion. Owen's words hung between them and he longed for Amy to claim them and take them into her heart. Finally she moved slowly toward him, closing the short distance. Owen unreservedly opened his arms and she willingly lifted her face, welcoming his kiss.

"Owen," she said softly when he lifted his face from hers, "it's raining."

"Is it?" he asked, looking up into the cloudy sky. "I didn't notice."

Together the young couple turned and, hand in hand, walked slowly through the soft rain back to the car.

Twenty-four

"I had a wonderful time," Amy told Owen when he brought her back home and walked her to her front door.

"I did, too," he said. "Thanks for being so spontaneous. I promise I'll call first next time."

"What if I'm not answering the phone?" she asked. "I'd miss your call."

"Why aren't you answering the phone?" Owen asked, capturing her eyes with his. "Is there something you're afraid of?"

"Not really," she said. Hesitantly, she searched for the words to tell him how she had been bombarded with calls from women's groups, the library committee wanting to dedicate a room to the memory of her mother and the small garden outside to her father. And, of course, there was the small business owners of downtown Summerwind taking in more members and wanting her involved as they formalized their organization. Mark Andrews knew to call Jim and Linda's if he needed to reach her about Covenant House. "It's just that I've had so many calls lately, I hardly have time to think. I've got a stack of correspondence to answer and I haven't even been able to keep up with that."

"Ever think of getting a service?"

"An answering service?" Amy seemed quite surprised by his suggestion.

"Who answered the phone for your father?"

"Mama. And, of course, people called him at the store, too."

"So, who's answering the phone for you?"

"I'm not answering, remember?"

"How does Aggie reach you?"

Amy shrugged slightly. "She can't unless I'm answering calls."

"Amy," Owen said, leaning casually against the railing on her front porch, "do you think you need some secretarial help? I mean, would you be able to let someone help you out with some of this and maybe help you get your life back?"

"So I can run off to the beach more often?"

"Exactly." He grinned widely and pulled her into his embrace. "If you're going to be my girl, I want to be able to reach you."

"Your girl?"

Owen overlooked her remark and continued, "Why not get a service for this number and have your home number changed to an unlisted one? That way you'd not miss any important calls, and we'd have our privacy, too."

"We?" she asked, still held close in his arms.

"I'm in your life, Amy Weaver. Get used to that idea, okay?"

"I'll try," she said before he kissed her good night.

———

Four days later, early in the morning on Sunday, April 3, 1960, Amy met with Jim and Linda Henry, Owen Sampson, and Mattie Sloan. She solemnly placed a large floral spray at the family headstone that had been put in place when Anna's grave was moved alongside her parents'. Jim read a simple Scripture, and holding hands in a circle, they recommitted Anna's body to the earth along with Amy's parents. When Jim pronounced the "amen," Amy stooped and traced with her finger the words added to her sister's marker. *Baby Anna*, it now read, with a new inscription in smaller letters underneath, *Beloved daughter, cherished sister. April Third, Nineteen Hundred and Thirty-Seven* .

The small ceremony didn't take much more than fifteen minutes. Leaving the cemetery, Amy looked into Owen's eyes. "Now," she said, her eyes shining with both joy and sorrow, "it's done. I feel better now. I won't need to come back here for a long time."

———

Jim and Linda agreed with Owen's idea that an answering service would give Amy the peace and quiet she needed, while making sure she got all the calls that were important. She could then return calls at her leisure. If she had a secretary, they reasoned, she could not only help answer the stack of letters that came each day, but answer the calls Amy didn't want to handle at the moment.

"You could use your father's office," Linda suggested.

"Or I could renovate his downtown office. He used to keep an office in one of the rooms upstairs over Mr. Brown's camera shop," Amy offered. "I'm sure it's still empty. My father moved his things home—he didn't want to be away from Mama after I went away to school. That's when he moved home."

"Are you going to become a working woman, Amy?" Linda teased.

"I already am," Amy said laughingly. "Whether I like it or not."

Plans were made and within two weeks Amy and Linda had thoroughly cleaned a small two-room office suite in the front of the building, upstairs over the camera shop. In the process they discovered another desk and an old typewriter hidden under a canvas in one corner. Amy decided to keep the desk but replace the typewriter. They bought and hung some readymade draperies, and after the carpet had been cleaned Jim, Owen, and Mark Andrews, along with some of Mark's men, moved John Weaver's desk, files, and a small sofa into the office suite.

Linda volunteered to work with Amy until she could hire a part-time secretary. Two weeks later, secretarial help had already lightened Amy's load considerably, and the answering service had given her the buffer she needed to regain her sense of privacy. Winifred Fielding, or Winnie as she was known to almost everyone in town, took immediate charge and brought order and organization to the myriad of details that clamored for Amy's attention. Winnie saw to it that a proper phone system was installed and some simple but attractive business stationery was ordered along with business cards for Amy "to have on hand, just in case. You never know when you'll need them. Gives things a more professional look." Winnie had such a way about her that Amy didn't even question her decisions and opened a small bank account for Winnie's office expenses.

Owen and Amy spent as much time together as possible and Mark came to visit her often at the office to discuss various details and give progress reports on the construction of Covenant House. Finally, he invited Jim, Linda, and Owen to accompany Amy and pick up Aggie to meet him at the site for a guided tour and progress report.

Of the small group in attendance, Aggie seemed to know the most about the project and could carry on the most informed conversation with Mark about the building itself.

"My dear husband, he was a carpenter of sorts. Quite a do-it-yourselfer in his day," she said affectionately.

"I'm impressed, Aggie," Mark said. "You know, if I didn't already have my heart set on Mattie Sloan, I'd be courting you."

The simple woman blushed and backed away from the compliment. "Get away with you, Mark Andrews. Mattie and I are both old enough to be your mother!"

When the tour was over, the six settled in a booth at the local A&W for root beer floats. In a momentary break in the lively conversation, Amy took a deep breath and decided to reveal a secret, something she had been hiding for a few weeks for fear it wouldn't be a possibility.

"I have something to announce," Amy blurted out almost as if she were embarrassed.

"Oh?" Jim said, smiling in Owen's direction. "Something we don't know about already?"

"Something no one knows about yet," Amy said.

"Don't look at me," Owen declared his innocence. "This is as much a surprise to me as to any of you."

"Well, I signed the papers a few weeks ago—you know," she addressed the comment to Owen, "the day you took me by Mr. Carlson's office before we went to the beach."

"I remember going to the beach, but not much else," he said, smiling affectionately at her.

"Owen," she said, poking him playfully in the ribs, "I'm serious."

"So was I," he said.

"Are you going to let me tell this or not?"

"Go ahead," Owen said and stuck a long-handled spoon of ice cream dripping with root beer in his mouth.

"Well, I applied for guardianship of Anna," she said. Five pairs of eyes stared at her with unbelief. "I did. I thought that since my father had passed away, she needed someone to look out for her. I couldn't let it be the state. They could move her from Aggie's if they wanted to. I knew my father wouldn't want that, and neither did I. So Mr. Carlson filed the paperwork and I heard from him yesterday. No one objected to the petition. It was granted."

"No kidding," Mark said with a low whistle. "That's quite a responsibility, isn't it, Amy?"

"Nothing more than my father was willing to take," she said. "There's something else," she said, looking toward Owen, who avoided her gaze. "I set up a trust fund that will pay a monthly allowance to Aggie for Anna's expenses and arranged for her to have hospitalization insurance. She is no longer a ward of the state, Aggie. She's your first *private* resident."

Later, when they were alone on her dark, ivy-covered front porch, Amy noticed how quiet Owen was, almost withdrawn and sober.

"Owen," she asked, "what's wrong? You haven't said much since we left the A&W."

Taking her hand, he held the inside of her wrist to his lips. Amy stretched her fingers to take in the feel of his face.

"Why didn't you tell me what you were doing about Anna?" Amy could see the tears building in his deep gray-blue eyes.

"Owen, have I done something wrong? Have I hurt you?" She sought out his eyes with her own. "Please, what did I do wrong?"

"You didn't tell me, Amy. You made a decision that will affect the rest of our lives, and you didn't even tell me." He came close, looking down at her intently. "Don't you think I should have been told what you were planning for Anna? Don't you think I care about this?"

"I didn't think it was any of—" She stopped and turned

away, not wanting to finish her sentence.

"Any of my business? Is that what you were going to say?" He took hold of her shoulders and turned her to face him. "You take on a lifelong commitment and you don't consider it any of my business?" He stood up and Amy watched him push his hands deep into his pockets. "I guess I see our relationship differently than you do." He shrugged his shoulders. "I thought you knew how serious I am about our relationship," he said. "Was I wrong?" Before she could answer, he continued. "You know, Amy, that day at the beach I told you I love you. You came into my arms and I *assumed* you might be falling in love with me, too. Was I wrong about that?"

"I don't know what to say," she said. "I—"

"I'd better go," he said roughly. Retreating down her front steps he paused, turned, and looked briefly over his shoulder.

"Will you call me tomorrow?" she asked, choking back her tears.

"I'm going to work tomorrow," he said, his voice sounding flat and distant.

"Then when you get off?"

"Look Amy," he said, turning to look up at her from the bottom of the steps, "it's time you gave our future some thought. I love you and I want to marry you. You think about that for the next four days, will you? And then you decide if you will let me into your life or not. Not just a part, but all of your life. You know good and well I'm not after your money. I like the way you live. It's the way I want to live. But I won't be left out of any part of your life and your important decisions. That's what I will expect from you. You have to decide if that's what you want from me. When you know, you call me, okay? When you know what you want from me, you let me know." He turned and walked away, then stopped in midstride. "And you take your time. This is too important to rush," he said, once again turning to face her. "I've waited a long time for you. I'll wait a little longer."

"Owen, wait!" Amy said, flinging herself down the front steps toward him. "Please don't be angry with me. I didn't mean to hurt you."

"Intentionally or not, you have. You need to think about

us, Amy. About me and you." She felt him resist her efforts to slip into his arms. "I get off at midnight on Wednesday. You have my number." Cupping her chin in his hand, he searched her upturned face. "This time," he said, his voice thick with emotion, "you call me."

Helplessly, she watched him slide behind the wheel, start his car, and back out of her driveway and into the street. A flash of wild grief and fear ripped through her, sending her running into her safe, secure, but empty house.

Twenty-five

Amy went to church late, slipping into the back row, and left as the last hymn was being sung. She hadn't slept well and didn't feel like talking to anyone. Once she reached her house, she put the family car into the garage and closed the door.

Inside the house, she changed into her robe and slippers, made some tea and toast, then making sure the back and front doors of her house were locked, barricaded herself in her TV room. Princess curled up next to her the moment she sat down on the daybed. Fred Astaire and Ginger Rogers danced and tapped their way through the afternoon *Matinee Showcase*, and Amy stared mindlessly at the flickering screen.

Restless and unwilling to be alone, she finally dialed Linda's number. Her sense of abandonment intensified when she didn't get an answer. In the late afternoon, she approached her mother's storage closet and tackled still another box of quilting squares and a variety of fabric remnants. She put the box with all the others on the back porch and determined to call Mattie within a week to see if someone wanted to finish still another of Charlotte's unfinished projects.

In the evening, she stared blankly at the *Ed Sullivan Show* and afterward would not have been able to tell anyone who was on that night. Only the *Hallmark Hall of Fame* episode was able to capture her full attention. When it was over, she turned off the set and headed for bed.

———

Amy spent Monday morning downtown, pacing the floor of her small inner office. Winnie was shielding her from all but the most important calls. That part of her life, at least, was beginning to settle down, becoming manageable, almost enjoyable. Linda called and persuaded her to go to lunch. Initially, Amy resisted the invitation, but the closer the appointed time came the more she looked forward to it.

At the restaurant she scanned the menu. She wasn't sure how the Mexican food would settle on her already tense stomach, so she ordered only sopa, a clear soup; a flour tortilla filled with melted cheese called a quesadilla; and hot tea. She nibbled at the tortilla chips from the basket in the middle of the table but avoided the fresh salsa, knowing full well the hot peppers would not only burn her mouth, but her empty stomach.

"Are you all right?" Linda asked after the waitress had taken their orders.

"You know me too well," Amy responded. How could she even begin to explain to her friend the humiliated, deflated feelings she struggled with? Remembering Owen's comments and the look on his face, an unwelcome blush crept into her cheeks. "I think I've made a terrible mistake."

"Good heavens!" Linda's voice carried a tone of mock severity. "What terrible thing have you done?"

"Don't laugh at me," Amy pleaded. "I've made Owen mad. I've done something without asking for advice from anyone. The hardest part for me is that I didn't even consider anyone's feelings but my own—except my father's, that is. And what good is that? He's gone. He doesn't even know what I've done."

"What are you talking about?" Linda pressed closer. "What have you done that's so terrible?"

"Anna," Amy whispered, leaning toward her friend. "It's Anna."

"Which one?" Linda tipped her glass of iced tea toward her lips.

"You know which one," Amy's whisper turned to a hiss. "The Covenant House Anna."

"Oh, that."

"Owen was—probably still is—furious with me. He said some pretty difficult and pointed things to me the other night."

"Like what?"

"He said that he loved me and that if we were to have a life together he wouldn't stand for being left out of—"

"He proposed?" A flash of humor crossed Linda's face.

"What's so funny?" Amy pouted. "We had a fight."

"You had a fight," Linda said in a statement rather than a question.

"Yes, a fight."

"He proposed and you had a fight? So did you fight after he proposed, or did he propose after the fight?"

"Well, during, I guess." Amy wished Linda didn't find this so amusing.

"He proposed to you in the middle of a fight—that's unique." Linda paused while the waitress served their lunch before continuing. "Let me see if I get this straight. You made a mistake with Anna, Owen proposed in the middle of a fight . . . and then what happened? What mistake did you make with Anna?"

"Do you think it was wrong of me to apply for guardianship?" Amy asked.

"No." Linda said through a bite of her taco. "Jim and I did wonder why you hadn't ever mentioned it. And we were a little surprised that Owen didn't know. And," Linda added as if she were reading from a list, "we thought it a fairly heavy responsibility. But setting up a trust fund will protect her if anything happens to you, right?"

"Right," Amy said flatly. "I have to have a designated administrator for the trust in case I'm unable to administrate it for any reason. But I can take care of that, I guess. I'd probably name Aggie as first choice, then I'll need to find someone else too, so it's set in place—you know, just in case."

"What does Aggie say to that?"

"What do you mean?"

"Haven't you discussed any of this with her?"

"No," Amy's eyes widened with innocence. "I just thought she'd want whatever is best for Anna."

"And you're the best judge of that?" Linda asked.

A cold, congested feeling settled across Amy's chest. Suddenly she felt irritable and unhappy with herself and her decision. Shrugging, she tried to hide her confusion.

Linda offered her a forgiving smile. "You know, Amy," she

said, lowering her voice to a comforting, smooth level. "There isn't anyone who loves you who doesn't understand what you did, or even why. What Jim and I, and probably Owen, maybe even Aggie, are puzzled by is why you didn't tell any of us what you were planning. We've been with you through so much. Jim is your pastor, Amy. If you couldn't have come to us for advice, you could have gone to Mattie, or even Mark Andrews. We're here for you, Amy. You don't have to make these decisions alone anymore. We love you and we want what's best for you. It's your decision, of course, but do you want to carry something like this all alone?"

"I'm tired of being alone," Amy said, pushing her half-empty soup bowl away. Unconsciously, she ripped at the quesadilla, tearing it into bite-sized pieces. "I wanted to talk it over with my mother—I miss her, Linda. I still have trouble believing they're both gone." Amy began rearranging the pieces of tortilla and melted cheese, putting them back together as if it were a puzzle. "I've never had anyone to talk to other than her."

"You have me," Linda said. "I'm your friend."

Amy's eyes filled with tears in response.

"And," Linda continued, "you have Owen."

"Owen," Amy repeated his name softly.

"So," Linda said squirming with anticipation, "he proposed, did he? What did you say?"

"Nothing." Amy felt empty.

"Nothing?" Linda's surprise registered in both her voice and her raised eyebrows.

"Nothing."

"And?" Linda gestured toward her friend as if she would have to pull any more information out of her.

"And—that's all. He said I could call him when he gets off duty on Wednesday night."

"You're not telling me everything, Amy. Do I have to yank the whole story out of you, or are you going to tell me what happened?"

Amy took a deep breath, then spilled her account of Owen's angry reaction to her surprise announcement concerning Anna. "He said if I wanted to have him in my life, you know, if we were to get married, he expects me to share my life with him completely."

"Sounds reasonable to me," Linda said, scooping the last bit of refried beans from her plate with her fork. "So what's the problem?"

"I don't know if—" Amy stopped and looked intently into Linda's dark eyes before continuing. "I don't know if I know how."

"To what? Let him in your life? Be open with him? What?"

"Linda, what if I mess up? What if I say I want to, but somehow make a mistake and shut him out without realizing it? I certainly didn't realize that I had left any of you out of my decision about Anna. I told you on Saturday—I thought I was letting you all in."

"You were," Linda said gently. "But after the fact. That's okay for someone in your life, say, like Mark Andrews. But Jim and I are your friends. We would have prayed about this— both with and for you. And what about Aggie, don't you think she would have thoughts, and even insights you don't have about Anna's welfare? Don't you see? You've picked up your parents' isolation. At least they had each other. Who do you have, except us?"

"Owen," Amy said, barely above a whisper. "Hopefully, Owen."

"Then you'll have to let him in, Amy. No one says it will be easy, but all you have to promise him is that you'll try. He'll help you. And God will help you. Do you love Owen?"

"Yes," Amy's face felt flushed and she knew her fair cheeks were flooding with color. "Yes, I do. And I don't want to shut him out, honest."

"Then you'd better tell him, don't you agree?"

"But what if—"

"Is he asking for guarantees? For perfection?"

"But what if I disappoint him?"

"You probably will. But then, he'll probably disappoint you now and then." Linda leaned closer and stretched her hand across the table to touch Amy's. "No life is perfect, Amy. Nobody expects you to be perfect. Can't you see that? All Owen is asking—at least my best guess is, he's only asking that you try. He's the one who has to tell you that for sure."

"Thursday is a long way off," Amy said wistfully.

"I thought you said he got off on Wednesday night."

"Well, yes. But midnight?"

"Be creative, Amy. Do something unconventional. Let's see . . ." Linda glanced at the ceiling and tapped her temple with one slender finger.

"You're too much," Amy said, reaching for the check. "I'll treat you today—but next time, it's on you."

"What a pal," Linda said. "What a pal."

———

When Owen reached his apartment after coming off duty, he chuckled at the large pink bow tied to his mailbox with a small note attached. Opening the miniature envelope, he read, *Please call PY2–6954 for an important message.* He recognized the number and knew he'd be talking to her service. "Wonder why she didn't have me call the house," he mused to himself as he opened the door with his key.

"Go to the north garden at the library immediately," the all-night operator said. "Come alone."

"Is that what she said?" he asked.

"Well, not exactly," the woman laughed. "I added the 'come alone' part."

Owen didn't hesitate, but simply grabbed his jacket and once again headed out into the night.

At the library, he looked around for Amy. His lightened heart grew heavy with disappointment tinged with fear when she wasn't there. Just before leaving, he caught the sight of another large pink bow in the shrubs. It was tied to the small memorial marker, placed in memory of Amy's father. Hanging from it was another tiny envelope containing a message that read: *In Summerwind Square you will find a phone booth. Who knows what else might be there?*

"Call PY2–6954 for another important message," he read aloud. The note was tied to the phone receiver with still another large pink bow. Taped to the note was a dime.

"Message number two, please," Owen said when the operator answered.

"Who's calling, please?"

"This is Owen Sampson."

"Oh, yes, Mr. Sampson, let's see. I know I have that message here somewhere." The operator was clearly enjoying the diversion from her usually long, lonely night routine. "Yes, here it is: Proceed to the south entrance of City Hall."

Tied securely to the brass handle of the south entrance door was another large pink bow and the now familiar small white envelope with another message.

"Hey," a uniformed patrolman called from his black-and-white police car. "That you, Sampson?"

"It's me," Owen called back, waving to the young officer.

"I thought I saw you running around downtown. What are you up to?"

"I'm on either a scavenger hunt or a wild goose chase," he said, holding up the pink bow with the note still attached.

"Need some help?"

"Nope."

"You sure?"

"Absolutely." Owen opened the small envelope and squinted in the dim light of the streetlamp to make out Amy's handwriting. *Call PY2–6954 for another important message.*

"All right," Owen said when the operator answered. "Let's just cut to the chase, shall we? It's the middle of the night out here. Is there a message four, five, or six?"

"No, sir," the operator said lightly. "Number three is all I have."

"Then let me have it," he said.

"Go to Matt's Diner," the operator said. "You know the place? It's out on—"

"I know where it is," he said, then hung up without saying good-bye.

Once inside the diner, he approached the all-night waitress at the counter. "I'm Owen Sampson," he said. "Do you have a message for me?"

"No, sir. I don't think so. I can ask Pete, but no one's said anything to me about any message."

Owen glanced around the empty diner. "You're sure no one left a message for me."

"There's nobody here," the waitress offered apologetically. "You can see that for yourself. Business is lousy tonight. Can I get you a cup of coffee?"

"No, thanks," Owen said curtly and headed out the door and toward his car. Before he could get halfway across the vacant parking lot, he saw the large pink bow tied to his radio antenna. He threw back his head and laughed. "Amy," he called loudly. "I give up. Where are you?"

Her gentle laugh rippled through the night air; Owen spun around to face the direction it came from. She stepped from the shadows of the shrubbery and walked slowly toward him. He walked forward, stopping in front of her, and she tilted her face up to his.

"You silly fool," his voice was husky and low. "You could get killed running around in the middle of the night by yourself."

"Don't be ridiculous," she said. "This is Summerwind, not L.A."

"Come here, you," he said, reaching out to take her in his arms.

"Wait." Taking a deep, unsteady breath, she stepped away from him. "I want to say something to you."

"We can talk later. Right now I just want to hold you."

"No," she said firmly, raising her hands in a gesture to stop him. "This won't take long."

Owen stopped and inhaled a deep breath, impatiently waiting for her to say whatever was on her mind. Owen noticed the soft, pastel blue woolen slacks and matching sweater set and thought they made her look almost angelic in the soft light. Her long blond hair was caught up on one side with a barrette exposing her ear, revealing a single pearl earring. She lifted her gaze to his, and the anticipation of what she was about to speak became unbearable. "Amy," he whispered. "Don't torture me any longer."

"I love you, Owen," she said, keeping her distance. "I want you to know that this is new for me. I didn't mean to shut you out, honest. And I'm sorry I hurt you. I don't want to shut you out. But—" She faltered and Owen felt his heart nearly stop before pounding back to life when she spoke again. "What I'm trying to say is, I didn't even know I did it. Can you ever forgive me? Will you give me another chance?"

Owen closed the distance between them and pulled her tightly into his arms. After kissing her, he realized they were both crying. "Amy, my beloved, Amy. I love you so much."

He covered the top of her head and then her cheeks with kisses. "Please, Amy, don't shut me out of your life. I want you to marry me. Will you?"

"On two conditions," she said quietly.

"Name it," he whispered into her soft hair. He would meet any condition she set up as long as she didn't shut him out of her life.

"First, let's tell Jim and Linda. If they think it's a good idea, I'll say yes. After all, he's our pastor and something as important as this—well, it might be a good idea to get some advice. Okay?"

"More than okay, sweetheart. Far more than okay." Owen ran his finger along her cheekbone and down to lift her chin. "What's the second?"

"That you help me learn not to shut you out."

"I promise," he said. Pulling her close, Owen searched her eyes deeply for the shadow he had noticed there far too often. All he saw was the sparkling moonlight reflected in her moist eyes. She closed her eyes briefly then met his gaze once again. Slowly, gently, he kissed her, closing his own eyes in an effort to keep his heart from bursting.

"You know what?" he asked, wishing he could hold her forever.

"No, what?"

"I'm hungry," he said. "And there's a waitress in there who's complaining about having no business nearly all night."

"Sounds good to me," she said, pulling slightly away from his embrace. "I'm hungry, too."

Before opening the door to the all-night diner, Owen gently pulled Amy around to face him and kissed her again.

"Hey, Sampson, that you?" the patrolman called from his car. "I guess it wasn't such a wild goose chase after all, was it?"

Owen smiled down at the beautiful young woman at his

256

side and waved the policeman on. "We'd better be careful, Miss Weaver. This is a very small town. I wouldn't want to sully your reputation or tarnish your name. I guess I'd better make an honest woman out of you and marry you as soon as possible."

He touched her mouth with his finger before she could respond.

"That is," he said smiling, "just as soon as the parson gives his blessing."

"And when will that be?" she asked.

"What time do you think he gets up?" Owen asked, checking his watch.

"Early," Amy said. "Very early. I'd say about four-thirty or five."

"Great, that gives us just enough time to eat before we go pounding on his door."